Rider of the Stars

Center Point
Large Print

Also by Robert J. Horton and available from Center Point Large Print:

Three Trails to Triangle

This Large Print Book carries the Seal of Approval of N.A.V.H.

Rider of the Stars

Robert J. Horton

CENTER POINT LARGE PRINT
THORNDIKE, MAINE

This Center Point Large Print edition
is published in the year 2023 by arrangement with
Golden West Inc.

First US edition: Chelsea House

The text of this Large Print edition is unabridged.
In other aspects, this book may vary
from the original edition.
Printed in the United States of America
on permanent paper sourced using
environmentally responsible foresting methods.
Set in 16-point Times New Roman type.

ISBN 978-1-63808-800-4 (hardcover)
ISBN 978-1-63808-804-2 (paperback)

The Library of Congress has cataloged this record
under Library of Congress Control Number: 2023934185

CONTENTS

Rider of the Stars

CHAPTER I

CHECK

Spring had wrought her miracle in the open country. The far-flung prairies were a sea of living green. In the west the outlines of a towering mountain range were limned in purple against a sky of clearest blue. To southward a fringe of stately cottonwoods marked the course of a river. Northward and eastward the limits of the plain were lost in the haze on the horizon's rim.

A rider broke through the timber screen of the brakes along the river, cantered up a long, gentle rise to the bench land above the bottoms, and turned westward. His bay gelding negotiated the pathless, open range at a tireless lope, while his master whistled or hummed simple melodies and ditties of the cow camps, with occasional snatches of popular airs.

Evidently horse and rider were keenly enjoying the crisp morning air and the mounting warmth.

The man lounged in the saddle with an awkward grace and rode with the deceiving abandon of an expert horseman. He was lean and rather tall, with clean-cut features and a skin which, though tanned almost to the color of horsehide, was smooth and clear. His gray eyes, filled with the sparkle and luster and keen alertness of youth, were half closed, as he gazed at the vast panorama of mountain plain, and sky about him.

His leather chaps, leather cuffs, the narrow leather band about his broad-brimmed hat, even the black holster strapped to his right thigh, were embellished with dull-silver ornaments. This penchant for simple decoration also found expression in his bridle and saddle, and the spurs on his polished, high-heeled riding boots were of silver, too. An expensive, but not obtrusive, outfit, which any man in the cow country would have conceded—and admired.

As he sped westward with the sun at his back, the rider's attention became focused on the river bottoms. Four men were working on a bunch of cattle which appeared to be beef steers. Two of the men were riding on the sides near the rear of the herd, which was grazing eastward, and two others were riding "on point" on either side of the cattle up ahead.

Urged by the riders behind, the herd gradually began to move faster; and with the increased impetus they began to converge and string out until the cattle ceased grazing altogether and moved forward, four or five abreast. The rider on the bench reined in his mount and watched the operation with indubitable interest. The two men riding point, almost directly below him now, were gesticulating to the other pair driving the cattle.

"Coming too fast for 'em," the lone rider grinned to himself. "Gettin' away from 'em, too."

As the long line of steers plunged between the two men riding below him, he now and then tied a loose knot in one of his reins. He could hear the men shouting loudly, saw the two who were driving the herd cease their efforts and try to slow up the cattle, which now were running.

Once more his gaze flashed to a point between the two riders below, and, as he picked out a big shorthorn, he tied another knot in his bridle rein. The cattle now had closed up and were moving between the pair below, almost in a solid mass. The two riders tried in vain to slow them and gave it up, as the last of the herd thundered on eastward.

"And thirteen," said the rider on the bench, aloud, as the space between the two men below became clear. Then he slowly untied the five knots in his bridle rein. He looked rapidly about and saw a steep trail leading to the bottoms, from a point on the bench some distance behind him. He whirled his horse and, riding back, turned into the trail and in a short time gained the bottom land.

He came out on the smooth, grassy surface flanking the river brakes at a point where the cattle were milling after their run. A big, wild-eyed steer, which he suspected should have been shipped two seasons before, broke from the bunch and came plunging toward him.

Spurring his horse ahead, he secured the rope which hung on the right of his saddle horn. The maddened steer came on, and the rider, swerving his horse to the left, sent the rope with its wide loop shooting over his left shoulder and tripped the steer with the difficult back throw. He jerked the rope free and rode on, as the steer scrambled to its feet and stood looking after him uncertainly, before turning and trotting back to the herd.

As the lone rider approached the quartet which had been working with the cattle, he saw they were watching him.

"Had an audience that time, 'Saturn,' " he said aloud to the horse. The animal pricked up his ears at the sound of the voice. It was as if he understood the words were being addressed to him, and he quickened his gait at the sound of his name. The rider noted that one of the four men, a large man who sat his horse heavily, evidently was in charge. Two of the others were plainly cow-punchers, and the fourth was a young fellow, barely more than a boy.

"Nice bit of ropin'," the big man commented, as he rode up.

"Have to keep in practice," replied the newcomer jauntily. "How'd you tally?"

The big man frowned and surveyed him sharply from under black, bushy brows.

"I got five hun'erd an' thirteen," continued the new arrival. "An' I'll bet my saddle that count'll stand straight up for the bunch."

"Where'd you count 'em?" demanded the big man, surprised.

"From the bench," replied the other. "They came pretty fast, an' I lost 'em once, but I picked 'em back up, when that locoed steer came after me."

"Spying," said the youth, who was eying him with apparent suspicion.

"Why so?" asked the stranger quickly. "Just ridin' along, saw you was goin' to count the herd, rode down to see if you had 'em right."

"You're about seventeen off," said the youth scornfully.

"No, he's not," declared the big man in a booming voice. "That's what I counted last night."

"Check!" sang the man of the silver ornaments. "I'll gamble we've got the figures on that herd."

The big man again was subjecting him to a searching scrutiny. "Cow hand?" he inquired.

"Occasionally, when I'm working," was the merry rejoinder.

"Then I take it you're not working," said the big man, scowling. "It's gettin' pretty late in the season for a man to be ridin' the line."

"Maybe he's lookin' for strays," the youth interjected.

The stranger laughed. "You got some queer ideas, son," he observed, sobering.

The youth's face flamed at the patronizing tone. "I didn't say what kind of strays," he retorted hotly.

"Fred, keep still," said the big man. "What's your name?" he demanded, turning to the man in the saddle before him.

"My name's Dane," was the smiling reply.

"Never heard of any punchers by that name around here," said the big man, frowning. "Where from?"

Dane waved a hand in a gesture which included the whole southeastern horizon, and the rays of the morning sun gleaming on the silver ornamentations of his gauntlet were no brighter than the flash of his smile.

"From down yonder," he answered, a bit grimly. And the look he directed at his interrogator caused the latter to hesitate before he put his next question.

"Are you as handy with your gun as you are at ropin' cattle," he asked finally.

"I don't reckon that's what you wanted to ask me," said Dane cheerfully, as he built a brown-paper cigarette. "I figure you was wantin' to ask me if I was packin' a copper iron. I'll stand a frisk." Again the smile, and then:

"I invented ropes," he grinned; "an' I perfected guns!"

A glimmer of a smile in the big man's eyes was quickly overshadowed by a troubled look.

"Maybe you've got a spare match, mister—" Dane put the question with his eyes.

"My name's Hughes," said the big man, nettled, as he handed over a match. "You're on my ranch, the Diamond H. An' I'd kind of like to know just what you're doin' here."

"Helpin' to count the cattle," retorted Dane readily. "An' I didn't know I was on your ranch, although it seems to me I've heard of your brand somewhere."

"Where'd you say you'd worked?" asked Hughes.

Dane lifted his brows. "I don't recollect mentioning that," he drawled. "But I ain't worked north of the river, nor very close to it, if that's what you're drivin' at."

The rancher scowled, frankly puzzled.

"He means he ain't had no regular address," the youth, Fred, put in.

"Lookin' for work?" queried the ranch owner, paying no attention to the young man's remark.

"That depends," was the laconic reply. "There's jobs I wouldn't touch at a hun'erd a month, an' there's others I'd take for nothin'. If you're askin' if I'm lookin' for a chance to herd cows, I'll say I ain't right particular."

Hughes grunted in disgust. Then he glanced quickly at the lithe form of the newcomer, his excellent horse, the worn leather chaps with their silver, the black holster, and the black butt of the gun protruding from it, and last at the cool, gray eyes of the man himself.

"I take it you're observing," he remarked casually.

"I reckon I am," replied Dane, as he snapped the match into flame with a thumb nail.

Hughes turned to the two cow-punchers. "Ease the herd east away from the line. An' stay with 'em.

"We're goin' in to the ranch," he said to Dane, as the two punchers rode away. "This is my son, Fred. You'd better come along in with us."

"Sure," agreed Dane, as he touched the bay with his steel. "An' I'm wonderin' if you noticed there was a couple of riders out west there by a big cottonwood, watchin' your operations this mornin'."

"I saw 'em," said Hughes, his face darkening.

Dane whistled softly, as they rode eastward in the bottoms; he passed the place where he had emerged from the brakes at dawn and headed for a patch of brighter green, some miles distant, where a windbreak of tall cottonwoods protected the fields and buildings of the Diamond H.

CHAPTER II
A NEW HAND

As they rode in silence, Dane had an opportunity to observe Fred Hughes. He doubted if the youth had attained his majority, and he fixed his age at about twenty. He was very light, having one of those skins which burn rather than tan. His blue eyes were clear enough, but Dane imagined he detected a depth to them which might indicate that the young man had a habit of serious thinking; that, or he had something on his mind. Plainly he was suspicious of Dane.

The elder Hughes was dark, with a swarthy complexion which was almost coarse. He had the large build, the open manner, and all the characteristics which ordinarily are associated with the successful stockman. Dane knew instinctively that this man knew his business.

All during the ride toward the ranch Hughes failed to speak. He glanced at Dane now and then appraisingly, Dane thought, but for the most part he stared moodily ahead. They left the bottom for the bench land to take a short cut where there was a big bend in the river. Dane drew a sharp breath, as they skirted the edge of the bench where the river once more turned north to straighten out again on its eastern course. Below them lay the ranch proper. There was a line of cottonwoods from the bluff, where the bench was cut off to the river. East of these trees was a fifty-acre hayfield, and beyond were more trees, and then the ranch buildings, clustered in the shelter of the high bench.

The ranch house was a large, rambling affair to which numerous additions evidently had been built. There were two large barns, a huge hay shed, and a network of corrals. There was a large bunk house and cook shack, a blacksmith shop, and many smaller outbuildings. Altogether it was mute evidence of the fact that the Diamond H was an important property, where stock raising was carried on on a big scale. They rode down a wide trail past the corrals and sheds to one of the barns. Here they dismounted.

"You can put your horse up in a stall," said Hughes to Dane.

As he was unsaddling, Dane noticed that Hughes looked the big bay over for brands. But the horse bore no iron.

"You'll probably want to drop in at the bunk house an' slick up a bit," Hughes told him, when the horses had been attended to. "Come over to the house to dinner when you hear the bell. I'll be on the front porch."

"Bunk house'll suit me all right for grub," Dane demurred, "if it's all right with you."

“I’d rather you’d eat at the house to-day,” said Hughes gruffly. “I’ve got my reasons.”

Dane nodded.

On the way to the bunk house he smiled to himself. He found the wash bench and soon was removing the coating of dust from his face and hands. Then, after a survey in the cracked mirror, which hung over the bench, he returned to the barn and secured his shaving outfit in the slicker pack on the back of his saddle. He went back to the wash bench and shaved. He combed his hair carefully until it shone with a dull luster of bronze.

“Goin’ to a party?”

Dane swung on his heel at the words and beheld an old man who evidently had been watching him from the doorway of the bunk house.

Dane scowled for reply, and the old man’s face wrinkled into a grin. He shuffled toward Dane.

“My name’s Marty,” he volunteered with a welcoming light in his faded blue eyes. “They call me Old Marty, but I ain’t as old as a lot of ’em think.”

He held out a hand, and Dane grasped it. No sooner had he done so than he looked quickly down at it. Instinctively he glanced at the old man’s other hand. Both hands were mere pads, with the thumbs and fingers missing.

“Frozen off ten years ago when I was drivin’ Esther into town, time she was sick,” said the old man rather proudly. “Ain’t hardly done a tap of work since, but I'll allus have a home with Gordon Hughes. You goin' up to the house to dinner?"

Dane nodded, retaining his grip on Old Marty's stump of a hand.

"I 'spected so the way you was fixin' up," grinned Marty. "I reckon you're goin' to work here, eh?"

"Nothin' been said about it yet," Dane replied.

"Well, I reckon you will," declared the old man, bobbing his head energetically. "Gordon needs good men right now."

Dane passed over the implied compliment, although there was nothing in Old Marty's tone to indicate he meant it as such.

"Why does he need good men?" he asked.

"Ain't for me to say. He'll tell you, if he ain't told you already. Want to put them there shavin' things away? I'll show you where to put 'em in the bunk house. I kind of look after the bunk house an' keep things straight. Anything you leave in the bunk house is safe, with me lookin' after it. Come along."

Dane picked up his belongings and followed Old Marty into the bunk house, where the old man placed the shaving outfit on a shelf in a box nailed to the wall.

"They'll be there when you want 'em," he declared with a convincing bob of his white head. "You a stranger round here?"

"I reckon I am," Dane confessed, somewhat amused at Marty's fussiness and eager interest.

"Best range west of the Rockies an' north of the Missouri," said Marty, who couldn't keep his eyes off the newcomer. "Man, you shore look like you could ride. I used to be one of the best riders in this country. An' I bet you can shoot, too. An' you ain't very old—you're young. I wish I was young." There was a wistful look in the eyes of washed-out blue. "I used to shoot, too. Once I—"

He was interrupted by the dinner bell.

"There ye be; hurry up now! An', boy"—he regarded Dane with fatherly regard—"you'll see a girl up at the house. That's all right—wrinkle yore nose. You'll come out scratching yore haid!"

Dane hastened toward the front porch of the big house, where he found Gordon Hughes awaiting him. The rancher led the way into the long, cool dining room. Dane first was introduced to Mrs. Hughes, a small woman whose hair, though plentiful and wavy, was nearly snow white. Her face retained signs of a wonderful beauty which had been hers in youth. Another elderly lady, a Mrs. Dawes, was introduced as Mrs. Hughes's sister. Fred Hughes entered, accompanied by a girl, and Dane's eyes flickered, as he looked at her.

"Dane, this is my daughter, Esther," Gordon Hughes was saying.

Dane bowed, and because he looked quickly

away he failed to see that she had stepped forward to hold out her hand.

The six of them sat down at table, as a Chinaman entered with several dishes.

"What's this, mutton to-day, Lee?" said Gordon Hughes in a booming tone, pretending to glare fiercely at the Chinaman. "We're runnin' a cattle ranch, Lee."

"Allee samee mlutton glo glood for chlange," grinned the Chinese.

"Sam's name isn't Lee any more than mine is," smiled Mrs. Hughes in an aside to Dane. "Gordon thinks every Chinaman should be called Lee."

"Good enough name for 'em," Hughes asserted.

Esther Hughes smiled at Dane. Evidently she felt a certain tolerance toward her father's views.

Dane observed her by means of surreptitious glances. She was almost directly an opposite to her brother, who plainly took after his mother. The girl was dark, with dark eyes and hair, and her features were sufficiently irregular to be most attractive. Indeed, Dane searched his memory for a recollection of any other girl he had ever seen who looked more attractive. It wasn't that Esther Hughes was beautiful, it was—Dane gave it up. Perhaps it was her eyes; or it might be something in her personality. But there was an unmistakable appeal and charm about her.

"Are you going to stay with us long, Mr. Dane?" she asked when they had been served.

"Dane's a new hand," Gordon Hughes put in.

"Oh, I didn't know," she said quickly, as her brother shot a frowning glance at his father.

"Maybe you're to be the new foreman," she speculated with a smile.

She couldn't understand his presence in the ranch-house dining room unless he was to have a position of importance. It was not customary for ordinary hired hands to eat in the house.

"I didn't know I'd been taken on till just now," Dane returned with a side glance at Hughes, ignoring her reference to the possibility of his being made foreman.

So Gordon Hughes didn't have a foreman. He directed a questioning look at the rancher, who read his thoughts.

"I've been runnin' things myself," said Hughes. "An' about time," he added with a scowl.

"Did you find the cattle all right, Gordon?" his wife asked.

"Found five hundred an' thirteen of the shorthorns all right," growled the rancher. "I don't know how the seventy-odd others of the bunch are, for I don't know where they're at."

"And we probably never *will* know till we clean up Bunker an' his gang," said Fred.

His father looked at him sharply.

"Fred, you mustn't jump to conclusions," his mother reproved.

"Maybe the boy's right," said Gordon Hughes.

"I'm beginning to think something besides the boundary is wrong on the west side."

His tone caused his wife to look at him apprehensively.

"We don't want any more trouble with them than we can help," she said.

"An' if we can't help ourselves, what then?" demanded the rancher. "Tod Wendell was shot at this morning."

His wife looked troubled. "You can't always tell who is to blame when a thing like that happens," she said.

"But we can tell who's to blame when they order our men out of Black Butte at the point of a gun," stormed Hughes. "I've tried to be peaceful enough, but, by thunder, if Williams is goin' to use guns, I'm goin' to start usin' guns, too!" He brought his fist down on the table.

Dane saw Esther Hughes looking at him, and he glanced at her again, as he detected a new light in her eyes. She was staring at him; and it seemed to him that there was disappointment in her look as well as awakened curiosity. Yes, she was staring at him curiously, possibly in disapproval.

"Do you believe in guns, Mr. Dane?" she asked suddenly.

The question startled him. He laid down his knife hastily and reached for his coffee cup.

"All men of the range believe in guns at times," said Gordon Hughes sternly.

"Gordon, what are you thinking of?" Mrs. Hughes asked in an anxious voice.

"I'm thinking that I've built this ranch an' am responsible for it," replied the rancher grimly. "An' I don't intend to let any outfit take it away from me, or stop my runnin' it, as I see fit. An' from now on I don't want any talk at this table about the affairs of the ranch. An' I don't want you womenfolks meddling or worrying. You run the house, an' we'll run the cattle."

It was plain from the look on Mrs. Hughes's face that something which she had feared had come to pass. Dane suspected that when Gordon Hughes put his foot down he meant business. And, whatever was in the wind now, it was plain he was thoroughly in earnest.

There was no further conversation concerning the ranch. Hughes's declaration had its effect, if he desired the topic dismissed. The rancher spoke casually of stock and feed, but Dane could readily perceive that his mind wasn't on his subject, and Dane didn't take the trouble to vouchsafe any comments. Esther didn't speak to him again, although he sensed that she was studying him furtively.

Fred was almost morose, and again Dane was inclined to believe that the youth had something on his mind, a secret, perhaps, which was not shared by the rest of the family.

Old Marty had hinted in the bunk house that

Gordon Hughes needed good men. Now at the table there was talk of cattle missing and of gun play. Very likely Hughes had forbidden further discussion of it because he didn't want the women to be worrying themselves in the matter. It was all too evident that everything was not exactly as it should be on the Diamond H.

After dinner Gordon Hughes led the way to the porch.

"Go down to the bunk house, an' I'll slip down there pretty quick for a talk with you," said the rancher.

Again Dane merely nodded and smiled. He was taking things as they came, and it appeared that they were coming fast.

"Marty," he said, as he entered the bunk house, "it looks as if I'd been hired."

"Shore, I knew it," the old man replied and looked delighted.

Dane walked to the open window and stood looking out at the weaving branches of the cottonwoods about the house. Try as he would, he could not help but ponder over the queer look he had seen in Esther Hughes's eyes at the dinner table.

CHAPTER III

"SOME JOB!"

Despite Gordon Hughes's promise to meet Dane at the bunk house in a short time, it was nearly two hours before he came walking briskly from the direction of the corrals. Old Marty had gone out and left Dane alone. There were few men at the ranch, and those few, the old man had said, would not be in until supper time. Consequently, when Hughes arrived, he and Dane sat down to talk in the bunk house without fear of being interrupted.

Gordon Hughes wasted no time in beginning.

"Look here, Dane, I don't know much about you except your name—if it *is* your name—an' that you seem to know range work. Maybe I'm takin' a chance—I've took 'em all my life, or I wouldn't have this ranch—but I'm bankin' you're straight; anyways you're straight enough, I reckon, to stick by any man you'd go to work for."

He kept his gaze on his listener who was nonchalantly building a cigarette.

"I knew you was hep to those two men who was watchin' us down there in the bottom," the rancher went on, "an' something told me you wasn't in with that gang out west o' here. I ain't never seen you aroun' here, an' I can usually get a line on a man in short order; been hiring 'em an' firing 'em all my life, seems.

"That's why I asked you to dinner. Wanted to watch you. That's why I sent you in here to see if Old Marty would put his O. K. on you. I sort of bank on what Old Marty says 'bout a man, too; he's a wise old duck in some ways. I don't care where you're from, or what you've done or been, or who you are; but I'd like to hire you for a right tough job."

Dane smiled. "Looks like I didn't make much of a mistake in comin' north," he observed. "I'm listening."

"You didn't make any mistake, if it's excitement you're lookin' for," said Hughes. "There's been a feud for years between this ranch an' the Flying W, just west of here. Old Oscar Williams an' I've fought like cats an' dogs over the boundary, which was 'bout a quarter of a mile west of where we was countin' cattle this morning. We never got a fence up because both of us knew that the minute one or the other of us started to build a fence, war would be on. There's a strip of land out there both of us claim. Dang it, if it wasn't for givin' in to him, I'd let him have it!

"I might have let him have it this spring, anyway, if it hadn't been for the way things has been goin'. He imported a new foreman this spring, feller by the name of Matt Bunker. He's a gunman an' a bad one. He started in tryin' to take men away from me, an' when he couldn't do that, he started ridin' 'em. He an' his crowd chased five of the boys out of Black Butte a month ago. They wouldn't have went, but I've told 'em to lay off the shootin', an' if they'd stayed they'd have had to unlimber their hardware good an' plenty."

The rancher rose and paced back and forth nervously.

"My wife hates trouble, an' I hate trouble for her sake," he went on. "I'd have give in to Williams that strip on her account, if he hadn't started goin' too strong. I've been missing cattle, too; not many, but enough to show that there's rustlers workin'. We can't run rustlers out of the country unless we all stick together, an' I get it from a roundabout way that Williams ain't lost any cattle. An' that looks funny to me, although I don't think Williams would deliberately start rustlin' to push along a grudge.

"But in a whole lot of other ways he's forcing the play. Bunker's the worst. He an' his gang claim they're runnin' the town of Black Butte, so far's the cow-punchers are concerned. I can't even send in a man for supplies but what, if there's one of the Flying W outfit there, they'll try to pick a fight with him. An' some of my boys is gettin' sore, an' I ain't goin' to be able to hold

’em in, an’ then there’ll be all kinds of trouble.”

He paused and frowned. “An’ I haven’t got what you’d call a gunman in the bunch.”

He looked at Dane thoughtfully. Dane was staring out the window at the flecks of white drifting down from the shedding cottonwoods. In his eyes was a dreamy look, as though his thoughts were far away.

“You takin’ all this in?” asked Hughes sharply.

“I’m listening,” answered Dane without shifting his gaze.

Hughes resumed his pacing. “I can’t have any trouble on the range this year,” he said with bitterness in his tone. “An’ I can’t afford to lose any cattle. We’ve had two bad winters, an’ I’m in to the American Bank at Black Butte pretty strong. Had to buy feed, an’ on top of that I lost quite a bit of stock. An’ hay was as high as fifty dollars a ton at a time when I had to have it.

“Sam Stevens, down at the American, ain’t acted as friendly this spring as he might. He’s got a pretty good hold on me, an’ he knows it. But he’s got good security, even if he don’t think much of the shorthorns I’ve got. I know white-faces are better than rustlers, but I’ve always had more hay that I needed till the last two years. Anyway, I can get back on my feet, good an’ stout, with this fall’s shipment, an’ if we have a good winter, I can clear next year.”

"Hasn't the Flying W had the same trouble the last couple of years?" Dane asked.

"Sure. Williams has had to buy feed same's I have. But he ain't got so many cattle. I'm runnin' better'n five thousand head, an' that's pretty good for this range. Have to take some of 'em to the foothills on forest-reserve range in the summer. I don't reckon Williams has got more'n two thousand head. We range north to the Canadian line. He ranges west o' here, an' I range east. We don't mix the stock."

"How's it come you ain't got a foreman?" asked Dane suddenly.

"I discharged my foreman last fall because I thought the Williams crowd was gettin' to him. An' I want to be out 'tending to things myself. An' I need new blood in here, too. That's why I looked you over so hard to-day. You said you wasn't particular about any job just herdin' cows, and I've got enough cow-punchers."

Dane looked at the rancher quickly.

"An' you ain't askin' for any recommends," he observed in a low voice.

"The only thing I ask of a man when he goes to work for me is that he works for me an' not for the other fellow," replied Gordon Hughes.

"Fair enough," said Dane quietly. "Why did your daughter look at me so—so peculiar this noon?"

The rancher's eyes widened. Then he surveyed Dane gravely.

"I dunno," he said finally, "unless it's because you're a stranger aroun' here, an' she didn't know just what you was goin' to do on the ranch.

"Anyway, Esther's peculiar since she got back from that school in the East," he added.

He turned to look at Dane again, and his own look this time held something Dane was unable to fathom. Dane reflected that this was the third member of the family whose gaze at times had him guessing.

"What was it you was wantin' me to do here?" he asked, rising from the bunk on which he had been sitting.

Hughes hesitated. He watched Dane walk to the window and lean on the sill. He noted that he rested his left elbow on the sill. The long, tapering fingers of his right hand were hitched in the cartridge belt above the butt of his gun.

"I was wantin' you to find out who is rustlin' my stock," said the rancher slowly. "An' maybe think up a way to keep peace on the range till I can get my beef shipped. An' you can name your own price, if you can fill the order."

"Puncher's pay suits me," said Dane. "That's all you want?"

"If you can show old Williams of the Flying W where he's makin' a fool of himself an' costin' us both money, so much the better," Hughes grunted. "You'll have to think out the rest of the job yourself."

A flashing smile from Dane rewarded the rancher for this speech.

"I been thinkin' ever since you started to talk," said Dane cheerfully. "Some job! An' it beats herdin' cows. I'll be on my way in the morning to start work."

"Where are you going?" asked Hughes curiously.

"To Black Butte," replied Dane, smiling.

CHAPTER IV
BLACK BUTTE

Whatever Gordon Hughes might have thought privately about Dane, whatever might have inspired him to acquire his services in the extraordinary capacity in which he had engaged him, he kept his motive and reasons to himself. The cattleman long had been a judge of men, and it may be that he considered Dane's arrival on the scene at such an opportune time as something more than mere chance; for the stockman was, in degree, inclined to be a bit superstitious. Anyway, having acted, he reflected no more upon the matter, but was prepared to await results.

At supper that night he announced that Dane had been hired as an "extra hand."

"What *is* an extra hand, daddy?" asked Esther.

"A man who ain't regularly employed," replied her father. "That is, a man who ain't hired for regular round-up work, you might say, or—"

"I see," Esther interrupted; "sort of 'cow-puncher extraordinary'?"

Gordon Hughes frowned. "That education you picked up in the East ain't goin' to help you any too much out here on the ranch," he observed irritably. "If I was you, daughter, I'd save the most of it to use on the town boys when they get fresh."

Esther colored. Her father never had quite taken to the idea of her going away to school, although he was very proud of her. She regretted that many of the utterances which seemed natural and appropriate to her were taken by her father as an attempt on her part to be erudite, or even snobbish! Yet she had to confess to herself that she was not exactly the same girl she had been before her advent East.

In this instance she bit her lip and refrained from answering her father. Her pretty brows puckered into a frown, as she thought of Dane. An "extra hand." Then he wasn't to be one of the men on the round-up; he wasn't a regular cow-puncher, and he wasn't foreman. She kept thinking of the title her father had bestowed upon him—extra hand. And he certainly was good looking. She couldn't easily forget the dreamy look in his eyes and the occasional flashes with which they lighted up. It irritated her that she should actually find herself interested in one of the men hired on the ranch. And the fact that Dane had been engaged to work other than in the capacity of an ordinary cow-puncher interested her more. She was puzzled.

Dane ate in the bunk house with half a dozen of the Diamond H men that night. Old Marty's announcement that he was a new hand practically made him one of them at once. They accepted his easy banter, and before they quit the table he was on good terms with them and the Chinese cook as well.

But they soon found that he was given to spells of long silences. Nor did he appear to hear the few veiled references thrown out as to where he had previously worked. Still, it was not the general rule that a man had to recite his past history when he came to a new place. It was the rule of the range that performance counted, and that what a man did would sooner or later show what he was. So, while Dane became a man of mystery, he did not lose caste thereby. Instead, he excited interest.

"Listen to me, you wranglers," said Old Marty that night when Dane went out of the bunk house for a breath of air, "there's a man as knows cattle an' hosses. An', what's more—an' don't forget who told you—there's a man as knows how to handle a gun."

"Looks like a lot of a kid to me," observed one Servais, a horse wrangler and breaker. "What's he goin' to do on the ranch?"

Old Marty was nettled. "He ain't as young as he looks," said the old man with considerable spirit. "I suppose he's goin' out on the circle. But I'll bet whatever Gordon Hughes tells him to do, he'll do it in right smart fashion."

Servais grunted. He was a small, dark man, not

given to speech to any extent. What he thought he blurted out and let that end it. It had frequently got him into trouble, and he had incited the wrath of his employer more than once; but he was invaluable as a man who knew horses from hoof to mane; how to manage them, break them properly, care for them. He was the only man on the ranch who could ride "Jupiter," the stallion—and that is saying much.

Dane, unaware that he was being discussed in the bunk house, and doubtless caring little whether he was the subject of comment or not, walked up the bluff in the moonlight. On the bench he halted and, removing his hat, permitted the cool night breeze, with its scent of the open spaces, to fan his cheeks and brow and hair. He stood for some time under the stars, looking about him, absorbing the beauties of the wild prairie night. He replaced his hat and stared down at the shadows of the ranch buildings below. All the lights were out, and he could not know that a pair of dark eyes were regarding him from a darkened window of the big ranch house.

After a time he returned to the bunk house and sought the bunk which Old Marty had allotted him; smiled when he found that the old man had seen to it that he had plenty of blankets and a pillow with a clean, white case!

Next morning he was in the saddle soon after breakfast. Gordon Hughes, who was going down to look after the beef herd in the bottoms, rode westward with him.

"Now," said the rancher, when they reached a point above where the cattle had been counted the day before, "there's the line. See that big cottonwood to the right? The road's up there, an' that tree marks the line, or what should be the line. Williams claims the line is a bit this side of the tree, an' I know it's a bit the other side. North of the road, about two miles, you'll see a clump of alders. There's a spring up there, and those alders is supposed to be on the line, too. I don't range west of there, an' Williams don't range east of there. An' we both try to keep out of the bad lands."

He pointed south, and Dane turned to look at the miles of brakes on either side of the broad, sluggish river, the Teton. It was a wild country of tumbled ridges, seamed with gullies and deep ravines, spattered with treacherous "soap holes," where cattle would venture upon an apparently solid surface, only to bog and sink down out of sight. The soap holes were as bad as quicksands.

The brakes or bad lands, were studded with gnarled, wind-blown, bull pines, bushes, occasional clumps of cottonwood, alder, quaking ash, and willows. It would be next to impossible to find and recover cattle wandering in that labyrinth of tortuous trails, blind paths, twisted ridges, gullies, ravines, soap holes, and cut banks.

Dane reflected that here was an ideal country for cattle-stealing operations, provided that the rustlers knew the bad lands.

"Are there any fords across the river down there?" he asked Hughes.

"Most of 'em are too dangerous to tackle because of the quicksands," replied the rancher. "But there's one just at the end of the line down there—you can't see it from here—where you can cross pretty good when the water's low. The river's high now, an' it'll be another month afore all the snow gets out of the mountains, an' it goes down much."

Dane took his leave of the ranch owner and proceeded westward, turning north for a short distance to gain the road. He had ascertained that Black Butte was about twelve miles away. He rode slowly, surveying the country. South of him he saw occasional bunches of cattle and surmised they were Flying W herds. He met no one, and it was late in the morning when he rode into the town of Black Butte.

That this was an old cow town was apparent at first sight. It was half hidden in a grove of cottonwoods on the banks of a little stream known as The Muddy. Its one short street was lined with one-story buildings, unpainted, or, if they had been painted once, the paint long since had faded and peeled. Most of the buildings flaunted false fronts, suggesting a height not compatible with the size of their interiors.

A small bank building, two stores, a hotel, several resorts which once had been saloons, but now bore the legends of “Soft Drink Parlor” or “Soda Emporium,” a candy and cigar stand, one short-order cafe, several smaller stores, and a blacksmith shop and livery barn made the business section of Black Butte.

The town was in the southern end of the county, some forty miles from a railroad. Small motor busses furnished connection with the trains and communication with the county seat, which was on the railroad in the north.

Dane put his horse up at the stable and entered the little hotel for dinner. He sat at the window in the small lobby waiting until the dining room opened. The street was practically deserted. There were no sidewalks, and swirls of dust blew past the window. Altogether it was a dead, desolate aspect, and Dane reflected that it would be easy indeed for Matt Bunker, gun-fighting foreman of the Flying W, to come into town with a number of his outfit and have things all his own way.

The ranch buildings of the Flying W were about seven miles southeast of town, he had been told. Little wonder that the Flying W crowd found it possible to spend so much time there.

After dinner he made the rounds of the various

resorts. He was not surprised to find that illicit liquor was being sold across the bars, and that gambling was carried on openly. The town was isolated, without a deputy, and small enough to assure the tolerance of the county-seat authorities.

In the largest resort, The Palace, he met with a surprise. The place was a veritable honky-tonk, with a big bar, lunch counter in the rear, small tables, card tables, a roulette wheel, and a big open space for dancing, with a small stage. The dancing space was to the left as one entered—opposite the bar. The stage was in the center on the left side. One had to pass the bar and the dancing space surrounded by little tables to reach the gambling tables at the lower end of the big room. The place was profusely decorated, and big oil lamps hung between streamers of varicolored bunting overhead. There was a balcony running halfway round the room.

He hardly knew this place when he entered it that evening after supper. It had been deserted in the afternoon, save for a few solo players and men working; but with the coming of night it took on a festive appearance and resounded with the music from a three-piece orchestra, the shouts and rough jests of men at the bar, the jingle of spurs and the clinking of glasses, the dull rattle of chips. Dane stopped stock-still before he reached the bar, and his brows lifted in genuine surprise.

A girl was singing.

He turned to look and saw her swaying near the orchestra, in front of and below the stage. She was a pretty girl, with large brown eyes, a wealth of dark hair, rosy lips, and cheeks which had been rouged. She was slight, but exquisitely formed. And she was dressed in a pale-pink thing which accentuated her charm. She possessed a good voice, and when she came to the chorus she showed that she could dance.

"Who is it?" Dane asked a man at the bar.

"That's Marie," grinned the other. "An' don't try to get fresh with her. She ain't that kind."

Dane smiled his thanks for the information volunteered and wandered back to the card tables, taking careful note of the men in the place.

For the most part they appeared to be ranch hands or cow-punchers, and Dane wondered if any of them were from the Flying W. He had heard the little, boisterous town was a rendezvous for all manner of characters, many of them shady, perhaps, for miles around. Certain it was that there were gambling sharks present, for Dane's practiced eye enabled him to pick out a number of "boosters" or house players at each of the two tables where stud poker was being played.

He stood looking on at a game and was astonished to see how rapidly the place filled up. He surmised that the hotel and the few houses, shacks and tent abodes must have been filled during the day with the sleeping night patrons of The Palace.

Other girls besides the singer appeared, and soon dancing was in progress. It then became apparent that the dancing feature of the place was kept apart from the other forms of entertainment in the resort. A short, thickset, placid-appearing man, who acted with the authority of a proprietor, was present on the floor, and when a dancer made too frequent trips to the bar to assure the equilibrium of his steps, he was quietly, but forcibly, guided through the spaces between the little tables and denied the privilege of dancing.

Dane strolled over to the roulette wheel, which was situated near a short flight of steps leading to the balcony. He divided his attention between the operations at the wheel and in surveying the patrons of the place.

During one of the dance numbers he saw the girl, Marie, in conversation with a man in leather chaps and broad sombrero. The girl appeared angry and resentful, Dane thought; and when the man attempted to induce her to dance, she drew away from him with flashing eyes. Dane remembered the admonition of the stranger at the bar and smiled.

But the girl plainly detested the man who wanted to dance with her in this instance, and finally the short, placid man interfered and introduced her to another, a younger man, with whom she immediately whirled away.

The man who had been talking to her said something to the floor manager and turned with blazing eyes which, because he was looking straight at him, stared into Dane's. At once the man moved in Dane's direction.

The latter noted that the man had a large face, with cold features; he was freshly shaven; his eyes showed plenty of white and appeared to bulge a little. They were of a greenish brown. He was stockily built, a little above average height. An ivory-handled six-shooter reposed in the holster strapped on his right.

He walked straight to Dane.

"Stranger in town?" he asked.

"Not exactly," Dane drawled; "town's too small for that. I've been here since mornin' an' got pretty well acquainted with it."

"So?" said the other, with the suggestion of a sneer. "An' where might you be from?"

"I see," snapped Dane. "You're takin' the census. I'm from the south."

"That's a lie!" retorted the other. "Two of my men saw you ridin' in from the east this mornin'."

"What was that you said?" inquired Dane in a mild tone, although his eyes were flashing coldly.

His interrogator read the signal and hesitated. They had the attention now of those at the wheel and others nearby.

"I saw you come in from the east."

"An' I didn't deny it," replied Dane evenly. "But I also come from the south of the river. Get that? Or can't your brain work that hard?"

The other's face darkened. "You workin' for the Diamond H?" he demanded.

"If I was I don't reckon I'd be reportin' to *you,*" smiled Dane.

"Then I figure I'm right," said the man. Two others at his back mumbled something.

"If you're Diamond H you're in the wrong place," he said, compressing his lips.

"It suits me," replied Dane. "Are you the majordomo here, or just takin' it on yourself to give orders?" There was a queer note of cheerfulness in his tone, and, though his face had paled under its tan, his eyes were dancing with a queer, steel-blue light.

"I'm tellin' you so's you can light out while you've got the chance," the other roared. "That isn't orders, that's good advice."

"I'm much obliged for the favor," said Dane, as the smile froze on his face. "I take it you're right generous to-night."

The man who had been overseeing the dancing pushed through the throng.

"You gents will have to settle your argument somewheres else," he said, visibly nervous. "There's county men in town to-night, an' I can't run any chances of a brawl. We're shuttin' down the games in ten minutes," he added with an appealing look at the man who was confronting Dane.

This evidently had its effect.

"You got the high ball," said Dane's accoster savagely, as he turned on his heel. A path to the bar opened like magic, and he disappeared.

"I'm Willis Brady," said the man who had intervened, to Dane. "I try to run this place halfway right an' keep set with the bunch at the county seat; but you fellers have got to help the play, if I'm goin' to keep open."

Dane nodded and was about to ask a question, when the other, turning aside, drew a small whistle from his pocket and sounded a shrill blast.

"Last roll, boys!" came from the man who was running the wheel.

Dane felt something drop upon his shoulder; then a chip fell upon the floor. He looked up and beheld the girl, Marie, beckoning to him from the balcony. After a moment of indecision he ran lightly up the stairs.

CHAPTER V
THE INSULT

When Dane reached the balcony he found that the dance-hall girl, Marie, was greatly agitated. Her eyes were bright, and her glances darted with the flashing swiftness of those of a hunted animal. Her whole body was trembling, and she twisted a bit of handkerchief in her fingers nervously.

"Come thees way," she whispered, drawing back from the rail of the balcony.

Then she led him to the front end of the balcony over the diminutive stage. Here curtains were hung, and, as they stepped behind them, she paused before a door and spoke again.

"They will not come here," she said excitedly. "Thees is my room in here. The man who talk to you—you are not afraid of him?"

Dane smiled at her anxiety. She was indeed a pretty girl. He saw that she was prettier, if anything, under her rouge. Nor was her manner coquettish or bold. Was this an attempt to involve him in a sordid lover's quarrel—a frame-up, perhaps?

"That man who talk to you," she repeated, her wide eyes staring at him in frightened wonder, "you stand up to him when ever'body run?"

"I'm not afraid of him, if that's what you mean," said Dane. "But I don't intend to let him get the drop on me."

"Ah!" She drew in a long breath, and her eyes were shining.

"He ees a ver' bad man," she said slowly. "Be careful to no talk too loud. You know who he ees? He ees Bunkair from the Flying Doubleyoo. His hand it itch to shoot. Myself, I see heem shoot—fast, ver' fast. Like thees!"

She snapped thumb and finger to illustrate the speed with which Bunker was supposed to draw his gun and fire.

He was standing just within the shadow of the curtain, peering down at the scene below. The wheel had been removed from the table at the foot of the stairs. The dealers at the stud tables were cashing the last of the players' checks, and already two innocent games, one of solo and the other of hearts, were in progress. The blackjack dealer, having closed his game, was walking toward the bar with his check rack. Most of the lights in the rear half of the room had been extinguished. The proprietor, tipped off long since, was ready for the advent of the authorities who happened to be in the town that night.

The crowd had thinned considerably. There were less than a dozen at the bar. Bunker was the center of activities there. He was roaring orders to the bartender who was serving the white liquor. Even as Dane looked, he saw the stout, placid man, Willis Brady, hold up a finger at the white-coated servitor. The bartender whispered something to the men before him who hurriedly downed their drinks. The glasses of near beer had hardly been set upon the bar for camouflage, when three men entered by the front door and greeted Brady.

Dane quickly drew further back behind the curtain.

"Those men," he said quickly to Marie—"they must not see me." He looked hastily about. "Perhaps they will come up on the balcony," he added, knitting his brows.

"Here," she said excitedly, as she opened the door behind her. "Go in." She pushed him within, followed him, and shut the door.

"No, they will not come in here," she said with a look in which he thought triumph smoldered. "Thees air my room."

There were really two rooms. Dane saw that the one they were in was a little sitting room, neatly appointed, with a phonograph in one corner and pictures on the walls. A door was open to the other room, evidently the girl's sleeping room. Dane could see a window through the doorway. What he could see of the other room indicated that it also was simply furnished.

"Those men—they look for you?" asked Marie, smiling.

"I don't think so," Dane replied. "But they might know me. Are you French?" he added curiously.

"But yes—my mother, she was French. But I am born in thees countree. I am American. See?" She pointed with a charming little shrug to the American flag which hung above a long mirror on one side of the room.

"You see—I am American." Her eyes were laughing orbs of dark, mysterious color.

Dane thought to remove his hat and frowned. He was puzzled.

"You know why I call you up?"

He frowned again at the dancing light in her eyes and drew away, as she put a small hand on his arm.

"Ah, the beeg, stron' man, he afraid of the little girl," she said in evident delight. Then she sobered, stepped to the door, and turned the key in the lock. When she returned she faced him squarely.

"I call you up here to give you the warning," she said seriously. "That Bunkair—I know what he mean by his look." Her face clouded angrily, and Dane remembered how she had looked when the Flying W foreman had tried to make her dance with him.

"Right now he has his men here," she continued breathlessly. "They watch. I see you not 'fraid of heem like other men. So I tell you. You can be careful—yes?"

"I can sure be that," Dane agreed. "An' I'm obliged to you for puttin' me wise, although I reckoned that was Bunker when he stepped up to me."

She was staring at him again. Suddenly she lowered her gaze in a disconcerting fashion, Dane thought. He stirred and looked toward the door. He had heard someone on the balcony. She, too, was listening. Then she caught his arm.

"They no come in here," she said quickly in a low tone. "You tell me—you come from Diamond H?"

Dane smothered an exclamation. Then she was merely after information, after all. A weak ruse, he thought to himself. Yet it was certain that it would only be a matter of time before Matt Bunker and the others learned he was indeed from the Diamond H. Why not learn the consequences at once—draw their fire from the start? Also, he was reasonably certain that Bunker *knew* he had come from the Hughes ranch that day.

He looked at the girl coldly.

"Yes, I'm from the Diamond H," he replied sternly.

Her face lit up, and her eyes sparkled. "I tell nobody 'tall," she said.

She continued to look at him, while he regarded her with suspicion. Twice she started to speak, but desisted. It was plain that she wanted very much to ask a question but was holding it back.

"Say," he said suddenly, "what more do you know about Bunker?" He was thinking of the scene he had witnessed a short time before.

"Ugh!" She shrugged. "You must use the care. He ees a ver' bad man. I guess they go now. I look."

She turned the key in the lock, opened the door, and looked out upon the balcony. Instantly she shrank back, and her gaze darted to him in fear. He pushed past her and looked down the length of the balcony.

Matt Bunker was sitting on the railing near the head of the stairs, swinging his left foot, gazing at them with a sneer upon his lips.

"Havin' a nice little party?" he called.

Dane imagined the girl behind him caught her breath in a sob. He walked rapidly toward Bunker, who rose and confronted him at the head of the stairs, still sneering. As he walked, Dane flashed a look below and saw that the three county men evidently had left, or were closeted in some private room with Brady, for they were nowhere in sight. There were only half a dozen men standing at the bar.

"I don't suppose you'd understand, or want to understand, so I'm not going to try an' explain," he said, stopping before Bunker.

Bunker was speaking over Dane's shoulder to the girl, and the insult in Bunker's tone was unmistakable.

"Bunker, you're a low-thinkin' rat!" said Dane hoarsely, leaning toward the other.

"It don't take much thinkin' when I can use my eyes," leered Bunker. "I got your number, an' I got the number of that kid."

Dane's right fist shot out and caught Bunker full on the jaw. The Flying W foreman toppled backward and crashed down upon the guard rail on the left side of the stairs, smashed through it, and fell to the floor just as Dane swung over the balcony railing and dropped.

As he hit the floor, stumbling against a table, Dane's gun flashed in his hand, and two shots rang out. There were crashes of splintering glass which rained upon the floor, and the pair of lights overhead went out.

Dane dashed across the deserted dancing space toward the front door. He kept one eye on the men at the bar who had swung about and were staring in astonishment at what was happening so unexpectedly. The bartender was running down behind the bar toward a closed door which doubtless opened into a private room in the rear.

Dane grooved the bar, two feet ahead of the running man, with a bullet, and he stopped dead in his tracks, whirling about and elevating his hands. A man at the bar recovered from his surprise and went for his gun. Flame streaked from Dane's weapon for the fourth time, and the man's right arm jerked back and then hung limp at his side. As Dane gained the door and flung it open, he shot a last glance in the direction of the stairway and balcony. He saw Bunker crawling from behind the stairs, gun in hand. Above he glimpsed the white features of the girl, Marie, leaning over the balcony railing, her eyes wide with fright, her hands clutching at her throat. Bunker was raising his gun.

Dane fired the two remaining shots in his weapon, and the bullets splintered into the floor, only a scant three inches from where Bunker's left elbow rested upon it.

With a laugh he darted out of the door, as Bunker emptied his gun in that direction.

But the light was too dim in the front of the room for the Flying W man to reach his mark in that flashing instant. Dane, being in the subdued light and shooting toward the bar, where the lights still burned, had had an advantage, when he stopped the bartender and wounded the man who had tried to come to Bunker's aid. And he had purposely shot into the floor in front of Bunker, for he had no desire to kill the Flying W foreman.

Outside, Dane ran swiftly down the street to the barn just beyond the hotel. He grabbed a lantern from the man and dashed for his saddle and bridle. In marvelously quick time he had the bay bridled and saddled and had reloaded his gun. He led the horse out of the rear door of the barn, mounted and rode into the sheltering shadows of the big cottonwoods.

Slowly he picked his way in the dark around to the south side of the town and, keeping close within the shadow of the trees, worked to the eastern end, where he rode southward, close to the timber along the banks of Muddy Creek.

Any one seeing him, as he rode with the moonlight shining on his face, would have marveled at the joyous satisfaction reflected in his eyes. And, considering the exciting and dangerous incident just closed, one would have marveled, too, at the steadiness of his hands, as he deftly rolled a cigarette, snapped a match into flame in his cupped palm, and lighted the weed, totally indifferent to the fact that the flare of light must certainly disclose his whereabouts to any who might be following.

Yet his manner did not betray recklessness, nor needless carelessness; confidence radiated from him—it was in his very poise in the saddle. He hummed lightly, as he guided his mount into the denser shadow and brought him to a halt.

He waited in the darkness, smoking. Before him the vast plain stretched eastward toward the Diamond H and beyond. In the south the rolling range of the Flying W reached to the black fringe of shadow which marked the beginning of the bad lands. The prairie was bathed in the flood of moonlight, alive with shifting shadows and the silvered crests of gentle rises—a mysterious land laved by the scented prairie wind which crept out of the northwest and sang in the quivering grasses.

Now the steady pound of hoofs came to his ears. He saw three riders bear down from the north and swing off southeastward.

"Bunker an' two of his outfit headin' back to the Flyin' W," murmured Dane aloud.

He finished his cigarette, while the trio disappeared to the south of him. Then he rode slowly back toward the main road leading eastward. He turned into the shadows again, as he heard a horse coming at a fast gallop along the road from the direction of the town. As the horse passed him, the moonlight shone full on the face of the rider. Dane whistled softly in surprise.

"Marie! Now where's she headin' for this time o' night?"

He waited until the girl was some distance ahead of him, then he struck out into the road and followed. He had to ride hard to keep the girl in sight, for she was mounted on a good horse and was going at a fast pace. Dane's wonder increased, as he saw her turn south at a point a short distance west of the imaginary line between the two ranches.

He turned south, also, but now the ground was broken by short ridges and miniature ravines, and much of the time he lost sight of her altogether.

Then she and her mount were swallowed by the shadow of the brakes along the river.

Dane guided his horse, as near as he could tell, to the point where she had disappeared. Off to the right he could see a herd of cattle—Flying W stock. To the left the bottoms were clear. Directly before him were the first tumbled ridges of the bad lands. In vain he searched for a trail. He rode back and forth, looking for a path leading into the labyrinth along the river which the girl might have followed. He found nothing remotely resembling an entrance into that mysterious land of shadow.

Then he ventured in. He followed a shallow coulee for a short distance, crossed a ridge at its blind end, entering a ravine, brought up at the edge of a soap hole, its thin, surface coating of alkali gleaming like the white of powdered skulls in the light of the moon.

Cautiously he circled the left side of the treacherous bog and went on. His horse stumbled in the darkness, and he swerved to gain the crest of a high ridge. In the north he saw the plain, but all about him were shadows with twisted, blunted pines rearing their hideous shapes, and the ghostly gleam of a soap hole showing here and there in the dim light.

It was folly to think that the girl had entered the bad lands, he decided. Whatever had prompted her to take that wild night ride, it could be nothing associated with this desolate, dangerous section of the brakes. She had probably ridden east or west in the shadow of the first ridges. Had she gone to keep a tryst? He sniffed at this as unlikely, but at the same time wrinkled his brows in perplexity.

Anyway, it was time for him to get out of the brakes.

He rode down the side of the ridge on the northeast, intending to take what looked like a short cut back to the plain. For some time he threaded his way with difficulty through ravines and gullies, across open spaces, through patches of scrub timber, and then, when he thought he had about reached the objective point, he climbed another ridge to make sure of his bearings.

The plain now was farther away and in an opposite direction from where he had expected it to be! He took new bearings and again struck out for the open country. He had to turn back several times when he reached the blind end of ravines which appeared to deepen and widen as he progressed. He mounted a ridge and strove to pierce the shadow which hemmed him in. The moonlight surface of the prairie and bottom land was nowhere to be seen. He was lost!

Unable to see for any distance in any direction, he concentrated his gaze on the territory near at hand. It was a land of dense shadow because of the straggling growths of timber. The moon seemed nearly overhead, and in his bewilderment he could make no headway toward determining direction from it. He snorted in disgust, and then his gaze froze, as he looked to the right.

A blaze! No, it was not the flickering light of a camp fire, for it was steady. A lamp or lantern—and it was stationary. Could it be there was a habitation in that wild, desolate country?

Dane took careful note of the direction in which he had seen the light and started for it, following a long ravine which led that way. When he climbed the next ridge he failed to see the light. He camped for the night in the bottom of the next ravine.

CHAPTER VI
NIGHT MAGIC

Dane was up with the first gray streamers of dawn. He went up on the ridge at the end of the long ravine, which he had followed after seeing the light the night before, and took a survey of the country. He saw the river through the interlaced branches of trees to the south of him, and could make out the bench land some distance in the north. He could not see the bottom lands below it.

All about him were the bad lands, and they seemed weirdly beautiful in the light of the rising sun—colorful, wild, almost awe-inspiring. Something in their mocking beauty and desolation appealed to him, and he stood for a long time looking about him dreamily. Here was a natural, trackless refuge for the hunted—man or beast.

His thoughts returned to the light he had seen the night before, to the dance-hall girl who had ridden so mysteriously he knew not where, to Bunker and his insolence. Dane felt now that it had been Bunker's intention to precipitate a gun play on the balcony. He didn't want a gun play with Bunker—yet.

As he reflected upon it, he saw that Bunker was endeavoring to force his attentions upon the girl, Marie. Doubtless it was Bunker's aggressiveness toward him, Dane, which had caused the girl to warn him. He wondered now if her warning had been sincere. Was Marie what she appeared to be—a clever and straightforward girl working on the dance floor for the wages it brought her? And how interested she had been in learning if he was from the Diamond H!

Dane gave her up temporarily as a mystery and smiled at the recollection that he himself was a mystery in that locality. He checked up on the bearings he had taken by moonlight and proceeded in a southwesterly direction, keeping on his course by means of landmarks selected ahead and behind him. Within an hour he gazed down from the crest of a high ridge into a little clearing where there was a rough cabin.

No one was in sight, and there were no signs of smoke. He dismounted and waited for more than an hour in the shelter of the scant timber on the top of the ridge. Still he saw no one; and there were no visible evidences that the cabin below was occupied.

Finally he rode down the ridge and tied his horse at the edge of the clearing. He crept silently to the cabin and looked in at the one window. It was deserted. He found the door secured by a heavy padlock. However it was plain that the cabin had been used recently, for there was a neat pile of wood chopped, and the branches thrown over a frame of saplings to form a roof for a little porch in front were freshly cut.

He looked about the clearing. The imprint of many hoofs met his eye. There had been cattle in here. Dane considered. It might be that he was on the trail of the missing Diamond H stock. For why should one or more men want a cabin in the heart of the bad lands, unless they were hiding out, or engaged in some nefarious undertaking which required the protection and secrecy of the wilderness?

There were numerous trails leading out of the clearing on its south side. Dane followed each of these a distance. In every instance the trails split up into dim paths that crossed and crisscrossed in such intricate and bewildering fashion that twice he experienced difficulty in finding his way back to the clearing. And cattle tracks appeared on all the trails! He had been told there were a few bands of strays in the bad lands, and it might be that the tracks had been made by one of these bands. But the presence of the cabin was in itself suspicious.

He decided to wait for a time to see if any one came to the cabin. He sat in a small bunch of quaking ash at the northern edge of the clearing and smoked, while his horse grazed on the rich grass which grew on the lower slope of the ridge.

The sun mounted to the zenith before he rose, a prey to gnawing pains of hunger, and prepared to go. He led his horse up the ridge where he got his bearings. As he rode down the other side of the ridge toward the flatlands in the north, he took out his pocketknife and cut small blazes on the north and south sides of the trees along his course. In this way he made a well-defined trail so that he could at any time in daylight find his way back to the cabin in the heart of the brakes. When he reached the bottoms he rode at a rapid pace eastward and reached the Diamond H ranch buildings in midafternoon.

A word to Old Marty resulted in a speedy and substantial meal served by the obsequious Chinaman. He asked Marty about the bad lands, but all the old man said about them was that they were "a good place to stay away from, unless one wanted to get bogged, or lost, or both!"

A man came in from Black Butte late in the afternoon with a load of supplies, and at the supper table that night Dane knew by the looks the men directed at him that the incident of the night before had been reported.

Fred Hughes passed him after supper without a word in the space before the bunk house, but he looked at him with that same curious, indefinable expression in his eyes which Dane had noted before. This trait of the boy's was irritating.

Dane retired to his bunk early, and next day

he rode out to look at the various brands on the cattle in the bottoms. Gordon Hughes owned several brands, and it was only the shorthorns which were all branded with the Diamond H.

Although he saw and talked with the rancher, the latter made no mention of Dane's expedition to town; nor did he intimate that he had heard what had happened. Dane suspected Hughes knew he had gone to town to get a look at Bunker. It was as if there was an unspoken understanding between the two.

After supper that night Dane walked along the bottom east of the house. The long twilight had drawn its purple veil over the land, and the first stars were gleaming faintly in the darkening skies. A breath of wind stirred the leaves of the cottonwoods, and the scent of sun-warmed earth was strong. It was that time of the year when summer hangs upon the heels of the short prairie spring and comes suddenly—seemingly in a single day! As Dane was walking back toward the house, he stopped suddenly at a movement among the trees, and his hand dropped instinctively to the butt of his gun. Then a bobbing blotch of white appeared against the shadow of the timber.

"Don't shoot, Mr. Dane," came a girl's voice.

"Good evening, ma'am," said Dane, as Esther Hughes approached.

"You seem to like to be by yourself," she

observed, as she joined him. "You walk abroad of nights."

She laughed at her own quoting speech.

But Dane didn't laugh. He looked at her curiously. Here was a girl, Western born, who had acquired much of the refinement of the East. She had a certain confidence; but it was not the frank confidence of the Western girl who can ride and shoot and take care of herself under most circumstances. It was the confidence of speech and manner, and Dane decided that it didn't jibe with his conception of what a Western girl, such as the daughter of the owner of the Diamond H, should be.

"I reckon I like to walk aroun' in the evenin', ma'am," he said soberly, remembering to doff his hat in salute.

"But you know what they say when a man walks around much alone," she taunted.

"I can't say as I do, ma'am."

"When he keeps by himself a great deal they hint that he may have a guilty conscience," said Esther with a quick look at him.

"Them as say that, maybe, has had some experience along that line, ma'am," he retorted with a vague smile. Esther's brows lifted in quick perception of the adroitness of his reply.

"It's plain to see, Mr. Dane, that you are no ordinary cow-puncher," she said severely. "I—I can't help feeling interested in you."

"You're a heap interesting yourself," he said with a drawl.

Esther colored. He thought to himself that she was very beautiful, as she stood in the half light, her face turned up to him frankly.

"I didn't know you included flattery among your other accomplishments," she said, looking away.

"Was that flattery, ma'am? Well, I reckon I'm learnin' then."

"Let's walk up on the bench," she suggested. "I rather want to talk to you; in fact there's something I want to ask you."

"Maybe I won't know the answer," he grinned, as they moved across the meadow in the bottom and began the ascent to the bench. She slipped on the trail, and he caught her to support her.

"Never mind, Mr. Dane," she said, disdaining his arm. "I can still climb a trail even if I *have* been East to school."

"I'm mighty glad to hear that, ma'am," he said, seemingly with enthusiasm.

She stopped surprised.

"Why do you say that?" she asked, curious.

"I'd thought maybe you'd forgot a lot about the West since you'd been away, ma'am."

She bit her lip and frowned, and they continued on to the flatland.

"I know what you mean," she said, as they gained the high ground. "You think I'm no longer Western; but I am—I just *am,*” she added stridently.

“I’m glad to hear that, too,” said Dane lightly, “and I didn’t exactly say what you mentioned.”

“But you meant it,” she accused, petulantly. “And in *some* ways I *am* changed,” she confessed. “There are lots of things I don’t look at in the same light I used to.”

“Like what, for instance, ma’am?”

She thought there was something patronizing in his tone and resented it.

“Like violence,” she retorted. “Our Western idea that disputes and differences and even injustice should be settled by violent measures is wrong and ridiculous; and a whole lot of it is nothing more than heroics and cheap melodrama. Look at the way your hand jumped to your gun when I came out of the trees!”

He started and stiffened.

“Why, I didn’t hardly know it did that,” he said slowly. “It sort of dropped down there by instinct, I guess.”

She had been mean, and she knew it. She had meant to be. Why should this man of the range be arguing with *her?* And why should she be irritated at him, one of her father’s hired men? That’s all he amounted to. But *was* it all he amounted to?

She looked at his strong, lean face, lit by the first light of the stars. He was staring dreamily out over the bottoms to the sky above the cottonwoods. She had seen those same eyes flash, when she had cut him with that remark about his hand dropping to his gun. And she had heard things.

"Mr. Dane, *why* should your hand go to your gun by instinct?" she asked quietly. If she expected him to be disconcerted, she was disappointed.

"Because I was brought up that way, ma'am," he replied in a soft voice.

She bit her lip again in vexation. There it was once more—the tradition and teaching of the West. Somehow his remark seemed pointed at her. And there he stood, seemingly oblivious of her very presence, gazing up at the stars.

"I thought, perhaps, there might be other reasons," she said; and immediately afterward she was angry with herself.

"There might be," he conceded, to her surprise.

Somehow his remark seemed definitely to close that topic of conversation. And, if anything, it increased the aura of mystery which surrounded him. Why was she finding it difficult to talk to this man? What was there about him which baffled her? Why, he interested her more than any man she had met since she returned to the West! She flushed at the realization, and then felt more than ever resentful toward him.

The night shades had fallen, and the high arch of the heavens was aglow with stars. A cool wind brought the tang of open country, and in the brakes to southward coyotes began their nocturnal serenade. Something of the spell of the night seized her. After all this was *her* country as much as his. She had been born here.

"Does the wind ever talk to you, Mr. Dane?" she asked suddenly.

"Why, yes, ma'am," he answered surprised. "The wind an' I are pals, I reckon."

"And the stars—do they talk to you, too?"

He laughed softly. "I don't just exactly know what the stars do, ma'am," he replied, sobering. "But they do something. I like to look at 'em an' ride under 'em. They seem to be sort of kiddin' me along."

She looked at him sharply and perceived at once that he was not joking.

"The wind and the stars and you seem to be a mystery all in one," she commented idly. "You've always lived in this country?"

"I was born here, ma'am."

"Near here? Near this ranch anywhere?" she asked in surprise.

He turned to her, and his white teeth flashed against the tan of his features, as he smiled at her. "This country takes in a lot of territory, ma'am," he said, including the rim of the sky in a sweeping gesture and leaving her question unanswered.

"Why is it you won't tell anyone anything about yourself?" she demanded impatiently.

"An' why should anyone want to know much about me, ma'am?"

She stamped a neatly shod foot in annoyance. "Do you know what the men are saying about you?" she flashed.

"No, I reckon I don't. An' I can't say I'm a heap particular."

"They're saying you're a gunman!" she retorted accusingly.

"Maybe they are—sayin' that," he reflected dreamily.

"And they call you 'Lightning' Dane," she went on scornfully. "Are you proud of that title—Lightning Dane, the gunman!"

"It *does* sound a little like the heroics you mentioned, ma'am," he said, smiling at her.

"It's ridiculous!" she stormed. "The West is becoming too civilized for guns and the like."

"But maybe everybody don't realize that, ma'am," he interposed quietly. "There's some that ain't been enlightened an' are workin' on the old principle. An' some of 'em are tough customers."

"Like yourself, I suppose I am to infer," she said tartly. "I don't take it that you would be ashamed of your calling, and I really am curious to know if you are what they accuse you of being."

She looked at him expectantly, her lips parted, wisps of hair fluttering in the wind.

"I reckon there's nothing quite gets a woman like bein' curious, ma'am," he said gravely, without looking at her.

"It isn't altogether curiosity with me," she snapped; "I have the interests of the ranch at heart."

"Just so," he agreed.

"We had better be going down," she decided suddenly.

They walked slowly down the trail from the bench land to the bottom and turned toward the ranch house at the farther end of the long meadow.

Esther Hughes could not resist her feeling of irritation, which was aggravated by the fact that something in Dane's personality, or the mystery about him, appealed to her.

She glanced at the lithe figure at her side. Her gaze dropped to the butt of the gun so near her. As she looked at his profile, she reflected that he was almost too young to be a professional killer. Her mood softened.

"There's something I wish to ask of you," she said, stopping and touching him on the arm. "Please promise you will not set—a bad example before my brother."

"That depends, ma'am, on what you take to be a bad example," he said, removing his hat.

"Oh, *oh!*" she exclaimed. "I believe I hate you!"

And she ran toward the house.

CHAPTER VII
IN THE BRAKES

While Dane was saddling his horse after breakfast the following morning, Fred Hughes came into the barn. Dane glanced at him curiously, and he saw that the youth was standing and watching him, and, to Dane's surprise, there seemed to be a more cordial look in the young man's eyes.

"Ridin' out this mornin'?" Fred asked with a smile.

"Thought I'd scout aroun' a little," replied Dane, wondering just how much the boy might know about his, Dane's, somewhat unusual position on the ranch.

"Which way?" the youth inquired.

"Aroun' south, I reckon," Dane returned. He didn't feel that it would be wise to tell the boy much about his movements, and he didn't care particularly to be discussing his activities with him.

Fred, however, was evidently in a friendly mood this morning. Dane noted with interest that the youth had a good face and was an excellent physical product of outdoor life. That he was young, with the aggressiveness and heedlessness of youth, was apparent; but it also was to be seen that he possessed the qualities, or many of them, which go to make a man.

As Dane was leading his horse out of the stall, Fred spoke to him again.

"Hear you had quite a time down in Black Butte the other day," he said casually, rolling a cigarette.

"There's those who'd talk about anything," Dane countered with a frown.

"I'm glad you lit into Matt Bunker," exclaimed the youth with vehemence. "He's got a lot coming to him."

Dane was surprised at the bitterness in the boy's tone.

"I take it you ain't fond of Bunker," he remarked.

Fred's face darkened. "Someday I'm going to kill him!" he said in a voice which shook, as he turned and walked away.

Dane looked after him, marveling at the passion he had displayed. He was inclined to smile at Fred's threat, but he did not discount the evident sincerity of the youth's hate for the Flying W foreman. Whatever the improbability of the youth's being able to keep his promise, there was no doubt as to the integrity of his desire.

Pondering over the matter, Dane led his horse outside, and left him near the barn, while he went to the cook shack for a sandwich or two to take with him on his ride. He could not deduce just what had inspired Fred's intense hate for Bunker. True, Bunker was causing trouble; he was Williams' mainstay in the feud against the Diamond H; he was dangerous and ruthless. Had he at some time driven Fred Hughes out of Black Butte? Danc was inclined to accept the latter theory. Fred was young and such a proceeding would seem terribly degrading and ignominious to him. He would not stop to reason that it would not be cowardice on his part to back down before a man who was notoriously fast with his shooting iron and not particular upon whom he used it. Such had been the reputation of Bunker, as described to Dane in town.

Securing the sandwiches he returned to his horse and was wrapping them in his slicker pack when he heard a man shouting at the rear of the barn. He ran through the barn and found Servais, the wrangler, standing in a corral shouting at a horse which was running westward under the lee of the bluffs. It was the big, black stallion, Jupiter.

"Took him out in the corral, an' he broke through," cried Servais. "Look at him go! An' I've got to breeze after him an' bring him back."

"I'll go along," Dane volunteered, as the wrangler went for his horse.

Shortly afterward they rode rapidly in the direction taken by the stallion, and soon they saw him cutting through the lower range toward the trees.

Servais was angry and drove his steel into his horse's flanks. "He's makin' for the brakes," he shouted to Dane. "There's a bunch of wild mares down there an' he's been there before. We've got to head him off."

But that was easier said than done. The stallion, seeing them coming at a mad gallop in pursuit, increased his pace. He made a magnificent spectacle, running as swift as the wind, with mane and tail streaming. Coming to a small ditch, which ran through the range, he leaped gracefully and literally seemed to flow through the air to a landing far on the other side. He tossed his head and went on.

Dane caught his breath in admiration of the splendid beast. He knew the stallion was Servais's especial pride, and that the small, dark man not only could handle him under most conditions, but was also the only person who had ever ridden him. He saw Servais was worried, and he suspected that the man, being an excellent wrangler of horses, might not be an expert with the rope; for specialties obtain in the cattle country as well as anywhere else.

The stallion plunged through a windbreak of trees at the lower edge of the range and cut across the bottom in a southwesterly direction, with Dane and Servais following some distance behind. Neither of their horses was a match for the stallion in point of speed, although both were fast mounts. As they spurred their horses to their greatest speed, Dane realized that there could be no horse in that country which could run with the big, black stallion. He even slowed up and looked back at them, as if taunting them, and then he sped on.

It now was apparent that the stallion was indeed making for the brakes; and, as he was running in a straight line, cutting toward the southwest corner of the bottom land near the visionary line between the two ranches, it seemed probable that he was heading for a trail which led into the bad lands.

This proved to be the case; for, when the stallion disappeared behind the outlying tumbled ridges of the brakes, and they reached the place, they found a dim trail leading south.

"We're in for it now," shouted Servais. "We'll have to go some to get him in there. But we've got to get him," he added, as he guided his horse into the trail and galloped along its twisting way. And Dane realized that the wrangler possibly never would return to the Diamond H unless he got the stallion.

It now was dangerous going, with roots and rocks in the trail and overhanging branches leaning low. Coming out into a clearing from a ravine, Servais brought his horse to a rearing halt on the edge of a white-lipped, treacherous soap hole.

"He wouldn't get into one of these, would he?" asked Dane, peering ahead.

"Him?" replied the wrangler scornfully. "He's too wise for that! He'll likely lead us along a ways an' then lose us."

They skirted the soap hole carefully and plunged on along the trail on the farther side, which now led up the side of a ridge. When they gained the top they could see the stallion some distance ahead. He had slowed his gait and was trotting along, superbly confident and disdainful of any pursuit. They followed down the ridge, and at the bottom Servais checked his horse.

"I hear you're a fair hand with a rope," he said to Dane. There was a pleading note in his voice, and Dane realized that, if he could succeed in roping the stallion, he would earn the lasting gratitude of the wrangler.

"I'll try to snare him," he said simply and pushed his horse past Servais.

Now in the lead, Dane held the pace down a bit. He knew that the stallion would be off again at full speed, as soon as he heard the sounds of pursuit, or saw them. The trail had a soft-dirt bottom, and they proceeded with a minimum of noise, except where they had to cross stretches of gravel, and at such places and where they encountered soap holes, Dane pulled his horse down to a walk. Mounting another ridge they saw the stallion almost directly below them. The big black was walking, shaking his head, on a piece of trail strewn with boulders.

Dane loosed his rope for a throw and, putting the spurs to his horse, dashed down the slope recklessly, the rope whirling over his head. Just as he was about to throw, the widened noose caught on the projecting limb of a dead tree above the trail and dangled behind. The stallion trotted off down the trail, tossing his head as if in derision.

"If you can get the rope on him, he'll stand," called Servais. "He ain't bad; he was excited this mornin', since he hadn't been out for a spell. Guess it was my fault for foolin' with him," he added in a worried voice.

Dane coiled his rope and urged his mount in rapid pursuit of the runaway. They didn't catch sight of the stallion again for some time. The trail had turned toward the west and wherever it intersected another dim path, Dane halted and made sure of the stallion's tracks.

As they rode through a ravine between two high ridges, a shadow came creeping over them. Dane looked up to see that the sky was filled with clouds, and that the northern horizon was black. The wind began to pick up, and the branches of the stunted pines on the higher pieces of ground twisted and waved in grotesque fashion. He increased his pace, with Servais pounding along close behind. The trail wound steadily westward, and Dane reflected that they must be nearing a point directly north of the place where Gordon Hughes had said there was a ford across the river. Could the stallion be making for the ford?

Dane didn't doubt but what the big horse could swim the swollen river; but the current would be certain to carry him downstream, and there was the danger of cut banks shutting him off, or quicksands swallowing him. He was too valuable a piece of horseflesh to lose, but Dane thought only of the splendid animal. Not only did he want to save him in the interests of the Diamond H, but for his own love of a good horse.

At the top of the next rise they were rewarded with another glimpse of the stallion trotting ahead. The wind was blowing harder, and the animal held his nose high in the air, scenting the approach of the storm. The sun now was obscured by the veil of clouds which had swept across the sky from the northwest, and in that direction an inky-black curtain was rising above the mountaintops.

They swept along the trail through another ravine and across an open space into a grove of poplars. At the farther end of this grove they emerged suddenly upon a meadow, and Dane reined in his horse, pointing ahead. The stallion was standing, snorting, in the center of the meadow. Some little distance ahead of him stood an old man, his white hair and long, white beard flying in the wind. He held out a hand and appeared to be speaking to the big black. Dane walked his horse ahead, and the rope whirled over his head.

In another moment the stallion reared back, with both front feet high off the ground, twisted about, and lunged for the southern edge of the meadow, as Dane's lariat sang. The wide loop shot straight for its mark, hovered an instant in mid-air a space ahead of the plunging stallion, then settled down over the animal's head.

As the noose tightened about his neck, the stallion came to a stop, looking about, as if bewildered, and shaking his head doubtfully.

"There he is! Go after him," Dane shouted. "He's got his halter on, anyway," he added, turning in his saddle toward Servais.

The little wrangler was sitting his horse, with popping eyes staring down the range.

"The hermit!" he ejaculated in a choking voice. And to Dane's astonishment he crossed himself.

Then he seemed suddenly aware of the issue at hand and, quickly dismounting, walked toward the stallion, with a halter rope in his hand. Dane looked down the range, but saw no one in sight. Servais crooned to the stallion, as he approached him, snapped the halter rope to the halter which the horse wore, and stroked the animal gently on the neck. Then he led him back to his own horse and began to remove his saddle.

"What're you going to do—ride the stallion?" asked Dane in growing wonder.

Servais nodded, and, while Dane looked on in astonishment, he saddled the big black and hung his horse's bridle on the saddle horn.

"My horse'll follow," he explained, quite as a matter of course. "We'll have to hurry to get back before the storm breaks," he added with a look of concern at the darkening heavens.

"Wait," called Dane. "Who'd you say that old fellow was who stopped the stallion?"

Servais's face clouded and he looked hastily down the meadow. "He's gone," he said with relief. "That was the hermit of the bad lands. Nobody knows where he lives or how, an' there ain't been many who's seen him. They'll think I'm lyin' when I tell 'em at the ranch, but you saw him too, didn't you?"

Dane nodded. He was amused at the other's agitation, but nevertheless he felt an impelling curiosity.

"Is that all you know about him?" he asked, riding slowly to the wrangler's side.

The other grimaced and looked at Dane rather sheepishly.

"He's supposed to be a spirit," he said in a low voice, looking about the meadow.

Dane laughed outright at this, for it was plain

that the little wrangler was of a very superstitious mind, although, for that matter, the appearance of the old man had been rather startling, and Dane realized he was a character to conjure with because of his mode of life.

"Where'd he go?" Dane asked the wrangler, searching the range with his gaze for a sign of the old man.

"I dunno," said Servais; "an' I don't care. I ain't lost any hermits! We better get goin', or the storm'll hit us sure."

"Go ahead," said Dane. "I'm goin' to look aroun' a bit."

He watched in admiration, as the little wrangler rubbed the big stallion's nose; and then without an instant's hesitation Servais mounted and was off, the stallion trotting along the back trail. They soon disappeared in the grove of poplars.

Dane rode to the lower end of the meadow and found a dim trail leading through another clump of trees. He could see another small open space ahead through the branches, and he was just about to emerge, when he checked his horse suddenly and sat in the saddle, peering between the leaves. He saw a small clearing, at the upper side of which was a tiny cabin. He pursed his lips in surprise, for it was the same cabin he had seen from the ridge and later visited the morning following his night in the bad lands. And standing before the open door of the cabin was the old, white-haired man—the hermit. A horseman was sitting his mount before him. Dane's lids narrowed over his eyes. The horseman was Matt Bunker, foreman of the Flying W.

CHAPTER VIII
THE HERMIT

In the shelter of the poplars and the tall grasses which grew among them, Dane watched the strange scene in the little clearing before the cabin. The old man was hatless, his long, white hair and beard waving in the wind. Faded overalls and jumper clung to his loose frame, and Dane could see, even at that distance, that his feet were bare, although browned to the color of old leather. He was gesticulating, and now and then he would stamp a foot, as if in childish rage. He looked very old, and his face appeared white. It would not take any great exertion of one's imagination to see in him a likeness to a spirit, as the wrangler, Servais, had hinted.

Bunker was leaning down from his saddle. He appeared to be threatening the hermit, for his attitude was aggressive and hostile. He apparently was talking loudly, but the wind in the leaves prevented Dane from hearing anything that was being said.

Once the hermit pointed south, and Bunker's gaze flashed in that direction for an instant. Then he waved the butt of his quirt at the hermit and half turned his horse. He said something over his shoulder, flipped the butt of the quirt into his palm, and cracked the short lash past the hermit's face.

With a few more words, accompanied by energetic nods of the head, he dug in his spurs and galloped across the clearing, disappearing in the timber at the foot of a ridge opposite.

The twilight preceding the breaking of the storm had descended and the wind was howling through the sparse tree growth and hurtling the ridges. In the north sky the lightning already was flashing—white tongues that licked at the black curtain of cloud. It was the first electrical storm of the season which was racing out of the north and west, sounding its warning in rumbling rolls of distant thunder.

Dane saw that the dim trail he had followed into the poplars petered out among the trees into a dozen faint paths which blended with the trampled grass of the clearing. Little wonder he hadn't found a trail at this point, when he had inspected the clearing on that day after he had followed the girl, Marie, to the edge of the bad lands.

But the pursuit of the stallion had shown him a direct trail to the clearing, and it had resulted in his ascertaining who inhabited the little cabin. Now the presence of Bunker convinced him that there was another trail leading to the Flying W Ranch.

The advent of the storm gave him a legitimate reason for visiting the hermit. He would ask for shelter. He rode slowly into the clearing and headed for the cabin. As he approached, the old man came running out with a rifle in his hands. He brought its stock to his shoulder and covered Dane, as the latter halted his horse before him, astonished.

Dane started to speak a word in greeting, just as there came a vivid flash of lightning, followed by a deafening crash of thunder. The old man dropped the gun on the ground and stood as if stunned, staring at Dane with eyes which were glittering dots of black. Then he groped with his hands, ran back into the doorway and motioned for Dane to come in, as the rain began to fall in sheets.

Dane unsaddled and took the bridle off the bay and turned him loose, knowing the horse would go in under the trees and graze. He hurried inside, carrying his saddle and bridle, as he saw no sign of a barn. The old man was busy pulling thick curtains of burlap down over the window. He lit a lamp and, hurrying to the door, closed it and fastened it securely. His hands were shaking, and he was mumbling to himself.

Dropping his saddle and bridle near the door, Dane surveyed the interior of the cabin. There was a bunk on the farther side; a table was under the window, with a stove in the corner beyond the door; a curtain was pulled across the corner at the foot of the bunk, where some clothes doubtless were hung; a bench stood on the side opposite the window, with three straight-backed, homemade chairs. Dane sank down in one of these, watching the dim shadows from the lamp play upon the walls, as the wind sifted in through cracks in the chinking.

The old man sat upon the edge of the bunk, peering with bright, reddened eyes about the dim room. Dane thought his teeth were chattering. He was clasping and unclasping his thin, bony, shaking hands. He curled back his lips against his yellow teeth, and his bare toes beat a restless tattoo against the rough boards of the floor.

Even with the window darkened by its coverings and the lamp lit, flashes of lightning could still be sensed, and the booming artillery of the storm seemed to shake the cabin. With each terrific crash of thunder the hermit would look at Dane out of frightened eyes. The thunder and the roar of wind and rain made speech impossible, as the mighty fury of the storm was unleashed.

Although he could not see it, Dane knew that the lightning flashes played incessantly, for the echoes of one clash of thunder did not have time to die away before there was another crash. The rain was falling on the roof with the force of a cloudburst, and the cracking of branches torn asunder by the wind could be heard in momentary lulls, when the storm seemed to pause briefly for a fresh outburst of even greater ferocity.

The old man cowered on the bunk, while Dane watched him and wondered. His abject fear of the storm was pitiful. And Dane sensed that the hermit was glad of his company at this moment. Then he began to doubt. The clutching fingers, the chattering teeth, and the twitching toes might well be caused by extreme nervousness. But the look in the eyes!

He regarded the hermit narrowly. It hardly seemed within reason that a man should be a prey to such terror of a storm, even though the storm be a bad one, as in this instance. There was something about the old man's eyes which fascinated and chilled him; it was more than the wide-eyed glimmer of fear. Dane imagined it was the piercing gleam and cunning glitter of insanity. Perhaps the old hermit was mad!

But Bunker hadn't been afraid of him; nor had he seemingly treated him with the tolerant and soothing tactics ordinarily adopted toward a demented person. Why had Bunker been angry?

The ferocity of the storm now began suddenly to diminish, as is the rule with electrical disturbances in the prairie country. The thunder was less violent and began to rumble distantly. The wind abated, and the downpour suddenly slackened until the rain merely beat upon the roof, with the gentleness characteristic of a passing shower. Finally the thunder died to a distant muttering.

"It's all over," said Dane, as cheerfully as possible.

The hermit looked at him doubtfully, stared for a moment at the floor, and then went to the window and pushed aside the curtain. It was now bright outside. The trees on the slope of the ridge were a vivid green. The rain ceased with the same abruptness with which it had come, and a ray of brilliant sunlight shot down through a rift in the lifting clouds.

Dane opened the door, and the first thing he saw was the old man's rifle, lying on the ground where he had dropped it. Dane went out and secured the rifle, brought it back to the cabin, and put it in the corner opposite the stove.

The hermit paid no attention to it.

"You live here?" Dane asked.

The old man looked at him vaguely; then his gaze shifted to the clearing, which now was again flooded with sunlight. The trees were dripping diamonds, and Dane saw his horse feeding on the farther side of the meadow.

"You live here?" Dane persisted, as the hermit came to the door and looked out.

"Yes, this is where I live," replied the old man in a matter-of-fact tone to Dane's surprise.
"Whose horse was that?" the hermit asked eagerly.

Dane assumed that he referred to the stallion he had seen in the meadow to the east. "Belongs to the Diamond H Ranch," he replied.

"Nice horse," the hermit commented shortly. "It was a bad storm," he added, caressing his silky, white beard. "Very bad storm."

Dane shrugged. He felt that his suspicions about the hermit's mentality were at least partially correct. And he was curious.

"Who was the man on horseback who was talking to you just before I came?" he asked, intending to feel the hermit out.

The old man looked at him quickly, with fear shining in his eyes. He wet his withered lips with his tongue.

"He is the master," was the puzzling reply. "He lets me live here. But he doesn't know," the hermit cackled; "an' he's afraid. I can tell. I know much, I do, and all the wild ones are my friends."

Dane shook his head impatiently. It was all so much dribble. The hermit *was* crazy. And why shouldn't he be, living there in the solitude, a slave to his fear of storms, alone with his warped thoughts.

However, the word "master" conveyed something. Bunker must have some kind of a hold on the old man. And for what purpose?

"Why does he let you live here?" he asked without expecting an intelligent answer.

"Because he has to," the hermit retorted fiercely. "Only he don't know that."

Dane reflected that this was reasonable. But did the old man mean it, as he had expressed it?

At this moment two horses broke through the timber at the right of the clearing and trotted a few paces toward the cabin. The hermit stepped out toward them, but they seemed to be looking at Dane. In a flash they whirled and dashed away out of sight. The hermit looked at Dane with blazing eyes, as the latter realized that the horses were wild mustangs which evidently ranged at will in the bad lands.

The fierce look in the hermit's eyes of faded blue died away. He appeared to inspect Dane thoroughly for the first time, and Dane found himself uneasy under the old man's searching scrutiny.

He thought it queer that the hermit did not ask him his name, or where he was from. Yet on second thought this did not seem queer, either. His own desolate domain was evidently sufficient for the hermit; his interest more than likely began and ended there. Yet the whole business was so unusual that Dane found himself probing his mind for some kind of a solution. It all resolved into one thing: The hermit was crazy, and Matt Bunker was in some way taking advantage of him for reasons of his own.

"Have you seen any stray cattle aroun' here?" he asked.

"No," snapped the hermit.

But Dane was instantly alert; for he had seen a look of cunning come into the other's eyes.

"You haven't seen any cattle a-tall?" he demanded sternly.

"Of course not," returned the hermit, and he turned and strode to the cabin.

Dane followed him. He stood undecided and looked on curiously, while the old man built a fire in the stove. Then the hermit pulled aside a piece of carpet in the center of the floor and opened a trapdoor. Dane caught his breath in astonishment. A small cellar was revealed. He stepped forward to look into it wonderingly. Hanging from a suspended wire were several hams and fully a dozen slabs of bacon, while below were case after case of canned goods and other provisions. There was a bin of potatoes. Enough supplies to keep a man like the hermit for more than a year!

The hermit climbed out with some things, shut the trapdoor, and replaced the bit of carpet.

Dane kept back the question which was on his lips.

"Will you show me the trail to the Flying W?" he asked at last.

"There is no trail," answered the hermit, busying himself at the stove.

"But that man who was here rode off toward the west," said Dane in an irritated voice.

"There is no trail," repeated the hermit fiercely.

Dane shrugged in resignation. Apparently anything to be learned from the hermit was to be learned accidently by the tedious process of baiting him in an irrelevant conversation. But Dane felt he had learned something of value. The presence of Bunker, the large amount of supplies in the hermit's cabin, the old man's quick denial of any knowledge of cattle or trails, convinced Dane that the cabin in the bad lands was the center of some kind of activity which could best be carried on in such a wild and little-visited section.

And he hadn't forgotten about the missing Diamond H stock. He left the cabin with his saddle and bridle and went to his horse. Later he rode to the west side of the clearing and explored the ridge on that side. He could find no trail, although he was sure one was there somewhere. He gave it up finally and crossed the clearing to the trees on the west side, where he speedily picked up the trail down which he and Servais had pursued the stallion. He had no trouble in following this trail to its outlet from the bad lands. It was afternoon when he reached the ranch. He saw Servais in the barn.

"Got soaking wet," grinned Servais, and Dane knew he had the little wrangler for a friend.

CHAPTER IX
BUSINESS

It was from old Marty that Dane learned something of the baffling history of the hermit. No one knew the old man's name, it seemed. He had appeared in the country many years before, had worked for a time on the Flying W before Williams had bought the ranch, and then had disappeared. Later a man answering his description had been seen in the bad lands. Marty had never seen the hermit, but he was of the opinion that he was the same man who once had worked on the Flying W.

But even Marty's attempts to explain the presence of the hermit in the brakes of the river were unconvincing. And Dane, for reasons of his own, did not make known what he had seen, or did he give any details of his visit to the cabin in the clearing. He approached Gordon Hughes that evening, however, with the request that he run about a hundred head of cattle in the bottoms, near the contested strip between the two ranches.

"You haven't lost any more cattle?" he asked the stockman.

"Not that I know of," Hughes replied, frowning. "But I ain't been missin' 'em in very big bunches, an' maybe some more are gone. I can't count every day or two. I'm runnin' the beeves east an' will take 'em on the north range toward the springs next week. We're through branding down here an' have got to head north, anyway. What's your idea in puttin' some over there in the bottoms?"

"That's where the most of 'em turned up missing, wasn't it?" Dane countered.

The stockman nodded with a look of understanding.

"Well, we'll give 'em a chance to get some more, an' maybe they'll trip themselves up," said Dane.

Hughes appeared on the point of asking a question, but he merely shrugged instead and favored Dane with a searching glance.

"All right," he said finally. "I'll put a mixed herd over there to-morrow. You'll have to keep an eye on 'em yourself, for we'll be on the north range."

Dane agreed and sought the bunk house. He didn't walk up on the bench this night, for he believed that Esther Hughes was watching him and might join him. He told himself that he didn't want to talk to her or listen to her newfangled notions about the West. And she had said she believed she hated him. So much the better. He had no time to bother with women, especially with women who were trying to balance the effete opinions of the East against the traditional judgment of the West.

Dane went out in the morning and helped Gordon Hughes drive the bunch of cattle into the bottoms west of the ranch buildings. When they were returning they saw a small car coming along the road from town. Hughes knit his brows in a scowl.

"That's Stevens, from the American Bank in Black Butte," he said shortly. "I wonder what *he* wants."

Dane could think of no reply, so he kept silent. But he decided to stick around the ranch that afternoon.

As Gordon Hughes rode on to the house, Dane, dismounting near the barn, saw a small man striding toward the porch. This, he assumed, was Sam Stevens, the banker from Black Butte. He walked nervously, and, as he removed his hat to wipe his forehead, Dane saw that he was bald, and that his face was a pale, pasty color. He was looking about with quick, darting glances, apparently missing none of the orderly details of the ranch's appearance.

Dane turned to put up his horse, as he saw Hughes dismount and greet the banker at the porch.

"How'd you happen to come out?" boomed the rancher. "Ain't none of my paper due yet, is there Stevens?"

"Not quite," replied the banker, nervously offering a lukewarm hand. "But I thought we'd better have a little talk."

"Sure," said Hughes, looking at the other closely. "How'd you like the looks of the place?"

Stevens's face brightened. "First rate," he answered, nodding. "Looks good. Cattle picking up and feed first class, I'd say. You'll have lots of hay this year. Now if we only get a decent winter—" He cut off his speech with a sigh.

"Bound to get one this year," said Hughes heartily, pulling out a chair for his guest and sitting down with him. "The weather's got to average up in three years out of four."

"I hope so," said the banker with a gloomy look. "Last two years have put the banks in awful bad, Gordon."

"An' they've hit us fellows harder'n the banks," said Hughes quickly. "But prices are goin' up, an' the cattle are doin' well; so we'll pan out all right. My fall shipment will leave me sittin' pretty, an' next year, with any luck at all, I'll pretty near clear."

"I hope so," said the banker again. "But unfortunately it is a case of needing cash badly with the banks. We have been very liberal in the matter of loans, as you know, and we are going to have to insist that obligations be met promptly."

"Now why do you come to me with all this?" Gorden Hughes demanded with a frown. "Do you figure there is any question about my meetin' my obligations? An' don't talk about the banks. Your American is the only bank I'm doin' business with."

"Quite so," agreed the banker. "That's fair. And it's in the affairs of the American that I'm interested, of course. I'm looking after the interests of my bank, quite naturally. And I haven't come to you alone; I'm visiting all who have heavy loans with the American. It is, of course, purely a matter of business."

"When is my first paper due?" asked Hughes with a scowl.

"You didn't have to buy hay this year until early in February," said the banker. "But you secured yourself for that hay in January—January the fifteenth, I believe. You will remember I told you I couldn't make the note for more than six months. It was for six thousand, if I remember correctly. That note is due the fifteenth of next month, Gordon."

"An' what of it?" said the rancher impatiently. "That isn't a marker to what I've borrowed. You see how the range is, an' how the cattle are lookin'. What're you worryin' about?"

"About cash, Gordon," replied the banker in a low voice. "It's cash I need. We've got to get in these loans; we must—"

"Wait a minute, Stevens," Gordon Hughes broke in. "Do I understand you're tryin' to tell me that you've got to have that six thousand by July fifteenth? Is that what you're tryin' to say?"

"That's about it, Gordon," said the banker soothingly. "Now wait a minute. Don't become angry, or we'll never get anywhere. I want to explain something to you. You stockmen never can seem to understand what a bank is up against. Take your own case for instance. When you bought the shorthorns, which I advised against—"

"There you go, harpin' about the shorthorns," Hughes interrupted in a loud voice. "That bunch of shorthorns is worryin' you to death, I take it. Well, we wasn't havin' such bad winters when I bought them cattle, an' I had more hay than I could use. I know they're not good rustlers an' have to be fed, but I had the feed for 'em. An' they make a bigger beef in the end. I'm goin' to start cleaning up on the shorthorns this fall, an' if it'll ease your mind any, I can tell you I'm off 'em an' am goin' to put in all Herefords."

"That's right," nodded the banker. "I'm glad to hear it—mighty glad. Very good judgment, because you can't always depend on the weather or your hay crop, an' a whiteface will find feed where a shorthorn will starve.

"But, nevertheless, when you bought the shorthorns I loaned you thirty dollars a head on 'em. That was all right at the time, and the security was good. Then came the first bad winter when you had to feed, and hay went up out of sight, and I had to loan nearly fifteen dollars a head more on those cattle to protect my security. And you had losses. By the next spring I had loaned, counting the reduction in the herd, something like fifty-five dollars a head on those cattle. And you had other cattle which had to be fed."

"Dang it! Can I regulate the weather?" stormed Hughes. "Was it my fault I had to feed? You was protectin' yourself when you was protectin' me."

"That's true," Stevens agreed. "An' I've had to protect you and myself to the tune of twenty dollars a head more since," he added grimly. "I've got around seventy-five dollars a head loaned on those cattle right this minute."

"An' I'll get better than fifty thousand dollars clear for the beeves this fall," retorted Hughes. "That's more'n you've got loaned on the whole bunch—almost."

"Exactly," nodded the banker. "I know all that. But I just wanted to show you how the banks—how the American got into the thing over its head, you might say. We've got too much loaned out, and we've got to protect ourselves. I'm merely warning you, Gordon, and others, that all obligations to the bank will have to be met promptly. We're in too deep."

"Sure you're in deep," snorted Hughes. "An' who's goin' to pull you out? I'll bet right now that the bulk of your loans ain't to stockmen at all, but to the dry farmers up north an' out west there. They was goin' to turn this whole range into a big wheat field, an' everybody was goin' to get too rich to live. You swallered it, an' you ain't seen a crop yet!"

"The dry-land farmers have had three years of drought, just like you've had three bad winters for stock."

"Is this a farmin' country?" demanded Hughes. "Did you ever see any crops raised up here? Did you ever see anybody tryin' to raise wheat here until those crazy homesteaders came in? Say, Stevens, I happen to know that you loaned thirty thousand dollars to a farmer to lease an' work an' seed two thousand acres of leased land, two years in succession, an' you ain't got a dollar back yet! An' you ain't got no security! But you've got security with the stockmen, an' the stockmen is the ones that'll pull you out of the hole, although it'll take three years to do it."

The banker was frowning. "There isn't a bank north of the Missouri that didn't try to help the farmers when they came in," he said irritably. "And most of my loans in that direction are secured by deeded land."

"An' what's the land worth?" cried Hughes. "The land's good for nothin' but stock raisin', and the last three years has proved that. An' land ain't worth no thirty or forty dollars an acre for range."

"That's beside the point," snapped the banker.

"I didn't come here to discuss that. Anyway I'm most concerned with those loans which are best secured. Your loan is one of them. There's just one point that I'll have to insist on being cleared up before I renew the note due July fifteenth. I suppose you'll want it renewed?"

"Of course I'll want it renewed," said Hughes. "I want it renewed until after I make my fall shipment. None of the rest of my paper falls due before October first. What is it you want cleared up? You want me to sign a new note now?"

"No," smiled the banker; "but I want the boundary between the Diamond H and the Flying W adjusted."

"What's that?" exclaimed Hughes.

"The boundary line between the Diamond H and the Flying W must be definitely established," said Stevens firmly.

"What in thunder has the boundary got to do with my business with the bank, Stevens?" Gordon Hughes thundered.

"It's a matter of protecting my security," explained Stevens in a hard voice. "The ranch is security for your loans as well as the cattle. But it isn't particularly good security when its boundaries are not all established, and when there is a feud between the two ranches, and a feeling present which might make it unpleasant for anyone who took over the ranch in—er—a case of necessity."

Gordon Hughes leaped to his feet. "Stevens, what are you tryin' to do?" he demanded, stepping close to the banker, who rose hurriedly.

"Exactly what I said—determine the boundary between the Diamond H and the Flying W for once and all. Establish that line, and I'll extend your note due next month for three months more, which will give you a chance to ship. It's almost the end of June now and I'd advise you to act quickly."

Hughes's fists were clenched. His lips were compressed into a menacing white line. His eyes glittered dangerously.

"There's something behind this, Stevens," he said hoarsely, as the banker hastily walked to the steps and down them. Then he went into the house without another word to the departing banker. Mrs. Hughes and Esther came into the little office in the front of the house to find Gordon Hughes strapping on his gun.

"Why, Gordon!" said his wife, surprised. "Why are you putting on your gun?" She saw the look in his eyes. "Gordon, what is the matter?"

He didn't answer her, but strode toward the front door.

"Gordon!" called Mrs. Hughes. "Where are you going?"

"I'm goin' to the Flying W," said Hughes grimly, as he went out.

CHAPTER X
ACROSS THE LINE

Walking to thc bunk house, Dane was surprised when Gordon Hughes galloped past him, looking grimly ahead, and flashed past the barns and corrals and on toward the lower bottoms. He had noticed, too, that Hughes wore a gun for the first time since he had known him. The big stockman ordinarily went unarmed, although Dane had suspected this would not be the case when the rancher went up to the north range.

As he turned again toward the bunk house, he saw Esther Hughes running toward him from the porch. Her hair was flying in the wind, her lips were parted, and her eyes shone with burning excitement.

"Mr. Dane!" she called breathlessly and held a hand up toward him.

He walked to meet her.

"Get your horse," she cried, as she came up to him. "I'll go with you," she said. "Oh, I'm afraid something terrible is going to happen. Mother is worried to death, and we don't know where Fred is—and it probably wouldn't do any good if he was here."

She had started walking rapidly for the barn with Dane at her side.

"Where are we goin'?" he inquired mildly.

"To get your horse. Oh, you must hurry. You must follow father as fast as you can!"

Dane remembered Gordon Hughes riding madly toward the west.

"Where has your father gone?" he asked, as they reached the barn, and he went in to saddle the bay.

"He's gone to the Flying W," said the girl, following him. "You must hurry, and—oh, Mr. Dane, do not let anything happen."

Dane whistled softly. "What's he gone over there for?" he asked wonderingly.

"Something the banker said, I guess," replied Esther. "They were talking on the porch—Mr. Stevens and dad—and father got angry and put on his gun."

Her worried gaze flashed to the weapon at Dane's side, and she turned half away. Then she swung about to confront him, as he tightened the saddle cinch and led the bay out of the stall.

"You can catch up with him," she said eagerly. "Maybe you can stop him from going there. It's dangerous for dad to go to the Flying W. He must be going to see old man Williams, or maybe that horrid new foreman. Oh, try to stop him, and if you can't stop him—*help* him!"

Dane smiled at the excited girl. What a beauty she was under the stress of her emotion!

"I reckon your dad knows what he's goin' over

there for, an' who he's goin' to see," he said; "an' I don't figure I could stop him. But if he needs any help, well, I'm workin' for him."

He swung lightly into the saddle.

"Go back to your mother," he advised. "Gordon Hughes is no fool. I don't reckon you've got much cause to worry about him."

There were tears of doubt in the girl's eyes, but she looked at him gratefully.

"Ride!" she called after him, as he touched the bay with his spurs, left the barn, and turned down toward the bottoms.

She watched him out of sight, then turned and ran for the house where she could see her mother standing on the porch.

Dane, as he rode westward, did not himself feel the confidence which he had endeavored to impart to the girl. Gordon Hughes was not riding to the Flying W on any peaceful mission. Esther's reference to the banker indicated that Stevens's visit had in some way brought some phase of the trouble with the neighboring ranch to a head, and Hughes was riding to see about it.

Dane didn't regard the incident of Hughes taking his gun along as necessarily important. He naturally would go armed on hostile territory. And it was hardly probable Hughes and Williams would get to shooting. They should have too much sense for that. Bunker, of course, was an entirely different sort of person. He was a gun fighter and made no bones about it. But if Hughes met him, his good sense ought to prevail, for the rancher certainly knew he would be no match for the Flying W foreman in a fast gun play.

When he reached the bottoms Dane could not see Hughes. Evidently the rancher's horse was fast, and Dane remembered it was a large animal. Inspection had shown him that Hughes had an excellent strain of saddle horses on the Diamond H.

Dane rode swiftly along the bottom until he reached the tall cottonwood which marked the logical dividing line between the two ranches. As he crossed the line, he turned south and passed through a big grove of cottonwoods and alders which shut off the view of the Flying W's lower range. When he emerged from the trees he saw a herd of cattle to the left some distance ahead. And then he glimpsed Gordon Hughes riding at a fast pace toward this herd.

Swinging to the left to be close to the tree growth which marked the beginning of the brakes, Dane rode in a semicircle toward the herd which plainly was Gordon Hughes's objective.

He saw the owner of the Diamond H ride south of the herd and pull up his horse near a rider who evidently was watching the cattle. He proceeded slowly and soon made out Hughes riding beyond the herd. Now he descried another horseman coming from the west. When Hughes met this rider he stopped again, and this time he did not ride on.

Dane turned his horse into the timber to avoid being seen and slowly proceeded westward in the general direction of Hughes and the others who were sitting their horses on the bottom some distance out from the screen of timber.

Gordon Hughes was looking steadily into the eyes of Oscar Williams, owner of the Flying W. If Williams was surprised to meet the Diamond H owner on his property, he did not show it. He returned Hughes's gaze with a coolly questioning expression. He was a smaller man than Hughes, with a lean face, much wrinkled, blue eyes that were small and cruel; they gave one the impression of craftiness and the ability to hate without compromise. He was supposed to have come from the Southland. He was round-shouldered and sat his saddle with a pronounced stoop. He had a habit of lowering his head and looking out from under thin brows. He fussed with his bridle reins nervously, and he was armed.

"Did Stevens see you to-day?" demanded Gordon Hughes coldly.

"Yes," replied Williams shortly. He had a high-pitched voice.

"Suppose he made the same proposition to you that he made to me," scowled Hughes.

"Don't know anything about propositions," said Williams. "He said he wanted the ranch lines fixed up."

Hughes glared at him. "Wonder how he got *that* idea so suddenlike."

"Dunno," said Williams, looking straight ahead. "It doesn't bother me any."

"I don't suppose you have to do any business with the bank," flared Hughes.

"I don't aim to let him run my ranch for me," said Williams.

"Then I reckon you don't care if the boundary is fixed up or not," said Hughes, his eyes narrowing.

"I don't need any fence to tell *me* where the line is," replied Williams angrily.

Hughes held his temper in check with difficulty. It was plain he was trying to keep whatever he was thinking to himself.

"Look here, Williams," he said finally, "this boundary business has got to be settled some time. We're both losing time an' money at present, runnin' our cattle away from the line an' leaving a lot of good range untouched. There ain't any sense to it. I reckon we'd be usin' our heads if we split the difference in land in two an' let it go at that. We've both got enough land, so we shouldn't have to haggle over a hundred foot or so."

"I had that land surveyed—paid out good

money to find where the line was, an' I found I own the big spring up north," Williams retorted. "I don't aim to lose that spring."

"An' I've had it surveyed, too," said Hughes harshly, "an' it was just the other way round. A survey can show anything, an' you know it. There ain't a cornerstone on a single one of those section lines. This country was all surveyed on horseback. Anyway we can both use that spring. If we split the strip, the line'll go through it."

"Might all be, but if you was to sell the Diamond H, the next owner mightn't be so agreeable," sneered Williams.

Hughes's eyes flashed. "If you hadn't said *that,* I might have *give* you the strip," he declared. "You've made trouble ever since you've been in here, Williams. I reckon you'd like to drive me out. You can't do it. I've been here a long time, an' I'm goin' to stay. If you don't want to come to an agreement about the boundary, I'll settle it one way or the other for both of us. *I'll fence it!*"

"An' be mighty careful where you build your fence," cried Williams, his face darkening with passion.

Dane, watching from the shelter of the trees directly south of the two men, saw Hughes's horse side-step. His eyes were glued to the strange scene, and some of the loudly spoken words had reached his ears. He was leaning forward in his saddle, and suddenly a thin shadow floated over him; he felt the sting of a rope against his face. Next moment he was jerked from his horse to the ground. He heard the echo of shots. Then his head seemed to explode, and the world was blotted out by black oblivion.

Gordon Hughes rode slowly up to the Diamond H ranch house on a lathered horse, spent by hard riding. Mrs. Hughes and Esther came out upon the porch, as he dismounted and looked at them wearily.

"Gordon!" cried his wife. "What is the matter? Oh, *what* has happened?"

The rancher turned a haggard face up to her.

"I've killed Williams!" he said dully, as he mounted the steps and sank into a chair.

CHAPTER XI
MISSING

Staring at the man in the chair, Esther Hughes and her mother stood as if stunned. The only sounds were the drone of the vagrant wind in the cottonwoods and the creak of the chair, as Gordon Hughes rocked slowly to and fro. Mrs. Hughes's sister came out and, struck by the sinister aspect of the scene, stood near the doorway.

"Don't look at me that way," said Hughes irritably. "It had to happen—Williams himself started it when he went for his gun."

"Oh, Gordon," sobbed his wife, as she dropped on her knees by the arm of his chair. "Oh, *why* did you do it? I knew something dreadful would happen when you put on your gun. All this trouble! It isn't worth it."

She couldn't keep back the tears. Her sister went to her side and stood over her, laying a hand upon her head.

"If that man Williams started it, it was his own fault," said Esther with heat.

She went to her father's side. "I know you wouldn't deliberately kill a man unless you *had* to, father," she said consolingly.

"Why, daddy, you're bleeding!"

Crimson drops were falling from Gordon Hughes's left hand which hung limp on the left side of his chair.

"Just nicked," he said with a vague look in his eyes. Evidently he still was thinking of his encounter with Williams on the Flying W range. "Don't amount to anything; but if my horse hadn't shied, I might have got it in the heart," he added, compressing his lips grimly.

"Are you shot, Gordon?" His wife was up in a minute and examining his left hand.

"Come into the house, Gordon," she said in a firm voice, her tears vanishing. "Your wound must be attended to. Come."

Gordon Hughes rose and walked slowly into the house. He was weary with the reaction from the excitement of the past few hours. He removed his coat and submitted without complaint to the ministrations of his womenfolk.

Mrs. Hughes bared his left arm, disclosing a wound just above the elbow.

"Thank God, it is just a flesh wound," she said and busied herself cleansing it, applying an antiseptic and bandaging it tenderly and carefully.

"There," she said when she had finished. "Now you want a cup or two of strong coffee, Gordon, and in a little while you must eat something."

The shock of her husband's announcement over, she had become practical. She went for the coffee which Hughes drank moodily.

"Now tell us how it happened, Gordon," said Mrs. Hughes.

"It just happened like those things happen, that's all," was the man's reply. "Stevens told me this mornin' I'd have to get the west boundary fixed up before he'd renew that note that's due next month. I'll bet Williams was behind it. He wanted the whole strip out west, because it'd give him the big spring up north. I'd have let him have it, but he went hintin' aroun', before I could tell him so, 'bout my sellin' the ranch maybe—only he meant I might *lose* the ranch." Gordon Hughes's face darkened wrathfully.

"I know what now," he declared loudly; "he wanted this place. I accused him of it after I told him I'd put a fence down the strip. Then there was some more words, an' he went for his gun. I heard two shots besides my own, an' Williams dropped from his horse like a sack of bran. I guess he was dead, the way he looked. I came on home with a cow-puncher who was herdin' cattle over there in the bottom."

"And where was Dane?" asked Esther who had been listening intently.

"Dane?" Gordon Hughes looked puzzled. "I didn't see Dane."

"Probably not," said Esther with a queer smile. "I guess he wasn't as anxious to go on the Flying W, as he tried to make me believe."

"Esther, what are you talking about?" demanded her father in a stern voice.

"Daddy, when I saw you were going to the Flying W, I was afraid you'd get into serious trouble," said Esther with spirit. "And I was afraid too, that they might try to take advantage of you over there. I told Dane, got him to saddle his horse and follow you. He said if you needed any help, he was working for you. It looks like it, I must say."

"You had no business to do that, daughter," said Gordon Hughes with a frown. "An' Dane had no business following me. If I'd wanted him along I'd have asked him, myself."

"I guess he knew his business then, because it's plain he didn't follow you as he promised," said the girl, her dark eyes flashing. "If he had been there, this thing might never have happened. Lightning Dane!" she scoffed. "They better change that Lightning to Lingering. I believe he's a *bluff!*"

"What do you mean by that?" her father asked curiously.

But Esther merely shrugged and evaded the question. Dane had failed her when she had asked him to do something which she thought was right in his line. And she couldn't forget his remark about working for her father. The day's events had, in her opinion, disproved that. If Bunker had been present at the meeting on the

Flying W, her father most likely would have been killed. Perhaps Dane had thought Bunker would be there—perhaps. Her lips curled in scorn.

"I wouldn't put too much trust or confidence in Mr. Dane," she said to her father. "He—"

"Look here, Esther, don't blame a man for minding his own business," Gordon Hughes interrupted. "He had no call to follow me onto that ranch, even if you did ask him to do it. He's takin' his orders from me, an' I didn't hire him for no bodyguard."

"What *did* you hire him for?" Esther couldn't resist asking.

"That's neither here nor there—now," scowled Hughes. "Go out an' find Servais. I think I saw him aroun' the barn."

Esther suddenly again was cognizant of the seriousness of the situation.

"Daddy, will they—will they be sending the sheriff?" she asked with a catch in her voice.

"Go an' get Servais," roared her father.

"Gordon!" exclaimed his wife aghast, as the girl went out. "Will they—will it be *that?*"

"It likely will," said Hughes grimly. "I'll probably have to go up to the county seat for a day or two until the bail can be fixed. I don't see how they can bring a charge of—" He paused thoughtfully. "I reckon there's still such a thing as self-defense in this country," he added, "although that cow-puncher who was takin' it in likely'll swear to anything. It's Williams' own fault; but I'd rather the thing had ended some other way."

Servais came in shortly afterward, and Hughes sent him out to the main herds to bring back Shay, the cow boss, and Fred. Meanwhile he ordered old Marty to be on the lookout for Dane and to send him to the house as soon as he came in.

With the arrival of Shay and Fred, the rancher began to give his orders for conducting the ranch during the period for which he expected to be away. He told Shay he would be in charge of the cattle. Fred was to keep his eye on things about the house and buildings and to keep in communication with his father. Servais was to have charge of the horses.

Even the most remote contact with the Flying W, or any of the Flying W men, was absolutely forbidden. There must be no more trouble, Gordon Hughes pointed out sternly.

Other details of the ranch management were gone into, and Hughes and Shay were in conference the remainder of the afternoon. The sputtering of the little ranch car was heard in the late afternoon, and Mrs. Hughes came into the office, a worried look on her face.

"It's Fred," she said, as the purr of the motor died away in the distance; "he's gone to Black Butte to find out what he can. I didn't want him to go, but he insisted."

"I don't think there'll be any trouble," said

Hughes. "He'll probably find the sheriff there when he gets in. Hasn't Dane shown up yet?"

His wife shook her head.

"I can't see, Gordon, why you rely on and seem to trust that man the way you do, when you know absolutely nothing about him," she said. "It isn't as if he was one of the old hands."

"I don't have to have a man's life history to hire him on this ranch," said Hughes. "What'd we know about any of the men we've got when they first came? We only knew what they told us, an' I didn't *ask* 'em that. A man'll show what he is sooner or later, an' I ain't got no kick coming on Dane so far."

"I suppose you know he receives a peculiar respect from the other men," said his wife. "If he is what they say he is, it's only bidding for trouble to have him here."

"Mary," said Hughes impatiently, "we ain't left the old conditions behind yet. It may be different in the towns, since the homesteaders have come, but it ain't much different out here. We're still runnin' cattle on a big scale, an' there's only one class of men as knows steers an' horses an' ropes an' branding irons an' guns—an' that ain't the class that'll ever turn this into a farming country."

Mrs. Hughes left the office with a sigh. Moreover she knew what her husband had said was true. If anything, the last years of the open range were more dangerous than the first.

At sundown Dane had not returned. Servais came back from a scouting expedition to the bottoms and near the Flying W, with the information that he had seen nothing of him. Marty appeared worried, which in itself was not a good sign.

Hughes was annoyed and puzzled. Considering what he had learned from Esther he thought it queer he hadn't seen Dane, and more puzzling that Dane hadn't returned to the ranch. And he wanted to see him before he went away.

They sat down to supper, but little was said during the meal. They were a silent crowd in the bunk house, too. The wranglers, wise in the ways of the range, anticipated trouble, although they could not predict how it would come. Loyalty to Gordon Hughes made them sympathetic for him. It was as if the shadow of tragedy had come over the ranch from an unexpected quarter.

Dane had not returned when night fell. The lamps in the house had been lighted, and the family was in the sitting room when the car was heard rattling down the road. Fred Hughes entered soon afterward, removed his gloves and hat and tossed them on the table. His father was watching him with a question in his eyes.

"Williams ain't dead," Fred announced shortly. "They've taken him to Conard in one of the stages."

Gordon Hughes straightened suddenly in his chair.

His mother sighed with relief. “Is—is he badly hurt, Fred?” she asked anxiously.

“Shot through the right shoulder an’ lung, I guess,” replied the boy. “Couldn’t find out much; everybody’s excited an’ talking. I don’t figure it’s so bad, though. Williams could ride in the seat.”

He sat down before his father.

“Dad, how was you sittin’ when Williams drew on you?”

“Sittin’ same’s I am in front of you,” said Hughes with a frown; “ ’cept I was on a horse, an’ so was he. An’ my horse shied when he pulled his gun—”

“Was you north of him or south of him, or how?” the boy interrupted.

“Why—I—he was between me an’ the brakes. I was north of him. What you askin’ that for?”

“He was sittin’ with his back to the trees?” said the youth with a vague look.

“Fred, tell us what you are talking about,” said his mother nervously. “Has the sheriff or anybody been notified?”

“I don’t reckon so,” said Fred Hughes with a grin. “An’ I don’t figure they’ll be callin’ in the sheriff or anybody else for a while.”

“Why do you say that?” his father demanded.

“Because old Williams was shot in the back!” declared the boy.

"In the *back?*" asked his father, bewildered.

"In the right shoulder, just under the collar bone, from behind," said Fred with emphasis. "Dad, your bullet never touched him, for that's the only place he was hit. The bullet struck a bone an' come out on the side, leavin' a jagged hole. He lost a lot of blood. I got that straight from Brady at The Palace who knows what he's talkin' about. You can't shoot any more, anyway, dad. An' everybody knows you wouldn't shoot a man in the back, no matter *what* you had it in for him for."

Gordon Hughes was staring at his son with an incredulous expression.

"It was somebody in the trees that shot Williams," Fred went on. "An' that ain't all. He was shot with a soft-nosed bullet. The hole it made shows that. Whoever wanted to get him, wanted to get him right!"

"From the trees?" Hughes muttered, wonderingly.

Fred nodded. "I guess we ain't the only ones that's got Williams' number," he said.

"Did you see Dane in town?" his father asked.

"No," replied Fred, looking interested. "Isn't he back yet?"

Hughes shook his head, and a sudden silence fell over the group.

"Tell Shay I'll want three men besides him an'

Servais in the morning," said the rancher, rising. "I'm goin' to bed."

Long after the others slept, Esther Hughes sat at her window, looking out over the moonlit open space of prairie and bottom land, thinking.

CHAPTER XII
MYSTERY

From far, far away came the "feel" of throbbing sound, gaining in volume, preserving a monotonous rhythm—as accurate as though it were regulated by the beating of time. It continued for what seemed ages, now farther away, now nearer, then suddenly close at hand, and Dane opened his eyes.

He was conscious first of a dull, aching pain in his head—in the back of his head and in his neck. He felt leaden, limp, spent. And he was fearfully thirsty. He twisted his head with a groan toward a faint light. He looked at this light without realizing what it was, as he strove to gather his shattered senses and his vague thoughts.

Then he remembered. Esther Hughes first, and her request that he follow her father to the Flying W. He saw her face, excited, flushed, fearful, as she urged him to "Ride!" He recollected the two horsemen on the bottom, just beyond the fringe of trees, where he sat his mount, watching. He saw the horse of the man on the farther side move suddenly, felt the sting of the rope again, the jerk and fall to the ground; heard the sound of shots, and then the awakening and the excruciating pain in his head and the thirst.

As he regained his mental faculties he realized that he was staring at the fading light of day through an open doorway. His gaze roved nearer where he lay, and he saw a pail of water on a bench.

He tried to raise himself and fell back with a groan, as the fiery lances of pain shot through his head. He raised an arm, heavy as lead, and felt his head. There was a great lump at the back, and his hair was sticky. His hand came away damp and slightly red from a blood clot.

He ground his teeth, shut his eyes, and fighting the pain the effort cost him, rose to a sitting posture. He knew, quite as an incidental matter of course, that he was on some kind of a bed. He got his feet over the edge, rested them upon the floor, reached for the pail on the bench near at hand.

It required both hands to bring it to his lips, but he managed to do so, and drank long and deep. The water was cool; it revived him somewhat. He removed his scarf, soaked it in the water, after he had drunk copiously again, and tied it about his aching head. He laved his temples with the water, bathed his face, held his hot hands in it—and it helped.

For the first time he took note of his surroundings. They seemed familiar. Then he remembered the bench, the table, the stove, the bunk. He was in the cabin of the hermit. He did not try to reason why he was there, nor how he had come to be roped, dragged from his horse, and dealt a stunning blow upon the head. He was too sick to reason—to think.

He moved back upon the bunk and lowered his head to the pallet of straw. And instantly he was in the throes of delirium. Riding, ever riding, with the thick dust swirling about him and the hot sun beating down upon his head. He could hear the bellowing of steers—a continual throbbing of sound which never ceased.

In a lucid moment he felt something cool against his feverish lips. Water! He drank long and eagerly. Water! Could he ever get enough water!

And then he was in a dance hall, and the girl, Marie, was singing to him; and there were many others, and the crack of guns—always that throb, throb, throb of never-ending sound.

During another lucid interval he again felt the cool touch to his lips and drank eagerly of the water. He saw vaguely through eyes that blurred and played queer tricks with his vision, and a lamp was burning on the table. He heard the wind whispering in the trees; and then he became unconscious. But the delirium had passed. He slept, and when he awoke his eyes were clear, the pain in his head was less severe, and he was not so thirsty.

The door to the cabin was open, and the bright morning sunlight was flooding in. He could see the green of the meadow and the trees on the slope of the ridge on its farther side. He was alone. A pail of water and a cup were on the table which had been pulled close to the head of the bunk. He took a drink of the clear, cold water, and it refreshed him. He found he could sit up without discomfort.

On the bench near the foot of the bunk were his hat, chaps, boots, spurs, cartridge belt, and holster. He frowned as he saw the holster was empty. His gun was gone.

He was startled by the sudden appearance of the hermit in the open doorway. The old man stood looking at him, fingering his white beard, mumbling in an undertone. Then he spoke aloud:

"How do you feel?"

"Pretty rocky," Dane confessed. "How'd I get here?"

The hermit advanced to the stove in which a fire was burning. "I brung you here," he said, inspecting a small pot on the top of the stove. He turned to regard Dane gravely. "You've been sick," he observed, quite as a matter of fact. "I thought maybe you'd die."

Dane scowled darkly. "Whatever put this lump on the back of my head was sure enough to put me out for keeps," he said. "How'd you happen to bring me here?"

"It's the only place I had to take you," replied the hermit gravely. "Where else would I take you?"

"But where'd you get hold of me—an' how?" snapped Dane, glaring at the hermit suspiciously.

"Found you under the trees west o' here, bleeding to death," the hermit replied soberly. "You must eat some of this." He took a bowl and dipped some of the contents of the pot into it; then he handed it with a spoon to Dane.

"Did you see my horse?" Dane asked.

"Yes; your horse followed me when I carried you here."

"Carried me!" Dane looked at the hermit; and then he saw that the old man was indeed sturdily built and undeniably was the possessor of great strength.

He tasted the contents of the bowl and found it to be a thick, rich gruel. To his surprise he ate hungrily. He could almost feel the strength returning to him. He looked over the steaming bowl at his belongings on the bench.

"Where's my gun?" he demanded crossly.

The hermit shook his head. "I didn't see it," he said loudly.

"Maybe it fell out of the holster when I hit the ground," said Dane, looking at the old man questioningly.

"I didn't see it," repeated the hermit with irritation, turning his back and pouring out a cup of strong, black coffee.

Dane looked angrily about the cabin, undecided what to say next. He saw the hermit's rifle leaning against the wall near the stove, saw a long, rawhide lariat hung on a peg near the door, saw a saddle and bridle on a peg below it. This surprised him. He was quite certain that the rope, saddle, and bridle hadn't been there on the occasion of his previous visit. He started to ask a question, but desisted. He felt that after all he was under obligations to the old man. Whatever the hermit's reason for succoring him, he had probably saved his life. Yet something convinced him that the hermit was not telling all he knew by any means. He suspected he could learn something of value if he could only some time get the hermit to talk. Now he took the cup of hot coffee which the old man held out to him.

"I'm sure much obliged to you for all this," he thanked him. "I guess you saved my life yesterday."

The hermit stared at him thoughtfully, mumbled something to himself, and turned away.

"Crazy as a bat!" Dane thought to himself. "Reckon he don't know half what he's doin'."

He looked again at the saddle and received another shock.

"Sufferin' coyotes!" he murmured aloud. "Am I cracked, too?"

The saddle was his own, and he saw his own lariat hanging from it. This seemed to explain why the hermit had carried him. There was no saddle or horse belonging to the hermit which Dane had seen. The hermit must have been afoot and had preferred to carry him rather than attempt to transport him on the horse. Dane knew by experience that the bay would object to carrying a dead-weight, and that he would not lead.

The hermit sat down to his own breakfast.

"Did you see anybody else out there where you found me?" Dane asked, putting the empty bowl on the table.

"No," answered the hermit shortly.

Dane wanted to ask if he had seen the meeting between Hughes and the other rider whom he suspected was Williams of the Flying W. He knew it wasn't Bunker. Yet, for reasons which were not quite clear to himself, he didn't wish the hermit to know he was interested in this meeting. What had the hermit been doing there?

"Did you hear any shots before you found me?" asked Dane, watching the hermit narrowly.

"No," was the reply.

From past experience Dane knew the old man was done talking. He swung down from the bunk and stood for a few moments unsteadily. He was strangely weak in the knees, and he didn't feel at all like himself. He pulled on his boots, buckled on his chaps, and, sitting on the bench, he affixed his spurs. He turned his hat thoughtfully in his hands before he put it on. He frowned, as he picked up the cartridge belt with the empty holster. Again he looked at the hermit with suspicion. Yet the old man's story had "listened" true enough. And there had been no attempt to hold him prisoner. It must be that whoever had dealt him that blow upon the head, had either left him for dead, or had some mysterious reason for wanting to leave him alive, but nearly dead, or had wished to conceal his identity.

But Dane couldn't see the sense, under the circumstances, in taking his gun.

"Your horse is out back," said the hermit without looking at him. "Your saddle an' bridle's by the door." Then he went on eating, apparently oblivious to the other's presence.

Dane took his saddle and bridle and rope, which he saw was his, and staggered out of the cabin, calling back his thanks.

He found his horse in a makeshift corral behind the cabin, saddled and bridled him, and mounted with what seemed the very last iota of his strength. He sat in the saddle, breathing heavily, for a short space and then rode out into the clearing. The hermit was standing in the cabin doorway. He made no sign that he saw Dane leaving, and the latter walked his horse toward the fringe of trees at the eastern edge, where he knew he would strike the trail leading to the Diamond H bottoms.

Just as he gained the trees he heard the pound

of hoofs across the clearing, the sharp crack of a gun, and a bullet whined past him. He put the spurs to the bay and, as he plunged into the trees, flashed a look over his shoulder.

Two men were riding furiously across the clearing. Hot lead clipped the leaves about him, as shots sounded. The bay dodged through the trees and dashed across the open meadow beyond, urged by the relentless bite of Dane's steel. They darted into the trail and around a ridge, as more shots came from the two who were riding hotly in pursuit.

On either side of the trail the timber was thick, and Dane, pushing the bay for all he was worth, increased his lead. Where the trail swung eastward at the upper end of the ridge Dane left it, swerved to the left into the timber, and rode over the end of the ridge, sheltered by the trees, into a deep ravine. He was now directly north of the cabin, and he looked hastily about. Soon he saw what he was looking for—a small blaze on a tree. He swung northward and soon saw another blaze. He rode northeastward, following the blazes which he had made on the occasion of his first finding of the cabin on the morning after he had followed Marie to the bad lands and had ventured in to become lost.

In this way he lost his pursuers. He thought steadily, as he rode along the difficult trail, marked only by the slashes on the tree trunks, cut by his knife. The lids were narrowed over his eyes, which were gleaming with a steel-blue light. In that fleeting glance over his shoulder, as he left the clearing, he had seen that Matt Bunker was one of his pursuers!

Had Bunker known that he was at the hermit's cabin? And, if so, how did it come that he was aware of the fact?

These thoughts caused Dane's face to darken, as he rode cautiously out of the bad lands to the Diamond H bottoms and galloped eastward past the hundred head of cattle grazing there.

As he approached the ranch he began to think about the shots he had heard after he had been roped and dragged from his horse. Had Hughes and the other man had trouble? Had the thing which he would have prevented come to pass?

There was little of the youthful, dreamy look in his eyes as he pushed on across the bottoms. He pulled his hat down against the brilliant rays of the early-morning sun. He felt very sick. His head was aching again. Then he saw a rider approaching. He smothered an exclamation, as he recognized Esther Hughes in the saddle.

CHAPTER XIII

"DON'T SAY IT!"

The very freshness of the morning was in Esther Hughes's face. The olive-tinted skin of her cheeks glowed like a blooming rose, with the exhilarating whip of the wind. She sat her horse, a splendid chestnut, with the graceful abandon of one born to the saddle. Wisps of dark hair caressed her ears from under the cap set rakishly on her head. She rode astride in riding breeches and boots, and a dark-blue blouse and flowing, red four-in-hand enhanced her natural beauty.

Dane gazed at her in frank admiration, as she pulled up her horse beside him.

His smile vanished, however, as he saw the coolly speculative look in her eyes.

"So!" she said with a lifting of her brows. "You're back."

"I expect it looks that way," said Dane. He did not feel in a mood for much talk. He was weak, and his head was throbbing. He felt hot and was again craving water.

"Father and some of the men were about to go and search for you," she volunteered, looking at him steadily.

The quality of her gaze irritated him—made

him feel uncomfortable. Why did she look at him like that? It was as if he had done something wrong. He sensed that for some reason he was being disciplined. He resented it.

"That's peculiar," he said. "I've been gone before without any search parties being sent out, or is this a posse?"

"This is hardly the time for sarcasm," she said coldly. "I can only say that I am surprised and mystified, Mr. Lightning Dane."

He frowned. "An' I can only say that I don't know what you're driving at, ma'am," he retorted, his irritation putting a belligerent note into his voice.

"After the events of yesterday I should think you would understand my—my disappointment," she said a bit haughtily. "I took you at your word, Mr. Dane, when you said if father needed any help that you were working for him. I took it to imply that you would follow him and try to prevent trouble."

"I followed him," snapped Dane. His head was splitting. He could hardly see. It was almost impossible to think.

She took his evident discomfiture for a mental rather than a physical state—misplaced its cause.

"Rather interesting that he didn't see you," she observed pointedly.

"I didn't aim that he should see me unless it was necessary," he returned.

"I suppose you were hiding in the trees, and that very likely explains it all."

"Meanin' what, ma'am?"

"I don't suppose you remember anything," she taunted.

"I don't remember very much, an' that's a fact," he said, putting a hand to his head. The world seemed revolving about him. He saw the green of the bottoms and the bright sunlight, as through a veil of mist which wavered before his aching eyes.

"It is surprising, Mr. Dane, how much has happened since you arrived," she said mockingly.

"An' you may have some more surprises comin' before I leave," he said in a voice which seemed to him to come from far away.

"No doubt. And father likely will get blamed for it all."

"I reckon I ain't tryin' to hang the blame for anything *I* do on anybody else's shoulders, if *that's* what you mean, ma'am," he said tartly, resenting her insinuation.

"Then I suppose you will, perhaps, be willing to assume the responsibility for what happened yesterday, Mr. Dane?"

Her words brought him to himself. "What was it that *happened* yesterday?" he demanded, scowling.

"Oh, it's ridiculous," she said impatiently, "but

I'll go on. Father met that man Williams, and there was trouble."

"I saw 'em sort of squarin' off," he said, momentarily shaking off the pain and fever which gripped him and exercising all his will power. "Who did the shootin'? I heard shots."

"Oh, you *saw* them. Then you *must* have been in the trees. And you *heard* shots! How extraordinary. Bravado! But I thought gunmen fought in the open, Mr. Dane."

"What're you talking about?" he cried.

"I'll explain it all to you," she said with a mocking smile. "Williams drew his weapon and shot father in the arm. Father shot to protect himself, and his bullet went wild. Then Williams fell from his horse, shot in the back."

"I *heard* three shots," said Dane wonderingly, half to himself.

"Williams' back was toward the trees," Esther pointed out, meaningly.

He looked at her thoughtfully. "Somebody shot him from the trees?" he said vaguely.

"Where you were, Mr. Dane. Is that the way you intended to protect my father? He will be accused of shooting a man in the back because you"—she looked at him with scornful accusation shining in her eyes—"you hid—"

"Don't say it!" thundered Dane, the world wheeling about him. "Don't say it—unless

you want me to have to remember I once told a woman—she *lied!*"

A pain, sharp, excruciating, shot through his head. The girl, sitting before him, was a dim figure with a hazy background. The fever mounted in his veins.

"Oh!" she exclaimed, placing a hand to her throat. The color left her face, as she saw the strange look in his eyes. They appeared bloodshot with anger.

"I don't presume I should expect a gunman to be chivalrous," she said icily.

"I'm chivalrous enough to warn you not to take advantage of the fact that you're a girl," he managed to say. "I might *kill* a *man,* if he said what you was goin' to say." His voice wavered, and he looked about unsteadily.

She mistook his apparent distress for rage and nervousness. It seemed proof conclusive of his guilt. Her lips curled in contempt. Without another word she whirled her horse and galloped toward the ranch buildings.

Dane urged his horse ahead. He leaned far forward, holding to the horn of his saddle with both hands. The landscape was whirling again; his vision was dim; the pains were shooting through his head, and his lips and tongue were dry; his throat was burning with thirst.

He thought no more of what the girl had said; forgot his resentment at her unjust accusation. He could think only of the pain in his head. He was fearfully hot. He tore his shirt open in front. He needed air and water.

He roused himself with difficulty; saw the dim outlines of the big hay shed ahead. Passed it, clinging to the saddle horn and swaying in his seat. His horse broke into a trot, as he neared the barn, and Dane pulled him up, fearful lest he should fall from the saddle. He went on past the barn to the bunk house. He saw, as through a fog, that there were horsemen near the barn. He thought he heard his name whispered on the breeze.

Old Marty came running out to meet him.

He halted before the bunk house, slowly rose in the saddle and lifted his right foot from the stirrup to dismount. Then his strength left him, and he fell backward into old Marty's arms.

CHAPTER XIV
"IN THE SHADOW"

There is something tragic about a serious illness on a ranch in the open country. It may be because the ranch is a little community by itself, set off from other habitations, many miles distant, perhaps, from a town, and the welfare of all, therefore, of concern to each individual. Or, it may be because medical aid is obtained with difficulty at the cost of considerable time and effort, and is more or less transitory. And, as sickness is not common among people who lead an outdoor life, an unusual importance attaches to it when it comes.

Thus, when Dane toppled from his horse into Marty's arms, there was curiosity and then consternation at the Diamond H.

"Carry him into the house," Gordon Hughes instructed Shay and Fred, when it was found that Dane was unconscious.

They carried him to the sitting room where there was a quick examination by the rancher and his wife.

They found a deep cut, clotted with blood, in the back of his head.

"Looks like it'd been done with the butt of a

six-shooter," said Hughes softly. Then, looking about: "Fred, go to town an' get Doc Ross."

Fred left hurriedly, and almost immediately came the barking of the little car, as the youth sped on his errand.

Dane was taken into a spare bedroom at the front of the house and put to bed. Mrs. Hughes washed his wound and bandaged it, her sister and Esther helping her.

Esther was bewildered. She bit her lips, as she remembered the conversation of less than an hour before. Why hadn't he *said* he was injured? Why hadn't he told her what had happened? Had he been injured in attempting to go to the aid of her father? Or, had he been injured after—after— She shuddered, as she remembered his look when she had hinted of what she had believed. He must have been in great pain when she was talking to him; his eyes had been bloodshot with the fever which was raging within him. Her lips trembled, and she left the sick room hurriedly.

Fred returned with the doctor in remarkably short time. Doc Ross, as he was known the length and breadth of the range country, was short and rotund, with a round, red face and mild blue eyes. He wiped his glasses and looked at Fred with disapproval, as he inwardly thanked his stars that he was alive after that fast ride.

"That boy'll string himself an' his passengers an' his car all over the prairie between here an' Black Butte one of these days," he said to Gordon Hughes, as he entered the house carrying his medicine case.

In the sick room his professional instincts were immediately uppermost.

"High fever—gettin' delirious—bad cut there—big shock—young, though—an' what a build!" he said, partly to himself. "I guess he's got a constitution that'll pull him through. Now you people get out of here, except you, Mrs. Hughes. Please get me some warm water."

He set to work, and the others went about the house on tiptoe, while Mrs. Hughes hurried softly in and out of the sick room.

Gordon Hughes went out and walked back and forth between the bunk house and the barn. Shay and the others were sent back to their work with the cattle. Servais was given orders to ride down occasionally to look after the small herd in the bottoms west of the barns, and to keep them this side of the line.

Old Marty approached Hughes anxiously. "What's the matter with him? How is he?" he asked anxiously, rubbing his stumps of hands.

Hughes explained gruffly.

"Queer doings," observed Marty. "Something's terrible wrong on that Flyin' W range, Gordon. Dane was over there somewhere, all right. I bet that man Bunker has got something to do with it. He's got a bad eye, Gordon. I can tell. I know when they're bad clear through, an' one peep at Bunker high-handin' it in Black Butte showed me what he was. An' he's a gunman, all right.

"An' listen to me, Gordon," continued the old man earnestly. "Dane's no slouch with his shootin' iron, either. That boy's lightnin' fast. I'd bank on it. I know. I can tell by the way he stands and holds his hands an' walks. He's like a cat. An' he ain't askeered of Bunker none, either. An' Bunker knows it, after that rumpus in The Palace at Black Butte. If Dane gets it in for Bunker, that feller better watch out, for I'd bet both my eyes the lad 'u'd get him."

"Well, we can't find out what happened until Dane gets so he can talk," observed Hughes moodily.

"I like that feller," Marty reflected. "He's quiet. He don't say much. They're dangerous, them kind, too, when they get started. Sometimes they're hard to start, an' then they're twice as dangerous. I dunno; but I've got Dane figured for one of them kind that's hard to start."

Hughes saw Doc Ross on the porch and hastened to join him.

"Very high fever," said the doctor shortly. "I dressed his head. Bad cut. Done with the butt of a pistol, maybe. How'd it happen?"

The rancher explained the circumstances which made it impossible for him to answer the doctor's question. Then he asked about Williams.

"Took him to the county seat," snorted Doc Ross. "Thought I wasn't good enough, I guess. Maybe I ain't, but I've put a lot of men in my day back in their saddles that was shot up worse than he was. Maybe they thought I'd be askin' too many questions. He was shot from behind. Something wrong. No, Gordon, don't look at me; I know you didn't do it."

"Why, are they talkin' 'bout me?" asked Hughes.

"Just mentioned you was there," soothed the doctor. "What's *your* arm done up in a rag for?"

Hughes told him, and he insisted upon looking at the wound which he said didn't "amount to shucks." Then he prepared to go.

"He'll be delirious to-night," he told Gordon Hughes and his wife. "That medicine'll quiet him some. I can't give him too much. He's had a bad shock; hit in a bad place, too. I'll come out again in the morning."

Fred drove up in the little car.

"Not so fast now, you young scoundrel," cautioned the doctor, holding up a warning finger. "I'm an old man, an' I've got a few other patients that need my moral support, if not my medicine. So long, Gordon. Keep the windows open, Mrs. Hughes, an' give him all the water he wants to drink. I'm a great believer in water an' fresh air—nothing to eat while he's got fever."

Gordon Hughes looked at his wife, as Fred

drove away with the doctor. She was calm, appearing coolly efficient and composed in her white dress and apron.

"He's resting easily," she said. "You mustn't go in. Sister and Esther and I will look after him. Stop looking so worried and angry, Gordon. What's happened has happened. After all we're still ranching, and the West is the West; we can't change it."

"I'm glad you realize it, little woman," said Hughes, putting his arm about her shoulders. "An' it seems to me that out of all this trouble there ought to come some good. I reckon the Big Range Boss over this world will look at it that way."

"You're a good man, Gordon," said his wife, patting his hand. "Perhaps Dane got hurt trying to help you. I wouldn't be surprised."

"Nor I," said Hughes quickly, his face clouding.

By sundown Dane was again in the throes of a raging delirium. Mrs. Hughes and her sister took turns sitting up with him. In the early morning Esther came down and took up the vigil in the sick room.

Through the early-morning hours Dane raved and muttered and tossed and turned restlessly in the bed. When he opened his eyes occasionally he apparently failed to recognize Esther, who watched him eagerly for signs of normality. He would lapse again immediately into delirium.

She listened intently to his ravings for some word which would give a clue to his past; but none came. His mind seemed to be occupied with recent happenings, and she could make nothing of the disjointed sentences and muttered exclamations, except one.

"You lie!" he cried, half rising in bed. "I tell you, you lie!"

Her hands flew to her breast. Did he mean her! Was his fevered brain dwelling on what she had said to him the morning before, or, rather, on what she hadn't said, but had really thought? A little cry of anguish escaped her, as she gently pushed him down upon the bed, smoothing the pillow under his head. She stroked the shock of hair—the color of bronze—which peeped through the bandages, and there were tears in her eyes.

Oh, *why* hadn't she been able to see that he had been injured, that he was ill? Why hadn't he told her? Then came the agonizing thought that *she* was responsible for his injury! She had sent him to follow her father. He had done so and had come back like this!

"You lie!" he repeated in his raging delirium. "You know where that gun is! I reckon you've *got* it—you white-haired ghost!"

Then it was something about a gun, she thought. A ghost? Whatever it was it evidently had no reference to her. She pulled the light covers about him, touched his burning temples with cold water and watched over him with a pain of misgiving in her heart.

Toward morning he quieted down somewhat. Thus Esther watched the coming of the dawn through the windows.

Fred left for town soon after daybreak and returned after breakfast with the doctor. The physician spent some time in the sick room. When he emerged he found Gordon Hughes, Esther, Fred, and old Marty waiting anxiously in the sitting room.

"Still got the fever," grunted Doc Ross. "Very bad shock—dangerous place—might come out of it a little off." He tapped his head significantly.

"Doctor!" exclaimed Esther. "You—you mean—" She faltered, as the others looked at her, surprised at her emotion.

Then she quickly left the room, ran across the porch and down the steps, and walked rapidly to the shelter of the friendly cottonwoods. There she paused under the trees, her hands to her breast, and stared unseeingly. She knew—had known without asking—what the doctor had meant. The blow upon his head might cause Dane to lose his mind! She dropped limply upon the grass, buried her face upon her arms, and gave way to tears.

All that day the doctor remained at the ranch house. In the evening Fred drove him back to Black Butte to visit a patient there and returned with him in the twilight. And that night, while Dane's constitution battled with the raging fever, and he lingered in the black shadow, the prairie man of medicine fought for his life with all the science he possessed.

Gordon Hughes remained up.

"You had better look through his things an' see if you can find out anything about him," said the doctor to Hughes.

The rancher knew what was in the doctor's mind. He had told him all he knew about Dane. And both men realized that Dane might die. So Hughes examined his clothes, his slicker pack, and his other belongings in the hope that he might learn the man's identity. He discovered nothing to indicate who he was, or whence he had come. He noted, however, that his gun was gone.

With the dawn Dane fell into a peaceful sleep.

"Guess the crisis is over," said Doc Ross wearily. "I'll get a wink of sleep. When he wakes up we'll know."

It was Esther who was in the room that afternoon when Dane opened his eyes. She looked at him, her heart seeming to cease beating, as he stared at her fixedly. His lips moved, and she bent over him to catch what he said.

"Water," he murmured faintly, and a sob of joy came to her throat, as she saw the look of reason in his eyes.

The doctor forbade him to talk; forbade the

others to talk to him. Rest and quiet, and after a time a little orange juice and later a wee bit of broth. His instructions were explicit.

For three days Dane slept and rested and swallowed nourishment. Slowly his strength began to return. He was on the mend. The fourth morning an automobile came along the road from town. Gordon Hughes came out on the porch to greet the visitors. He scowled, as he recognized the sheriff of the county.

"Sorry I ain't here on a personal visit," said the sheriff. "Ain't got no say in the business, you understand." There was a note of apology in his voice.

Mrs. Hughes and Esther were standing pale-faced in the doorway.

"You don't have to explain, sheriff," said Gordon Hughes. "I was sort of expectin' you."

The official looked relieved. "I'm glad you look at it that way, Hughes. My job ain't always a right pleasant one."

"I know," nodded the rancher. "You want me to go back with you this morning?"

"You?" said the sheriff, surprised. "I ain't lookin' for *you,* Hughes. I've got a warrant for a man named Dane."

The little group on the porch stared incredulously.

"Dane!" Hughes exploded. "What do you want him for?"

“Charge is shootin’ a man in the back with intent to kill,” said the sheriff, nettled at the rancher’s tone.

“The dirty blackguards!” stormed Hughes. “Williams, I suppose.” And then, as the sheriff nodded, he quickly explained Dane’s condition.

“Can’t take him then,” said the sheriff, frowning. “But I’ve got to serve this warrant.” He stepped upon the porch.

“You can’t go in there, sheriff,” said Hughes sharply.

The sheriff looked at him severely. “I reckon you forget I’m sheriff of this county, Hughes,” he said, turning back his coat to reveal the star pinned to a suspended strap.

“Sheriff or no sheriff, you can’t go in that room until he’s *well,*” thundered Hughes, stepping before the official. “An’ if you draw that gun you’re goin’ to have to shoot!”

The sheriff hesitated, his brows puckering. “I’ve got my duty to do, Hughes, I figure you want to be fair.”

“I do that,” replied Hughes. “You can give me your warrant, an’ I’ll be responsible for Dane.”

“All right,” said the sheriff finally. “I reckon your word’s good.”

CHAPTER XV
AN ULTIMATUM

Dane's rapid strides toward complete recovery surprised even Doc Ross. He explained somewhat vaguely that the shock had caused "nervous complications" which had—here he had recourse to a number of baffling medical terms which meant nothing to the Hughes family, but convinced them that Dane had been very near death, as was indeed the case.

A week after Dane began to mend, word came from town that Williams had been brought back from the hospital at the county seat and was at the Flying W ranch, recovering from his wound.

As soon as Dane was permitted to talk to any extent, Gordon Hughes closeted himself in the room with him and heard the story of what had happened the day Williams had been shot. Neither he nor Dane could solve the mystery to their satisfaction, nor did they arrive at any conclusion which carried the force of sound logic. They decided it was best to keep what little they did know to themselves.

Dane was incensed at the thought of the loss of his gun.

"Whoever's got that gun knows who shot Williams," he told Hughes.

The rancher nodded, and then he told Dane of the warrant and the visit of the sheriff.

"That's Bunker's work," Dane declared. "He knew I was at the hermit's cabin that mornin'. Only thing I can't understand is why he didn't come in the night."

"He went into town with Williams," explained Hughes. "I reckon Bunker knows who shot Williams."

The two men looked at each other knowingly.

Nothing further was said about the matter that day, and Hughes announced at the supper table that he would go to Black Butte and the county seat on the morrow.

"I told Williams I was goin' to fence the strip," he said; "but I reckon I can't do that while he's on his back." He frowned heavily, remembering the warning of the banker from Black Butte that the boundary would have to be decided before he would renew the note due July 15th.

"I've got to see Stevens," he continued. "I reckon the American Bank owes me as much good will as I owe them."

However Gordon Hughes was not thinking so much about prospective financial difficulties as he was about the strange way Dane had received his injury. There had been a reason for swearing out the warrant. Hughes believed Bunker knew

Dane had nothing to do with the shooting of Williams. Did Bunker wish to put Dane out of the way to further some design of his own or of Williams? He might have thought Dane would have to remain in jail for a time. He knew Bunker had been enraged after the incident in The Palace in town, but he felt it would be more like the Flying W foreman to endeavor to take revenge with his gun.

Shay was instructed that afternoon to start north with the beef herd and the other cattle in the eastern section of the bottoms. Servais was looking after the small bunch in the bottoms to westward. He reported that no Flying W cattle could be seen near the contested strip between the two ranches. Williams or Bunker evidently had ordered that all Flying W men keep away from the line.

Old Marty shook his head and told Mrs. Hughes "there was sure something in the wind."

Gordon Hughes went in to see Dane before he started for town next morning.

"You're goin' to Conard?" Dane asked with interest.

"Yes, I'm goin' to the county seat," said Hughes.

"There's reasons why I wouldn't want to go up there," said Dane softly, looking out of the window to the green of the cottonwoods. "That is—not just yet," he added with a peculiar smile.

Hughes looked at him quickly. "You don't want to see the sheriff then?"

"No, I don't," replied Dane with a direct glance. "An' I wouldn't want to put in any amount of time as his guest, either."

"That won't be necessary—so far as this *Williams* business is concerned—anyway," said the rancher, watching him narrowly.

But there was nothing in Dane's look or manner to indicate that he didn't wish to see the sheriff for other reasons. He merely smiled cheerfully.

"Look here, Dane," said Hughes suddenly, "I want you to know that I'll stand behind you any time you might need me. If there's anything—"

He paused. Dane was shaking his head.

"You won't have to be no guest of the sheriff because of that warrant," continued Hughes, driving his fist into his palm. "I'll tend to that. I'll have a bond up for you before night."

"Aren't you takin' a chance?"

"No!" Hughes exploded. "An' if I *am,* it ain't the first chance I've taken. An' I'll bring you back a new gun."

Dane's smile broadened at this. He described his missing .45.

"I'll get its twin brother in Conard," Hughes promised.

Dane looked at him curiously, and neither spoke for a time. Hughes stared out of the window thoughtfully.

"Old Marty's got you pegged for a gunman," the rancher remarked in a casual voice without looking at Dane.

"Old Marty's got some queer ideas," said Dane, frowning. "But he's a good sort."

"There's been times when I wished I had a man that was handy that a way with his gun on the ranch," said Hughes. "But I ain't never hired a gun fighter because he was one. I don't believe in gun play—unless the other feller starts it, an' you can't get away from it."

He looked at Dane squarely.

"I reckon that's the right idea," said Dane.

Hughes rose to go, as Esther came in with Dane's breakfast. She flushed, as she looked at her father, and he paused a moment, regarding her queerly. Then he went out.

He started with Fred for town in the car shortly afterward. They took a road leading northward before reaching Black Butte and drove northwestward to the main road to the county seat, cutting off several miles. In the late afternoon they returned to Black Butte.

Gordon Hughes proceeded straight to the American Bank where, after knocking loudly on the locked front door, Sam Stevens appeared, let him in, and led him to his little private office in the rear of the building.

"I signed a five-thousand-dollar bond with the judge for the appearance of my man, Dane, when the court wants him," Hughes told the banker. "I thought maybe you ought to know."

"Bad business," said Stevens. "How do you know your man won't beat it out of the country?"

"I don't know," scowled Hughes, "but I don't figure I'm takin' much of a chance."

"Maybe you ain't, an' maybe you are," returned the banker. "It wouldn't be exactly fortunate to have to make that five thousand good this fall."

"I ain't worryin'," said Hughes, as the banker sat down and motioned him to a chair.

"There's something else on my mind," he continued, taking a seat. "You know about Williams, of course. I was down there to see him the day you came down to my place. He wants the whole strip we've been on the outs about. Wants the big spring. I'd let him have it, if he hadn't hinted aroun' that I might lose the ranch."

The banker's eyes were gleaming points of light in his pasty face. He switched his gaze to the window.

"Couldn't come to any agreement with him," Hughes went on, avoiding the topic of the shooting. "Told him I'd fence down the middle of the strip, if he wouldn't make terms. And *I'll do it!*"

The banker looked at him quickly. "That would make trouble, wouldn't it?" he asked in a smooth, monotonous voice.

"Probably would," said Hughes shortly. "But I

hate to do it while he's laid up. 'Twould sort of look as if I was tryin' to take advantage of him. We've got to get around that boundary till he gets on his feet again."

"I want the boundary determined," said Stevens tersely. "I'm within my rights in demanding it."

"Then let the county send a man down here an' survey it on an order from the court," exclaimed the rancher.

"But that isn't the point," was the suave reply. "The boundaries of your ranch are defined, more or less, in your patents from the government. But, as long as you and Williams are fighting over the matter, a prospective buyer, say in an emergency, would be frightened away, and—"

"Why are you always hinting about prospective buyers an' such?" demanded Hughes with a darkening countenance.

"Because I'm holding your paper to the amount of nearly sixty thousand dollars," retorted the banker loudly.

Hughes became suddenly calm. "If the line ain't fixed up by the fifteenth of next month you'll refuse to renew that six-thousand-dollar note?" he asked coolly.

"It's the only way I can see of getting you to do something," Stevens evaded.

"Then I'll go to the Cattlemen's Association!" cried Hughes, leaping from his chair.

"What good will that do?" asked the banker, rising.

"It'll put this business of financing where it belongs," thundered Hughes. "It'll mean that the association men who're doin' their banking with you will look outside of the county for the accommodation they need. I've got influence enough to put that over, Stevens; I can do it. An' I can get the six thousand, too—an' you *know it!*"

The banker's eyes were flashing angrily. He compressed his lips.

"Wait a minute," he snapped, as Hughes started for the door. "In any event the affair of this bank will not permit me to extend that note more than three months. I can do that, and the most of your paper will be due October fifteenth. I'll extend that note till then, Hughes, and then you'll *have* to make good the notes which are due. That's final, association or no association. It seems to me that your threat was a queer one in view of the accommodations this bank has given the stockmen in this county."

Hughes shook a forefinger at the banker. "The stockmen's notes are the only notes you've got right now that are secured," he said sternly. "With three years of drought behind us this land hereabouts ain't worth a dollar an acre for farming. All we ask is a chance to ship on a rising market. If we don't get that, there'll be no

American Bank in Black Butte—only you ain't wise enough to see it."

Stevens filled out a note blank and handed it to him to sign. While Hughes was signing, Stevens went out into the banking room and returned shortly afterward with the old note which he gave to the rancher. His face was cold and set.

"That ought to settle our business until the fifteenth of October," he said grimly. "But I'm expecting that you will get that boundary matter fixed up in the meantime."

Hughes looked puzzled. What had the boundary to do with it now? Why should Stevens be anxious about the boundary when he could be reasonably sure of getting the money due the bank when it fell due? The Diamond H beeves would be shipped in time to take care of the notes. The rancher shrugged and gave it up.

"Quit worryin', Stevens; you'll get gray-headed," he said with a laugh at his own joke, for the banker was bald.

Stevens showed him out with a bow and a sarcastic smile. Then he stood at a window of the bank and watched Gordon Hughes walk away. The banker's eyes were glittering points of flame, and there was no suggestion of mirth in the smile which played upon his thin lips.

Gordon Hughes walked jauntily enough, but he was uneasy in his mind. The banker had given in readily when he had threatened to take the matter to the Cattlemen's Association. The rancher knew Stevens didn't want any trouble with the association at that time. And he hadn't been bluffing when he said he had influence with that body. But there had been something in the banker's manner which indicated he had something up his sleeve. Hughes pondered on this as he walked down the short street.

Although the car was at the hotel, Fred was not there. The rancher turned and looked back the way he had come. He stiffened, as he saw two horsemen ride up to The Palace and dismount. One of the men was Matt Bunker. The other he did not know.

He reflected that Fred was very likely in The Palace. After a moment's hesitation he frowned and started toward the resort.

As he entered, he heard Bunker's voice:

"An' I'll tell that to the first Diamond H man I see," the Flying W foreman was saying loudly.

Gordon Hughes walked to where Bunker was standing at the bar.

"All right, Bunker, you can tell it to me!" he said quietly, as the foreman whirled upon him.

CHAPTER XVI

"I SAW HIM!"

The two men stood facing each other. They were about equal in size; if there was any difference in their weight it was in favor of Hughes, who was a bit taller than Bunker. Hughes's eyes, clear, coldly inquiring, looked straight into Bunker's which were gleaming fiercely. The Flying W foreman half sprawled with one arm—his left—upon the bar behind him. The suggestion of a sneer played upon his thick lips.

It was the first time Gordon Hughes ever had spoken to Bunker, and Bunker recognized the challenge.

"I was talkin' about your gunman," he sneered.

"Who do you mean?" demanded Hughes, although he knew to whom the foreman referred.

"That rat Dane," said the other, his face darkening. "He's your gun toter, ain't he?"

"You're takin' a lot for granted, Bunker," said Hughes evenly. "What was it you was goin' to tell the first Diamond H man that came into the place?"

"That I'm goin' to cure that gunman of yours of shootin' a man in the back from under cover," snarled Bunker. "I'll make him exercise his trigger finger in the open, an' I'll show him how a *man* shoots."

Gordon Hughes smiled. "Funny you'd want to put Dane in jail where you couldn't get a chance at him," he said sarcastically.

Bunker's eyes blazed wrathfully. He sputtered in an effort to speak, then compressed his lips tightly, holding back the burning words that were on his tongue.

"Or, maybe, you thought it would make trouble for me," Hughes went on amiably, smiling his tantalizing smile which was driving the other mad.

"I ain't runnin' the Flyin' W alone," flashed Bunker.

"That's what I thought," said Hughes in a tone of triumph. "I reckoned you only *thought* you was."

It had been Williams then who had sought to jail Dane and thereby made it necessary for him, Hughes, to put up a stiff bond. Williams was playing to hamper him, either by the loss of Dane's services, or by compelling him to risk the amount of the bond.

Bunker took a step toward him.

"You ain't wise to all that's goin' on on this range," he said darkly.

"No; I reckon you know a lot more'n you want to tell," retorted Hughes. "I figure you know who shot Williams, Bunker, an' both of us know it *wasn't* Dane!"

Bunker's popping eyes, always more prominent when he was in a rage, flashed red fire.

"That's a lie!" he roared. "An' you don't know one thing about it."

Hughes remained cool, shrugged his shoulders, smiled again. "I didn't say *who* shot your boss; I said Dane didn't shoot him," he replied calmly. "I ain't accusing you, Bunker; I wouldn't accuse *any* man till I had the goods on him; but—"

"You *can't* accuse me," shouted Bunker, while the few others in the place stepped quickly back away from the bar. "If you say I'd shoot a man in the back, I'll—" His hand hovered clawlike over the butt of his gun.

"Don't forget that I am not armed, Bunker," said Gordon Hughes sharply. "This is still a country where men respect fair play. An' you're takin' a lot for granted again. You come here with a string of killings behind you for a hole card. This has been a peaceful range, Bunker, an' it's goin' to be a peaceful range again. No one bad man is goin' to run this county!"

Bunker's face had purpled. The fingers of his gun hand were twitching with the itch to close like lightning on the butt of his weapon and shatter Gordon Hughes's logic with a bullet. But the Flying W foreman knew that the Diamond H rancher had friends; he knew he spoke the truth when he referred to fair play; he realized, even in the white heat of his anger, that this would be no ordinary killing if he went through with it—that he would be hunted the length and breadth of the State.

The fire in his eyes smoldered, as his anger gave way to a saner impulse. He didn't want to be chased out of the State—yet.

"Of course you ain't accusin' me," he said at length in a voice trembling with passion. "Good reason for that, too. It wouldn't be good policy, eh? Not knowing much that a way about your gun toter. You ain't what I'd call plumb observin'." He leered, as he said this.

"I take it you never was noted for sayin' what you meant, Bunker," said Hughes. "You shoot words like somebody shot Williams—from under cover. You can play your hand any way you want to, but I'm goin' to call it!"

"You want plain talk?" cried Bunker. "Get this: You been losin' cattle. *We've* been losin' cattle, but you didn't know it. When does this Dane show up on the scene? After the cattle begins to go. Where does he come from? Nobody knows. What's he hangin' aroun' the bad lands for? Tell me that. Why's he sneakin' aroun' of nights? Why'd he hide when the county men was right here in this place? How'd he come to be in the trees out there when Williams was shot?"

"How'd you know he was there?" Hughes's

question came like the crack of a whiplash.

"I saw him!" declared Bunker.

"Well, then, how'd *you* happen to be there?" Hughes inquired mildly.

"I was lookin' after cattle down there," replied Bunker readily.

"What became of him after you saw him?" asked the rancher.

"He lit out, same's you did. That was a fine play, Hughes," sneered Bunker. "You say I'm a bad man, but you don't have to worry about gettin' shot in the back from *me.*"

Hughes's face darkened at the veiled accusation. Bunker was trying to make it appear that he had had Dane in the trees to shoot Williams in case of trouble. He was suspicious of Bunker in connection with the shooting, but he could not fathom why the Flying W foreman should wish to kill his employer.

"The judge will probably be right interested when he hears you was hangin' aroun' when Williams got shot," Hughes said pointedly. "I'm still layin' my bets that you know more about that business than you want to tell."

Bunker's lips twisted into a sneer. "Two of us saw you draw on the old man, an' we ain't tellin' what else we saw," he said, affecting a drawl. "The play's gettin' out of your hands, Hughes."

He stepped toward the door. The man who had been standing near him at the bar followed him.

"There's just one thing, Bunker," Hughes called. "You can tell Williams that when he gets on his feet again, I'm goin' to fence the strip."

"An' he'll give you his regards when you start," replied Bunker over his shoulder, as he strode out the door.

A smothered exclamation came from above. Gordon Hughes looked up to see Fred standing on the balcony near a curtain at its forward end. There was a six-shooter in the boy's hand, and he was staring at the door. At his side stood a girl. She had both her hands upon his right arm; her lips were parted, her eyes bright. She said something to the boy, and he put up his gun, his gaze shifting to his father.

Hughes realized the youth had been ready to fire at Bunker, if the man had gone for his gun. He smiled with the knowledge, but his smile quickly gave way to a frown.

The boy disappeared behind the curtain. Hughes hesitated and then started for the stairway to the balcony, as Fred reappeared and came down.

Willis Brady, proprietor of the place, approached Hughes, as they turned to go.

"I've tried to hold Bunker down," he said with a shrug, "but I can't always make it stick. I'm afraid there'll be trouble, if that man of yours gets in here when Bunker's in town. I'd hate to have any trouble, and—"

"You've got to *expect* trouble in a place like

this," snapped Hughes. "I've told my men to keep out of it, an' they've backed down more'n once. I reckon you know that. All I'm expectin' of you is that you try to see fair play—if you can."

He turned his back on Brady and walked out with Fred.

As they sped toward the Diamond H, with the setting sun at their backs, father and son were silent. Hughes knew the boy had heard the conversation he had had with Bunker. He experienced a thrill when he thought of the youth standing by the curtain on the balcony ready to shoot if it should be necessary. He frowned a bit perplexed, as he remembered the attitude of the girl. She had seemed to be restraining the boy. There was something about her actions which caused him to wonder just what influence she had with Fred.

"Who was that girl with you on the balcony?" he asked Fred.

"That's Marie," the youth replied, flushing.

"What's her last name?" asked his father with another frown.

"I dunno what her last name is," Fred confessed. "Everybody just calls her Marie."

"I see," said Hughes, twisting in his seat and looking at his son. "Well, if you want to hang aroun' a dance-hall girl, I suppose I should say I expected it. You're the age when a young man tries to rope a little excitement."

"Marie's a good kid," said Fred stoutly. "She's better'n a lot of 'em that think they're too nice to go into a dance hall."

"Good friend of yours?" asked his father, rubbing a hand over his big, smooth chin.

"Yes," replied Fred. "An' a good friend of the Diamond H, too."

"Seems to me that one night this spring when I happened in there at The Palace, she was dancin' with Bunker," observed his father. "Maybe she's got lots of friends, eh?"

"If she was dancing with him it was because she figured she *had* to," Fred flared. "She's workin' there, an' she ain't always her own boss."

"She didn't want you to take a shot at Bunker to-day, did she?" his father inquired.

"If she hadn't been there, I'd have shot Bunker when he made like he was goin' for his gun," said Fred with venom in his tone.

Gordon Hughes was startled. "Don't let girls and your six-shooter get on your mind, Fred," he said soberly. "Don't get in any shootin' scrapes. Shootin' is sure bad stuff."

"Well, you got a gunman on the place."

"I don't know that Dane is a gunman," said Gordon Hughes sternly. "I didn't *hire* him for a gunman, an' he ain't said anything to me to make me *think* he's one. An' I don't want you talkin' about his bein' any such thing."

"Well, he didn't show that he was much afraid

of Bunker when he was in The Palace that night, an' I'm glad of that," said Fred. "An' it wasn't very slow the way he shot the lights out an' punctured one of Bunker's men when he tried to draw. I've got him spotted. He's no slouch with the women, either."

Hughes stole a look at his son. "Is Dane one of Marie's friends, too?" he asked.

Fred scowled darkly. "He wouldn't let Bunker run her down, that's all I know."

"Well, maybe it's enough," said Hughes.

Fred opened the gas throttle to its last notch, and the little car careened around a curve near the big cottonwood between the two ranches and shot ahead. There was no conversation during the rest of the ride to the ranch. Gordon Hughes always declared, after one of these final spurts, that he was going to scrap the car. He made the same statement this day when they drew up at the porch.

After supper he sat with Dane for a time and told him of the words he had had with Bunker.

"I reckon it'd be wise for you to sort of steer clear of town for a while," he said, as he finished.

Dane was silent. Then: "I'd hate to have Bunker think I was keeping out of town on his account," he drawled.

The quality of Dane's tone caused Hughes to hold back the advice which was on his tongue. He was not altogether sure that he knew the reason, but he realized that as a feud had developed between Williams and himself, so had a feud developed between Dane and Bunker. Considering Bunker's ruthlessness, his confidence in his gun hand, and his jealousy of his self-confessed and self-vaunted reputation, this feud had a sinister aspect. He looked at the man lying on the bed. Youthful, slim, alert with a dreamy look in his eyes, Dane more than ever gave that appearance of mystery.

"You're comin' aroun' fast," said Hughes by way of breaking the silence.

"I'll be ridin' again in a week," said Dane with a flashing smile.

And such proved to be the case. Hughes went up on the north range to look after matters there, taking Fred with him. Dane moved from the ranch dwelling to the bunk house, where old Marty insisted on "babying" him, as Dane accused. He saw little of Esther, and she in turn felt that he was avoiding her. As soon as he could remain in the saddle any length of time he took to going on long rides in the bottoms.

It was on one of these rides at night that he saw a girl ride out of the bad lands. As he swung along past the big cottonwood he recognized Marie. He put the spurs to his horse and galloped toward her.

CHAPTER XVII
NIGHT RIDERS

As Dane rode swiftly in pursuit of the girl, she saw him and gave her horse the spurs, veering straight north toward the road which led to town. He cut past the big cottonwood and dashed northwest to head her off, or catch up with her, as she gained the road.

She evidently was depending upon the speed of her mount and continued on her course. Dane could not help but admire her riding. She was superb on a horse—glued to the saddle, as the saying goes.

But the bay was in fine fettle this night, and Dane gained in the spurt. When Marie came close to the road she encountered a bank of earth, checked her horse in momentary indecision, then turned westward. The brief pause enabled Dane to overtake her below the road. She reined in her mount, staring at him out of widened eyes.

"Oh!" she exclaimed with a glad look. "It is Mistair Dane. I thought it was some bad man maybe—no? Riding in the night like this?"

" 'Pears to me that you're out kinda late yourself, Miss Marie," Dane drawled. His eyes were sweeping the dim plain to southward, where a shadow was moving in the direction of the

Flying W ranch house. They were not the only riders who were abroad this night.

"Do you make a regular practice of riding down into the bad lands at night?" he asked, regarding her keenly.

"But no, Mistair Dane," she said quickly, appearing agitated. "It is the cool air I like, an' the trail is good out here."

"The road is better goin' out of Black Butte on the other side," he scowled. "An', besides that, you don't stick to the road—you switch off south."

"I do not have to tell why I ride where I please," she said with a shrug. "Thees ees countree what I like." She swept an arm about in a vague gesture. "If I like ride here, why not? I cannot stay in that dance hall all night with the smoke an' not get no air. So I ride."

"But you ride the same place all the time," Dane accused.

She seemed startled and eyed him shrewdly. "You see me ride before thees time?" she asked.

"Yes," he replied. "You've come down here before. Marie, you can trust me. I want to be your friend. Why do you ride down here? Who do you come down here to see?"

He thought she looked frightened. "I no come to see nobody," she asserted firmly. "You are not the gallant man to watch me. If I see somebody I no have to tell."

"You must have come to see somebody to-night," Dane persisted. "I saw a man ridin' away from down there. You must have—"

He paused, struck by the wild look in her eyes, as she gazed quickly southward.

"You see some one?" she asked, plainly disturbed.

"I saw another rider way down there goin' west. Look here, Marie, you can trust me. Who was that rider?"

"I didn't see him," the girl retorted convincingly. "Maybe he ride an' watch me, like you. Why am I to be watched thees way? I am ride for pleasure an' the air. I say it."

"But that sounds queer just the same," said Dane skeptically. "An' I wasn't watching for you to-night. I just happened to be ridin' for exercise. Don't you know it isn't right safe for you to be chasin' around these prairies near midnight? Who do you know might be watchin' you?"

"I am not afraid," she said stoutly. "I have thees to keep me by myself."

From within her blouse she drew forth a small, pearl-handled six-shooter and smiled in dazzling triumph.

Dane snorted—but with admiration, nevertheless. "I know you are brave, but you ain't showin' good judgment. If you ain't coming down here to meet anybody on these rides"—he looked at her suspiciously—"you're takin' a chance just the same. This is a wild place for a girl, a pretty girl like you, to be ridin' aroun' in late at night."

"Ah, it ees night only I like to ride," she said petulantly. Then with a saucy look: "You are like to ride at night, too, Mistair Dane."

"You might better ride this way in the daytime," he told her with a feeling of irritation.

He was convinced she had a definite purpose in coming to the bad lands. He had followed her to the same place once before. And this night he had seen a rider going west after she had come out of the shadow of the trees and struck off for the road. But his questioning was in vain. Her guileful answers were suspicious. She was cleverly avoiding telling him anything.

"I'll ride along a way with you," he told her.

"Oh, eet ees not necessaire." She smiled. "I am not afraid."

Nevertheless he rode two miles with her, while they talked of irrelevant things.

"You must watch Mistair Fred," she said suddenly after a long silence. "He ees maybe get killed if don't be careful."

"Eh?" exclaimed Dane, startled. "How is that?"

"He has the great hate for that Bunker," said Marie, "an' he will maybe try to kill him. But Bunker will not let him do it, for he will—what you say?—stop him with a bullet. He will not fool, that man, he ees ver' bad."

"How do you know all this?" Dane inquired curiously.

"I have the eyes, an' I hear the talk," she said soberly. "An' Bunker say he will kill you, too. I hear him when he think no one can hear. He ees ver' angry at you."

"Yes, I guess you hear a lot in that place in town. Why does Fred want to kill Bunker?"

Marie shrugged again. Dane was puzzled by the dancing light in the eyes she turned upon him. The girl was a beauty, he thought to himself.

"You know Fred?" he asked.

"But, yes," she answered laughingly. "I know ev'body. They all come to The Palace—even you." She glanced at him roguishly. Then she sobered. "Eet is bad place for you to come now, Mistair Dane. That Bunker he look for you, an' he make trouble sure. You are not come now for a time?"

"I don't know," answered Dane, checking his horse. "I'll leave you here an' ride back. I've rode more'n I intended already. I guess you'll get in all right, but you'd better ride fast. I'd cut out these night rides out here if I was you—unless there's somebody you've *got* to see out this way."

"Mistair Dane, you have been seeck," she said softly, putting a hand on his arm, as she leaned toward him in the saddle. "You are pale. Maybe you ride too much to-night."

"No, I'm all right," he replied. "You go on now."

"Good night," she said with a flashing smile. "You are watch me so I am safe?" She giggled, as she gave her horse the rein and galloped away.

Dane looked after her, frowning. Mysterious actions, these. What could take the girl down there near the bad lands, if she did not go to meet someone? And who could that someone be? The coincidence had a bad look on the face of it; for he could not forget that the rider he had glimpsed in the south had been riding *west* on the Flying W range. There were no cattle in sight, and therefore he could not have been looking after stock. And it was midnight!

He turned about and rode back toward the Diamond H, pondering the problem. He kept to the road and arrived at the barn very tired. Before he fell asleep in the bunk house, deserted now save for old Marty, Servais, and himself, he had resolved to ride every night to the vicinity of the big cottonwood. When the girl Marie came that way again he would follow her. Sooner or later he would discover the secret of her midnight pilgrimages into the shadow of the bad lands.

During the days which followed he recovered practically all his strength. He practiced much with the new gun which Gordon Hughes had brought him from the county seat. And every night he rode down to the bottoms.

Esther Hughes came upon him several times, as he was getting the "hang" and "feel" of the new weapon. She told at the table in the ranch house of Dane's proficiency at drawing and shooting with marvelous rapidity and *hitting the mark.*

Her mother looked a bit worried.

"I'd like to see him and Bunker matched," said Esther one day.

"Why, Esther!" exclaimed her mother. "*How* can you say such a thing?"

"Well, if he has to be a gunman he might as well be a good one," said Esther with a shrug. "An' I'll bet he's faster than Bunker!"

"I thought you told me you couldn't tolerate men who believed in guns," said her mother with a queer smile. "Isn't that what you said when you came back from the East?"

"I don't believe in gun law," said Esther calmly, "any more now than I did when I got back this spring. But I don't see where what I think makes much difference around here. We've had one shooting, and one of our men was nearly killed since I returned, and it looks as if we would have to protect ourselves some way."

She left her mother mystified at her change of sentiment. Esther herself felt mystified at some kind of a change which had taken place in Dane. Apparently he avoided her studiously. He adroitly circumvented the various subterfuges to which she resorted in the attempt to be with him and get him into conversation. She had tried to apologize for her words and what they conveyed that morning when he had returned to the ranch so ill, but he had shut her off with a hard laugh and a baffling look in his eyes.

He had been silent during the hours she had sat with him when he was recovering from the fever, merely thanking her for what she did for him. He had repelled with that peculiar, quizzical look of his her repeated friendly advances. He had all but verbally refused to ride with her!

This left her piqued and resentful, but more curious about him than ever. She conjured up all manner of conjectures as to his past. Was he merely a cow-puncher who happened to be an expert with his gun—or was he a killer, an outlaw, perhaps a fugitive?

During the wildest moments of his delirium he had said nothing which would give her a clue to any incident of the closed book of his life before arriving at the Diamond H. It was as though he had dropped from the sky. And night after night, as she watched from her window, she saw him ride forth with his face turned up to the stars. His attitude of aloofness hurt her pride, too. She came to feel that he was deliberately snubbing her. Thereafter she ignored him. And then one night she, too, rode abroad under the stars.

Instead of going down in the bottoms she cantered up the road to the bench land and sped northward. It was a peculiar night, with choppy clouds riding the skies and the moon drifting in and out in feathery formations, casting weird shadows upon the hazy surface of the plain.

She rode thus for an hour and then turned back. The mood of the night cast its spell upon her; she felt nervous, strangely excited without reason. She reached the road at a point beyond the disputed strip between the two ranches and rode slowly back. She dismounted by the big cottonwood, patted her horse's nose, and spoke to him softly to bring back her composure.

It was then that she saw a rider coming on the road from the direction of town. The moon disappeared behind a cloud, and when it emerged the rider was close and was turning southward off the road. She recognized the girl who had been pointed out to her in town as "Marie of The Palace." If the girl saw her, she gave no evidence of it, but sped swiftly southward and vanished.

Then Esther saw another rider, whom she recognized instantly by the posture in the saddle, dart out from the shadows far below and ride madly for the place where the girl had disappeared.

For some moments Esther stood staring, her eyes wide and glowing with amazing comprehension. The second rider was soon out of sight in the shadow at the edge of the bad lands. Still Esther stood, holding her reins and looking vaguely about her. Her lips trembled, then curled in fine scorn.

"So *that* explains his night rides," she said aloud. "Keeping a rendezvous with a dance-hall girl! I might have known it."

She mounted in disgust and rode back to the ranch house at a furious gallop.

CHAPTER XVIII
RUSTLERS

As Esther Hughes rode down from the bench land, Dane had watched her wonderingly. He saw her enter the shadow under the cottonwood and had lost sight of her when the moon disappeared. And when the moon had come out again he saw Marie coming on the road from town. He forgot Esther.

He watched Marie ride down the strip, and he marked as well as he could the spot where she vanished in the shadow. A few moments later he dashed to the spot and pulled up his horse in wonder. The girl was nowhere to be seen. He could see for some distance up and down the bottoms near the edge of the bad lands, but she was not in sight.

There could be but one explanation of this: she had entered the bad lands!

Dane rode back and forth, again searching for a trail into the brakes at this point. It was the same place where the girl had eluded him the night he had followed her from town. This fact convinced him that there was some kind of a trail leading into the fastnesses along the river from that spot.

He rode in in the same ravine he had entered

the night he had become lost, studied it by the fitful light of the moon—abandoned it. He took to the low ridges which began at that point, and again he had to turn back. He paused to listen and heard only the whisper of the wind in the stunted pines and buckbushes. He entered a wider and deeper ravine a little to westward and brought up against a barrier of trees and undergrowth.

Again and again he ventured into the shadows of the wild lands toward the river, only to emerge defeated. He could not find a trail. He could hear nothing but the chant of the wind. He gave it up at last and, withdrawing into the shadow at the base of a ridge, where he had a good view of the bottom in both directions, sat in the saddle to wait until Marie should come out.

If there was a man with her, he would find out who he was. If she were alone—He frowned as he recalled his last effort to get her to speak.

For an hour he waited, longing for the company of a smoke, but fearing to disclose his presence by the flare of a match or the glow of a cigarette. Then sounds were borne to him on the wind. He looked about and listened intently, endeavoring to determine from which direction they came. Gradually the west and north stretches were eliminated, and Dane decided that the sound he heard came from the bottoms eastward.

He rode slowly in that direction, keeping close in the shadow. As he rode cautiously along the edge of the bottom land the sounds became more distinct; but they were farther away than he had thought. He halted again to listen and then rode ahead at a swifter pace. He still kept within the shadow, and his right hand rested on the butt of his gun. He crossed the strip of unknown land and then swerved quickly into the deeper shadow and halted. He had seen the dim outlines of a horse and rider ahead.

The volume of sound riding on the wind had increased, although it still was of a subdued nature, punctuated by a dull, rhythmical pounding. Dane's practiced ear at once caught the significance of the sounds. They were caused by the impact of many hoofs upon the soft ground.

He dismounted, trailed his reins, and, leaving his horse in the shelter of a clump of buckbushes beneath the trees, climbed to the crest of a low ridge which jutted out of the fringe of the bad lands. From his new point of vantage he had a good view of the bottoms, and he caught his breath at the sight revealed in the dim moonlight.

The whole herd of a hundred cattle, which had been run in the bottoms at his request, was on the move. And the cattle were rapidly disappearing in the bad lands! Dane saw three riders working the herd. He could not determine who they were, and their work was aided by the clouds which continually obscured the moon, breaking only occasionally to flood the scene with light for a few fleeting moments.

As Dane watched, the last of the cattle drew close to the shadow at the edge of the brakes. The rustlers were running off the entire herd! Despite the seriousness of the situation, Dane smiled at the intrepid boldness of the cattle thieves. Lucky he had seen them—had been on the spot. It would take time to get the herd through the bad lands and across the river, if such was the plan of the rustlers, and he could think of no other logical course for them to pursue.

It was a foolhardy piece of work, he reflected; for, even if the cattle had not been missed until morning, there would still have been time to scour the brakes, pick up the trail, and follow at a far greater speed than the cattle could be driven.

What were the rustlers thinking of? Were they rank beginners at the game? As the last of the herd and the riders disappeared, Dane climbed down from the top of the ridge and mounted. He rode back a short distance and then cut north to the road. He did not fear pursuit, even if seen, as the three men would have their hands full guiding the cattle through the brakes. Perhaps it was their intention to set the herd adrift in the bad lands, split it up and scatter it. He scouted this theory, however, when he recalled that there had been other cattle run off the Diamond H that spring.

He rode rapidly back to the bunk house and woke the little wrangler, Servais. He explained matters to him hurriedly, and Servais hastened to the corral for his horse, saddled and joined Dane in front of the barn.

They rode swiftly to the lower edge of the bottoms and proceeded westward. Dane had judged that the cattle had been run into the trail which the stallion had taken—the only good trail leading into the bad lands thereabouts, of which he knew. He asked Servais if there was another good trail, and the wrangler shook his head. Cautiously they approached the beginning of the trail, keeping well in the shadow of the trees, skirting the ends of the ridges, which here flattened out on the floor of the bottoms.

Dane held up a hand and checked his horse, as they drew near where the cattle had been driven in. He listened, but the movement of the herd was no longer distinguishable by sound. All was silence, save for the murmur of the wind. He spoke to Servais in a low voice.

"Our play is to trail 'em," he said softly. "Follow 'em an' find out who they are, an' what they figure on doin' with the cattle. Maybe we'll find out where the rest of the missin' stock went to. They can't get that bunch across the river before daylight, if that's where they're goin'. We'll take it easy, only keep your ears an' eyes open, for they may have left a man behind to take a shot at anybody that might come moseyin' along."

Servais nodded that he understood and agreed with the wisdom of this course. The wrangler's eyes were gleaming brightly with suppressed excitement.

"This trail cuts south to the river from the meadow where we saw the hermit, the day we chased the stallion," he told Dane in an undertone. "Better let your horse pick the trail, for it'll be dark among the trees, an' watch out for the soap holes."

Slowly they rode into the trail and walked their horses into the dense shadow ahead. Dane rode in the lead, with the wrangler following him closely. They halted occasionally to listen; while Dane thought he could hear faint sounds ahead, he was not sure of it.

They waited a short time before venturing around the first soap hole, the surface of which gleamed ghostly white, as the moon shone through a thin film of cloud. The cattle had gone round it on either side, as their tracks showed. But the negotiating of this difficult place had slowed up the movement of the herd temporarily, and Dane and Servais now could hear sounds ahead.

Dane judged by the sound that the rustlers were trying to hurry the cattle. They would probably be less cautious now that they assumed they had run off the herd without being seen; or, if they had seen him when he started back to the ranch, they might show haste in an effort to get the cattle away ahead of pursuit. Dane would not have gone back for Servais, had it not been for the fact that, while he had nearly regained his normal health and strength, he still was subject to spells of weakness. Hard riding, or a running fight with the rustlers, might bring on one of these spells and place him at the mercy of the cattle thieves, in which event his knowledge of their operations would be worthless.

As he rode slowly along the trail, he suddenly was struck by the remarkable coincidence that the running off of the cattle should take place on the occasion of one of Marie's visits to the bad lands. He had forgotten her in the new trend of events. What had become of her? Was she in some way connected with the strange happenings of the night? His suspicions, smoldering before, now flared into flame. If she was in league with the rustlers it would explain her mysterious rides. But he could not determine in what way she could be of any use to the thieves.

They waited again at the second soap hole. They could hear the pound of hoofs close ahead and occasionally a shout, as one of the riders apparently strove to hurry the stragglers, or to keep the cattle to the trail. The movement of the herd was slow, necessarily so because of the winding trail and the darkness. Just below the soap hole the trail swerved to the west toward the meadow and the clearing wherein was the cabin of the hermit. As they reached this turn in the trail there was a flash on the ridge to the right above them, and a bullet whined over their heads.

Dane's gun leaped into his hand, and he fired twice at the spot where he had seen the flash, whirled his horse about and dashed into the trees, as two more shots came from the ridge, and bullets clipped the leaves about him. Servais was firing from somewhere to his right. Three bullets the little wrangler sent whistling up the ridge before he, too, sought the shelter of the trees.

Now the firing ceased. There were no more shots from the ridge. The sounds ahead became fainter. Dane guided his horse through the trees and underbrush until he found Servais coming toward him. After a wait of a few minutes they again proceeded cautiously along the trail, keeping well within the shadow of the trees on either side.

Dane would have preferred to dash ahead, give battle to the rustlers, kill or capture them if possible, and recover the cattle at one stroke; but he thought by following them it might be possible to find out what had become of the cattle stolen earlier in the season. And the result of a fight with the rustlers now would be doubtful, as the moon had disappeared behind a thick veil of lowering clouds which had spread over the entire sky, obscuring the stars and leaving the bad lands in utter darkness.

They felt, rather than saw, the meadow near the hermit's clearing when they reached it.

"We better wait here till it gets a little light," said Servais in a whisper. "It's almost mornin', an' then we can tell which way they've taken the cattle."

"Why, I heard 'em south of here," said Dane.

"I know, but the trail there splits up like a Chinese puzzle," returned the wrangler. "We can catch up with 'em fast enough when we're sure just what way they're goin'. Maybe they'll divide the herd, an' you'll have to go one way an' me another. Best to wait. It won't be long."

Dane realized the logic of this and gave in. They sat their horses under the trees for a time and then dismounted to stretch their legs. Dane was feeling the reaction from the exciting events of the night, but he said nothing to Servais. In a short time a drizzling rain began to fall. It filtered through the branches of the trees, and both men put on the slickers which had been tied behind their saddles. The rains increased as the first glimmer of dawn showed in the gray skies, and they again took to their saddles.

The trail left by the stolen herd was plainly observable. It led south from the big meadow, and Dane and the wrangler started in pursuit.

The way now led straight toward the river. Their horses soon were splashing through puddles of water in the trail, as the rain became a downpour, with the rising wind whipping it into their faces in blinding sheets.

Intersecting trails in large numbers appeared, but they had no difficulty in following the tracks left by the cattle. In time, however, these new tracks became harder to distinguish from old tracks, and several times the pair had to stop and make sure they were on the trail of the stolen herd. Then came a sudden interruption.

Sounds could be heard ahead, sounds which indicated the rustlers were having trouble with the cattle. And from a bend in the trail a short distance ahead came the crack of a gun, and bullets whistled past them.

Again they took to the trees, as their guns blazed at a figure which vanished round the bend. Then Dane moved forward in the timber at the left of the trail, while Servais did likewise on the right side. They came to the bend, cut through the trees to the trail, and were met by another fusillade. One of the bullets cut through the skirt of Dane's slicker. He saw a rider some distance before him whirling his horse in the trail for flight, and his gun roared.

The rider ahead slumped in his saddle. His horse turned and started down the trail. The wounded man fell on the left, his boot caught in the stirrup, and the horse plunged on, kicking and dragging him.

Dane shoved his gun into its holster and loosed his rope, dashing in pursuit, with Servais close behind him. The rope whirled in the air, its noose shaking out, and then the horse ahead broke loose from its helpless burden.

Dane and Servais dismounted beside the man on the ground. The wrangler was the first to reach him, and after a quick examination he straightened and looked about grimly.

"Shot in the side an' kicked to a pulp," he said. "He's dead."

It was true. Whether Dane's bullet had been fatal or not, the man's horse had finished him. His face was literally torn to pieces by the shoes of the horse. It was not recognizable. The features were literally obliterated.

Dane drew the body in under the trees and searched the dead man's pockets. He found nothing save tobacco and matches and a few odds and ends, such as might be found in any cow-puncher's pockets. There was nothing to identify the rustlers.

"Can't do anything here," Dane muttered. "He pretty near got me, too, as I shoved through the brush back there at the bend."

Mounting, they again took up the trail. They could hear sounds ahead, but these sounds were rapidly becoming fainter, despite the fact that Dane and the wrangler were riding fast.

Had the rustlers reached the river? Were they swimming the cattle across? They galloped ahead, entering a wide place where the trail ran straight between two high ridges. High on the right came the crack of a gun, and a bullet spattered the mud in the trail under Dane's horse's hoofs. Again they swerved into the protection of the trees, as another shot sounded, and a leaden messenger of death whined past them. They looked up the sharp slope on the right. Another shot greeted them, but the aim was wide. Then both Dane and Servais shouted in surprise.

Standing on the rock-ribbed crest of the ridge, hatless, his white hair flying in the wind, which was hurling the rain against him, bracing himself against the ferocity of the blast and holding a rifle in his hands, ready for action, was the hermit of the bad lands!

He was looking down in their direction, and, even as they stared at him in astonishment, he brought the gun to his shoulder and sent a bullet crashing toward them. Then he disappeared behind the rocks, as Dane and Servais fired simultaneously.

They remained motionless for a moment, staring at the bleak spine of the ridge; then they sent their horses dashing for the steep slope and began the ascent, as bullets whistled over their heads.

CHAPTER XIX
THE SOUVENIR

Taking advantage of every bit of cover which offered on the side of the ridge, Dane and Servais made difficult targets, dodging in and out of the trees, under overhanging rocks, behind outcroppings and boulders, zigzagging about, hunting a trail.

By the time they were halfway up the slope the firing from above ceased. The going became harder, and finally they brought up at the base of a series of cliffs. They rode southward under the cliffs until they came to a place where they could again climb. It was so steep here that they dismounted and led their horses.

The last slope was strewn with huge rocks which offered them protection from the fire of the hermit on the top of the ridge. It enabled them to make fast headway without fear of being shot down by a chance bullet. They redoubled their caution, however, as they approached the summit, and finally, with Dane in the lead, they rode out upon the crest of the ridge, with their guns in their hands, ready to return the fire which they expected from the hermit.

But no shots came. Nor was the hermit anywhere in sight. They rode against the wind and rain along the crest of the ridge, winding in and out among the boulders and rock outcroppings, searching for some sign of the old man who had been shooting at them. But they couldn't find a trace of him.

Dane saw some empty shells on the ground where, he assumed, the hermit had stood when he was firing at them, but that was the only tangible evidence that he ever had been there.

They next searched along the west side of the ridge. They knew their quarry could not very well be on the eastern slope which they had ascended, and the western slope offered excellent cover for a get-away. It was thickly timbered below the rocks, just under the summit, and Dane realized it had been easy for the hermit to slip down into the trees and make his escape.

"He's gone, hide an' hair," he said to Servais. "No use lookin' for him down there. I reckon that old coyote knows every foot of these bad lands, like a stud fiend knows his ace in the hole."

Servais was looking southward. "No sign of the herd," he said. "Looks to me sort of like that old devil worked a game to pull us off the rustlers' trail. There's the river—you can see the slope leadin' down to it, an' not a cow in sight."

Dane's brow wrinkled in thought. There was something in what the wrangler had said. It *did* look as if the hermit had stopped them and brought them up the ridge on a wild-goose chase. If that was the case, the hermit was working with the rustlers. Dane remembered the enormous supply of food in the hermit's cellar and scowled darkly. Supplies for the rustlers, of course. And this, too, explained why the hermit lived in the bad lands.

"Wasn't crazy after all," he muttered to himself. "Well," he said to Servais, "now that we've got the old man's number, we know where to find him—if he ever goes back home. I know where his cabin is. Let's hit down toward the river an' see if we can catch up with the rustlers. There's only two of 'em now—if the hermit ain't along."

They rode across the ridge and back down to the trail. By this time the rain, still falling in sheets, had obliterated the tracks of the cattle, and where they still showed it was impossible to determine whether they were new or old tracks.

However, it was only a short distance from the lower end of the ridge to the slope which led down to the river. The trail was broad, and the trails intersecting it were narrow and seemed to be merely leading into it. They were approaching a well-defined ford of the river. They took to the shelter of the trees and rode slowly. But they saw nothing. The wild desolation of the broken, tumbled country was as if its solitude never had been violated by man. The rain fell with less violence, and the wind abated somewhat. There was no sound, save the splashing of their horses in the water which filled small depressions in the ground, the patter of the rain on the dripping leaves, and the whistle of the wind in the branches.

In a short time they came to the slope which led down to the river. It was now a veritable mud flat. The mark of the recent high water still showed upon the trunks of the trees, and the horses sank to their knees in the mud under the trees and about the bushes. They rode out to the firmer ground on the beaten trail.

When they reached the edge of the river slope they halted and looked up and down stream. No one was in sight; nor were any cattle to be seen. There were no tracks which looked fresh, even on those pieces of muddy ground near at hand which were free from water.

"Don't look like they got 'em across," observed Servais.

"I don't reckon they'd 'ave had time anyway," said Dane, looking puzzled. "We were pretty close behind 'em when the hermit butted in. They couldn't have got 'em across an' out of sight over on that clear bank over there in the time they had. What do you think, Servais?"

Servais shook his head. "Don't believe they could have made it," he replied. "They've drove 'em off the trail an' have got 'em cached aroun' here somewhere. Or, maybe, they tried to scatter 'em an' left 'em, knowin' we was close behind."

"They was havin' a hard time with 'em a little while back by the sounds we heard," Dane reflected aloud. "It might just be that the herd bolted on 'em an' struck into the timber."

"In any case they'd have to cross one of those ridges back there," Servais pointed out. "An' I figure they'd have to be driven to take to the ridges. Anyway we better look aroun'—you go east, an' I'll go west. But look out that you don't get lost. If we cut back up to the ridge, where the hermit was shootin' from, we ought to find tracks somewhere under the trees where the rain didn't come down so hard."

Dane readily agreed to this method of procedure, and they separated to search for signs of the missing herd. Dane entered the bad lands to the east and, after going in a short distance, swung directly north. He held his course by landmarks established on the tops of three small ridges which he crossed. And finally he came to the wide ravine below the ridge from which the hermit had shot at them. He had seen no tracks which looked as though recently made; none which appeared like the trail which would be left by a herd of a hundred cattle. He frowned impatiently as he waited for Servais.

The wrangler followed Dane's system. He rode westward from the trail and also cut north up a broad ravine. He came to a barrier of trees—jack pines which grew very close together—and climbed the slope of the ridge to the west. This ridge was thickly timbered, and, unlike other ridges in that section, its crest was overgrown with trees and underbrush. He was unable to see down on either side, as he rode along this ridge, but he saw no tracks upon it and knew the cattle hadn't crossed it.

Continuing north he eventually recognized the tall ridge where they had hunted for the hermit on his right. He cut up through the timber on its western side and down its steep eastern slope and joined Dane. He smiled in resignation, as he saw the look in Dane's face.

"Nary sign," he said. "You didn't find anything?"

Dane made a negative gesture. "Whatever they did with that herd is past me," he said, confessing his perplexity. "They couldn't have got 'em across the river—I wonder now if they *could* have got 'em across the river."

"Not a chance," said Servais with absolute conviction. "They didn't have time, in the first place; an' did you notice how swift that water was runnin'? It would have carried those cattle downstream. An' there's steep banks on the other side below here. They'd have one big time gettin' 'em out. An' if they'd drove 'em in an' let 'em go, some of 'em would have showed over there. They've cached those cattle in here somewhere."

"Maybe so," Dane ruminated. "But where? That's what we want to know."

Servais shrugged. "I reckon those fellers know this country better'n we do. We'd have been able to track 'em if it hadn't been for the rain. An' now that it's cut us out of gettin' 'em, it's goin' to stop."

Dane noted that the rain was indeed about over. The wind had died down to a whisper. He felt tired, weak, and he was hungry.

"There's one man aroun' here that can tell us where those cattle are, an' I'm going to make him talk," he said savagely.

Servais nodded. "I reckon you mean the hermit."

Dane scowled darkly. "We'll hit back for the meadow this side of his clearin', scout aroun' for a look, an' then we'll pay him a visit," he said, putting the spurs to his horse.

They rode back along the trail to the big meadow. Here they turned west and entered the little grove of alders which separated the meadow from the hermit's clearing. They peered through the branches, but could see no one in sight. There was no smoke coming from the cabin; there were no horses about.

"We'll make a run for it," decided Dane.

He struck out in the lead, and they dashed

around the edge of the clearing to the cabin. Dane flung himself from the saddle and kicked the door open. The cabin was deserted.

"Didn't expect no such luck as findin' him here," he said, as he stepped inside.

"Maybe he'll beat it now that we're on to him," said the little wrangler, following Dane in. "I reckon he spread that story about him bein' a spirit himself just to make folks leery of him."

Dane sat down on the bench and took a drink of water. The night's ride and excitement had told upon him—drawn heavily upon his newly recruited strength. He felt weak and a bit dizzy.

Servais noticed this. "Reckon this has been a big order right on top of that sick spell of yours," he said, looking concerned. "That was a bad crack on the head somebody dealt you."

Dane started. It was the hermit who had picked him up after he had been hit. And now it was the hermit who had prevented them from overtaking the rustlers. A coincidence? Dane smiled ruefully. He might have known it.

"I'm goin' to make some coffee," said Servais, going to the stove. "Maybe by the time we get some coffee an' something to eat he'll show up."

Dane reclined on the bunk, while the other built a fire, found the coffeepot and coffee, cut some bacon from a part of a slab on the table, discovered some cold potatoes and bread, and went speedily about getting breakfast.

As the warmth from the fire in the stove permeated the cabin, Dane fell asleep. He awoke to find Servais shaking him by the shoulders.

"C'me on an' eat," said the wrangler. "I've puttered aroun' an' held off an' let you sleep two hours, till I'm scared I'll go to sleep myself. If that old devil an' his pals would show up an' find us both snorin', it might turn out bad for us."

Dane rose with a laugh. He felt better, rested. The nap had been just what he needed most. They sat down to a breakfast of fried bacon and potatoes, bread and sirup, and steaming cups of strong, fragrant coffee.

Dane could almost *feel* his strength returning. He even joked about their failure to locate the cattle and get the rustlers, saying that they could not get jobs as detectives with the Cattlemen's Association on the strength of their night and morning's work.

Servais raised his coffee cup with a grin and held it out, as if to toast the other. A gun barked on the slope of the ridge behind the cabin, there was a splintering of glass, and the cup was shattered to bits.

"Somebody's sent us a souvenir," said Servais, as they leaped away from the table.

"The hermit!" Dane exclaimed.

"An' more of 'em!" cried the wrangler, as several bullets crashed through the windowpane and embedded themselves in the log wall opposite.

CHAPTER XX
"DON'T HURT HIM!"

The little wrangler crouched upon the floor at one end of the table trembling with anger, looking at Dane, white-faced.

"They'd have shot us down like dogs!" he exclaimed. "Hidin' up there in the trees an' tryin' to pot us!"

"I don't figure they wanted to hit us," was Dane's surprising reply. "They could have got us if they'd wanted to. Look how deep in some of those bullets went. The old hermit, anyway, has got a rifle, an' I reckon he can shoot pretty straight. He didn't try to hit us from the ridge, I take it, an' he figured to scare us here. I'm believin' they don't want a pair of killings, but would powerful well like to capture us."

"Maybe you're right," growled the wrangler; "but shootin' the cup out of my hand is gettin' too close for me. I'm goin' to show 'em we're still up an' wigglin'."

He emptied his six-shooter through the window toward the slope.

"That won't do any good," said Dane. "Might as well save your shells. Might need 'em before we get out of this."

He went to the door and put the bar across it.

"Keep out of line with that window, Servais," he cautioned, as the little wrangler strove to peer out. "I don't understand their play a little bit," he went on in a lower tone. "They're either tryin' to throw a scare into us, or figure to keep us here till dark an' then pull off whatever stunt they've got in mind. I've got it in my head that they was watchin' us all the mornin'. Anyways, they haven't gone away with the cattle, an' that's worth knowing."

"Listen," said Servais, sitting on the head of the bunk well to one side of the window. "The two rustlers couldn't have been watchin' us. They was caching the cattle somewheres. But I'll bet the old hermit had his eye on us. They met up with him after we left down there an' started back for the cabin. Then they saw the smoke, when I was gettin' breakfast, and sneaked around on the slope to get a look at us. Now they're keepin' us in here till they figure out what they're goin' to do to us, or with us."

"Or till they ask somebody else what to do," said Dane, his gaze narrowing. "I've been countin' right along that there was something more behind this business than just runnin' off with a hundred head or so of cattle. There's some kind of a gang workin' in here, Servais. We've killed one of 'em, an' they'll more'n likely have it in for us for that, an' we've seen two others an' the hermit. But Gordon Hughes told me that Bunker said the Flyin' W was losin' stock, too. That means they're *workin'*. An' they must be pretty sure of gettin' away with the cattle to steal 'em as wide open as they went at it last night."

"If they're so sure of themselves, that's all the more reason they wouldn't care if they plugged us," said Servais, examining his gun after reloading it.

"No, a double shootin' would stir up too much fuss," said Dane. "I don't reckon they want to make things any harder for themselves than they can help, at this stage of the game. Anyway, I'm goin' to try 'em out."

Servais looked at him with concern.

"Where are the horses?" Dane asked, with a glance at the two saddles which they had brought into the cabin.

"They're in that little corral out behind," replied Servais wonderingly. "Look out close to that side of the window, an' you ought to be able to see 'em."

Dane looked and gave a nod of satisfaction.

"They made one mistake," he said grimly. "They didn't get the horses before they let us know they were aroun'. Now if they try to get 'em they'll put themselves in hittin' range."

"We'll take turns watchin' the horses out that side," Servais suggested. "How was you figurin' on trying out those gents on the slope?"

For answer Dane held his hat partially in view at the side of the window. A shot came from the timbered slope, and a bullet buried itself in the window casing just above the hat. Dane withdrew the hat immediately and smiled knowingly at the little wrangler.

"You see?" he said. "They ain't shootin' to kill anybody. I tell you they're holdin' us here an' waitin' for something or somebody."

"I don't see why they wanted to make a target of that cup, while we was eatin', to let us know they was aroun'," grumbled Servais who plainly was not convinced.

"I've got it thought out that the half-crazy hermit did that an' started the ball rollin'," replied Dane. "Sore, maybe, because we had the cabin an' was eatin' his grub. Maybe he didn't have any orders. There's grub enough under this floor, Servais, to feed fifty. That's another reason why I think there's a bigger gang than we know anything about."

Servais watched him moodily, while he built a cigarette.

"Does look as though they was kind of bungling the play because there's nobody aroun' to boss the job," he conceded at last.

For some time they were silent. Dane kept watch in the direction of the little corral, where the horses were, and Servais looked out the side of the window toward the slope. There were no more shots. An ominous silence prevailed.

Although the rain had ceased, and the wind had died down, the sky still was overcast with drifting gray clouds. It also had turned cold. Dane fed wood to the fire from a box behind the stove.

In half an hour Servais changed places with him, and he looked about the cabin to see if the hermit had any letters or other papers which might shed some light on his identity and activities in the locality. However, he found nothing of any importance. Then he got down on his hands and knees, pulled aside the piece of carpet on the floor, and lifted the trapdoor to the cellar.

Servais whistled, as he looked down at the provisions stored in the cellar. Dane slipped down and made a quick examination. There were several sacks of potatoes, many cases of canned goods, bacon, ham, vegetables, sugar, flour, salt, and cartridges for a forty-five-caliber six-gun and a thirty-thirty rifle. There were also four pack sacks which were strapped full. He emptied these and found they contained such provisions as a man would need on the trail. He repacked them and put them back. After a final look around he climbed out and replaced the trapdoor and the carpet. An hour passed, and nothing eventful happened.

Dane suddenly had an idea. "If they've sent for somebody, or for orders, there can't be more'n one man with the hermit," he said, staring at Servais with evident inspiration.

"An' those two can shoot us from the trees, if we got to movin' aroun'," was the sensible rejoinder. "We've got to play their game an' wait for dark, if that's what they're waiting for."

Dane lapsed into silence once more. Servais was right, but the inactivity necessitated by their position irked him. He would have welcomed an attack on the cabin—anything to break the monotony of the long wait for darkness. But at any cost he was resolved to make a break for it with the coming of night.

As the afternoon wore on, seconds became minutes, and minutes became hours to the two men in the cabin. They took turn and turn about, maintaining a vigil at the side of the window, where a watch could be kept on the corral. Servais, ever alert to the care of horses, complained that their mounts had not been watered. This, and the fact that they should be feeding, seemed to worry him more than anything else. To divert his thoughts Dane got Servais to talk about the big, black stallion, Jupiter.

"How'd you ever come to be able to ride him?" he asked.

"I made friends with him," replied the little wrangler with a touch of pride. "He knows me, and he'll do most anything I want him to do. There's a *horse*."

Dane listened casually, while Servais cited with enthusiasm the stallion's good points. Later he again held his hat at the side of the window. But this time there was no answering shot. He sat on the bunk and swung his legs restlessly.

"Maybe they've gone," he said finally.

Servais's teeth flashed against his dark countenance in a smile. "Open the door, or stick your head out the window an' see," he said.

For answer Dane rose, walked to the door, removed the bar, and deliberately threw it open, stepping quickly to one side.

This bold move was instantly answered by hot lead, as a bullet whistled through the open doorway and plunked into the wall above the bunk. Dane kicked the door shut and dropped the bar from the side.

"They wasn't shootin' high *that* time," Servais observed, and Dane saw that the bullet had indeed been on a line with his chest.

"That came from a rifle, too," he deliberated. "Maybe they mean business after all." He scowled darkly, and Servais noted that his eyes were flashing with a steel-blue fire.

It was the first time the little wrangler had seen this look in Dane's eyes. He watched the other curiously, as Dane squared away from the door, his hand dropping like a flash to the butt of his gun. He remembered what old Marty had said about Dane—that he had the bearing and the poise of a gun fighter. And the face, which ordinarily had a youthful appearance, now was drawn into grim lines, the lids narrowed over gleaming eyes, as Dane fell a prey to his thoughts.

"Keep your eye on the corral," said the wrangler. "I'll get a little supper."

The coffeepot had been kept on the stove, and he soon had a meal ready, drawing upon the provisions which were at hand. They did not eat at the table under the window; nor did they relax their vigilance on the corral where were their horses.

The wind came on again, as darkness began to settle. There would be no twilight this night and no moon or stars, for the sky was thick with clouds.

"They'll be after the horses at dark, probably," said Dane. "We've got to beat 'em to it, or stop 'em."

Servais nodded silently. He had a premonition that events would begin to transpire with the failing of the light.

Whatever plans the rustlers had would doubtless soon be put in operation. Both Dane and Servais were restless and nervous, as the darkness descended swiftly. Under the lowering skies the curtain of the night spread quickly—a black, inky void.

They got their saddles and bridles ready, and, when the darkness was complete, they removed the bar and opened the door stealthily, picking up their saddles, throwing them over their left shoulders, holding their guns in their right hands.

It was a pitch-dark night—impossible to see a foot ahead. They crept silently around the side of the cabin to the corral and felt their way to the loose bars of the gate. Dane stood ready with his gun, while Servais went in and bridled the horses. He led them out. Dane grasped the reins of his bridle, for Servais had been able to tell the horses by their height and feel.

They led the animals a short distance away from the corral, carrying their saddles, and then saddled rapidly. Dane stepped back, preparing to mount, and bumped into a man in the black shadow of the timber. Instantly he struck. The man staggered back, so that Dane could not see him. Then came a blinding flash almost in his face, and his hat was whipped from his head by a bullet. He leaped low and caught the man about the waist and twisted him about, as the gun roared again.

"What's up, Dane?" Servais called near at hand.

Dane secured the man's arms, as they rolled over and over on the ground, wrenched the pistol from his grasp, and dealt him a blow on the head with its butt. From somewhere down the meadow came more shots, and bullets sang in his direction.

He groped about for his horse, felt the dangling

reins against his hand, stepped around to the left side, and swung into the saddle. More shots came from down the meadow, nearer at hand this time. Servais mounted and closed in beside him.

"Into the timber on the other side," said Dane in a whisper.

They rode at a walk, their horses making practically no noise on the soft turf of the clearing. Suddenly Dane's horse shied, and Dane could dimly see the shadowy outlines of a mounted figure ahead. He raised his gun.

"Who is eet?" said a voice, which he recognized at once.

He pushed forward and swung in beside the horse ahead.

"Marie!" he exclaimed softly in astonishment.

"Do not make the talk," she warned in a low, excited voice. "Follow me—come."

She turned her horse, as Servais closed in on the other side.

Dane reached out and caught her reins. "Where do you want to take us—to the rest of the gang?"

"I show you a trail out," she replied. "You must come quick."

Shots broke the stillness of the night across the meadow. Dane looked behind and saw several flashes. The rustlers were firing blindly in the dark at the place where they thought he and Servais might be.

"You see?" said the girl in a loud whisper.

"They are know you are out an' look for you. You must hurry with me."

"Go ahead," said Dane; "but if we meet anyone we're goin' to ask questions with our guns."

They rode slowly behind the girl and turned into the timber. They felt a hard trail under their horses' feet. And, although they could not see their horses' heads, because of the impenetrable darkness, the girl held to the trail, as it wound over ridges and through ravines, about soap holes and through patches of timber, with an uncanny instinct, aided no doubt by her horse's familiarity with the path.

Dane thrilled as he reflected that the girl probably was following the trail by which it was her custom to enter the bad lands. She *was* in league with the rustlers then. But he could not solve the mystery of why she was guiding them away from danger—or was it a trap? If it was a trap, however, the outlaws would have scant advantage over them in the darkness.

They rode in utter silence, save for the sound of their horses on the trail and the drone of the wind in the trees. Dane could hear the girl's horse ahead, but could not see her mount or her. Servais was following close behind. The echoes of the shots back in the clearing died away. He realized that the rustlers had been waiting for darkness or reenforcements, probably both. The man he had knocked senseless, had been creeping up on the cabin. And the flashes of the guns in different places had shown there were more than the original trio. If it was a trap they were being led into, it had been well staged, although he could not see the reason nor the wisdom of such a course.

They mounted a high ridge and then rode down a long gentle slope. At the lower end of this they pushed through a tangle of buckbushes and trees. Dane sensed there was no trail here, but his horse followed the one ahead. Then suddenly they came out upon level ground and rode rapidly ahead. The darkness now was not quite so dense and all-enveloping. He could see the shapes of the other two riders more and more distinctly, and for some distance his gaze penetrated the veil of the night.

"Now," said the girl, checking her horse, "you can go home. You are safe."

"But why did you bring us out?" asked Dane, realizing they were on the bottoms, probably near the strip between the Diamond H and the Flying W.

"I no want to see you killed, Mistair Dane," she said softly. "An' thees other mans, he ees your friend—no?"

"Do you know those men back there who were shooting?" Dane asked.

"I am not to answer the questions," said the girl with a pout. "I am to ask the favor—for I do you the favor to-night, do I not? Those mens might killed you. You will do me the favor?"

Dane knit his brows. It was true that he was handicapped because they were under obligations to the girl. But why?

"Those men back there are cattle thieves, Marie," he said in a stern voice. "They stole a hundred head from the Diamond H last night, an' they've stole other cattle before. You have done us a good turn, yes; but, if you aren't in with the gang, you should tell us what you know."

She laughed softly. "Mistair Dane, you are so, so severe. I tell nothing till I want. There is one I tell you about an' ask the favor. You must do it for me," she added fiercely.

"Who is he?" Dane asked with much curiosity.

"He ees the ol' man—what you call the hermit."

"An' what about him?" demanded Dane in a hard voice.

"Don't hurt him!" said the girl in a passionate voice. "You must leave him alone!"

"Why, that old devil is one of the worst of the lot," exclaimed Dane.

"No, no," said the girl quickly. "He ees not. But you do not know. Some time you will know everyt'ing. I promise that. See, I give the proof!"

She dropped a gun in Dane's lap, put spurs to her horse, and was swallowed by the deep shadow.

Dane raised the weapon with growing wonder.

As he grasped it, he cried aloud in astonishment. He knew it instantly. It was his own missing gun which he had lost the day Williams had been shot!

CHAPTER XXI
ESTHER ACCUSES

After explaining to Servais and swearing him to secrecy, Dane rode toward the ranch with his thoughts in a turmoil. He did not hear the little wrangler's comments and observations. He struggled with the problem presented by Marie's friendly offices of that night, her request that the hermit be not harmed and her return of his gun.

On the face of it it was plain that she knew much. How had she been on hand to rescue them, or, rather, to enable them to get away quickly, if she had not known of the rustlers' movements? Why did she ask that they spare the hermit, if not because she was aware that he was working with the cattle thieves? Did not the coincidence of the return of his lost weapon show that she knew it was *his*—and that he had lost it in some unusual way? Wasn't it logical to assume that she knew what had happened to him that day, and who had struck him down from behind?

"Here is proof," she had said. Proof of what? Proof that some time he would know everything, as she had said. And she had promised! Did she then intend to tell him all she knew? Could he trust her? Why was she so interested in the hermit? Was all this merely a ruse to quiet him, to put a check to his activities until the gang in the bad lands had had ample time to carry out their nefarious schemes?

Her strange request concerning the hermit intrigued his interest most. Why was she so solicitous about him? Could it be that the old man, who had exhibited unquestionable signs of insanity during the electric storm, when Dane had sat with him in the cabin, was in reality the brains of the rustler band? Did Marie on her night rides go to the cabin in the bad lands to confer with the rustlers? Dane confessed to himself that it looked that way. The girl was "playing" him, he decided with rising anger.

He would round up the hermit and—Then he remembered that they had no actual evidence against the hermit except that he had fired at them when they were following the men with the herd. They had not seen him with any cattle, or with the other men. No, he would have to catch him and the others red-handed at their work of stealing cattle, or find them with the cattle they already had taken.

Progress toward capturing the rustlers was effectively blocked until the stolen herd could be located, or till they renewed their activities. They would have to go on the north range for cattle now, he reflected, and that would not be so easy.

Then he remembered that the Flying W still had cattle in the bottoms.

He shrugged and gave it up for the time being. Anyway, he knew more than before. He knew for a certainty that the hermit and Marie were in some way associated with the gang in the bad lands.

They had been riding along the bottoms with the deeper shadow of the tree growth at the edge of the river brakes on their right. Soon they saw the lights which marked the location of the ranch buildings, in the lee of the bluffs below the bench land. They made for them at a gallop.

Old Marty listened eagerly, while Servais during supper recounted their adventure. Marty, however, was the only one in whom they confided. Dane announced his intention of going up on the north range the following day to report to Gordon Hughes.

But this did not prove necessary, as the rancher came down the next morning with Fred to remain over Sunday. Hughes was for taking a force of men at once and combing the bad lands for a trace of the rustlers or the stolen cattle.

"We'll string that old hermit up, if he don't talk," he said angrily.

Dane argued against this. He held that it would be wiser to let the rustlers regain their sense of security and resume operations, when it might be possible to take them by surprise. And he particularly urged that the hermit be left alone. He was the connecting link between the rustlers and their deeds, he pointed out, without disclosing his remarkable experience with Marie. He felt that Hughes would not respect the girl's request that the hermit be left alone, and that he would scorn the idea that she might be acting in good faith. Dane himself felt inclined to give her a chance to make good her promise that she would tell what she knew at the opportune time, although he was, nevertheless, suspicious.

In the end he prevailed upon the rancher to permit him to handle the matter in his own way.

The skies cleared during the day, and once more the far-flung land was flooded with sunshine. Dane rode down the bottoms again that night, waited for hours in the shadows of the timber, but saw nothing unusual. The girl did not come. Nor did she come the next night or the next.

Meanwhile during the day Dane and Servais made two trips into the bad lands, venturing cautiously to the river slope, but they saw no one and saw no signs of the missing cattle.

On one occasion, when Dane crept up the ridge behind the hermit's clearing, he watched until he was sure the cabin was deserted.

It became a waiting game.

One evening, as he was saddling the bay, Esther Hughes came to the barn. She hesitated when she saw him, disregarded his nod of greeting, and finally spoke.

"It must be rather lonely—riding by yourself at night," she said, looking at him keenly.

"I reckon I sort of like it, ma'am."

"Very likely," she said in a severe tone. "Perhaps you are not always—*alone*."

He looked at her quickly. Then he remembered. She had ridden down to the cottonwood the night he had pursued Marie to the edge of the bad lands. During the strenuous events which followed he had forgotten the incident. She had seen him, of course. Perhaps she had recognized Marie and had assumed he had ridden down there to meet the girl.

He laughed boyishly. "Maybe not," he retorted, his eyes sparkling, as he saw the humorous side of the situation. Esther, then, resented what she thought were his clandestine meetings with the girl!

His laugh irritated her. She flushed and spoke accusingly:

"I had come to think there might be some extenuating reason for you being a gunman," she said in superior tones: "but I hadn't thought you were the kind to—to take up with a dance-hall girl!"

It was his turn to flush. Her disgust was all too apparent. He resented it, and it angered him. She insisted upon putting herself on a higher plane, he thought, and she was ready to jump to any conclusion not in his favor. He saw her, not as the square-minded Western girl which she should be because of rightful environment, but as a Western girl who had been spoiled by the notions of the East. In absorbing the viewpoint of those who did not know her own country, she invited merely the tolerance of such as he, who had never lived anywhere else.

"There are even dance-hall girls who are not a bad sort, ma'am," he said gravely, his eyes mocking her. "An' they ain't always finding fault with somebody."

Esther looked up haughtily at the rebuke. "I should have known better than to mention it," she said disdainfully. "Anyway, it's none of my business whom *you* associate with, and I'm sure I'm not interested."

She walked away with her head in the air. Dane continued saddling, his face cold and hard.

Next day Fred passed him with a stare. Dane looked after him, troubled. What was the matter with the boy now? He never had understood Fred; and this day he had seen again that mysterious look of antagonism and suspicion in the youth's eyes. Was it because of something which his sister might have said to him? Or was he merely suspicious of Dane after the loss of the herd in the bottoms?

From the first, Fred Hughes had been none

too cordial, he reflected. But the cause was a mystery to him. He was further mystified late that afternoon.

Esther sought him out near the bunk house before supper. She seemed excited, nervous, high-strung. She stood twisting a small handkerchief in her hands after she called to him. He went up to her with a cool, questioning look in his eyes.

"I wish to ask you to do me a favor," she said hesitatingly. "It may appear a peculiar request—under the circumstances, but I'm worried."

He waited without speaking, although he was seized with curiosity.

"Fred is going in to Black Butte," she went on, her voice gaining strength.

"If father was here, I'm sure he wouldn't want him to go, and mother has asked him not to. I don't know what's got into him these days. He acts so queer. He insists on going and won't let me go with him. I'm so afraid there'll be trouble. It's a dance, and there's bound to be Flying W men there. It's dangerous for Fred to go, and I would like to be there to try and keep him out of trouble, *some* way."

Dane was thinking rapidly. Yes, there likely would be Flying W men there; perhaps Bunker himself. And Marie would be there of course.

"What was you wantin' me to do, ma'am?" he asked.

"I—I—would you take me in, Mr. Dane?"

He did not show his surprise. “It might not be the best thing for you to do, Miss Esther,” he said seriously.

“But I want to go. I *do,*” she said. “If you won’t go with me, I’ll go alone.”

“Very well, ma’am, I’ll take you,” he said quietly.

CHAPTER XXII
AT THE DANCE

When supper was over, Fred Hughes saddled his horse and rode away toward town. He had brought the little car down from the north, where he had been driving his father about the range, but the car was now under repairs. Fred saw Dane in the barn but did not speak to him, and Dane knew it would appear presumptuous on his part if he were to advise the boy not to go to Black Butte.

And Dane had a thrilling feeling of anticipation, as he thought of the visit to town. His eyes were bright with excitement as he saddled Esther's horse and his own. He had been warned by old Marty to stay away from town for a spell, but he didn't think of that. One thing was sure: he wasn't going to let Esther ride in alone.

She had spunk, anyway, he thought with a grin. And she had asked *him* to accompany her. Evidently his supposed relations with Marie did not prevent Esther from looking to him for protection in a time of need. And she had rather condoned his supposed profession of gunman, while accusing him of meeting Marie in the bottoms.

Still she was not asking him to ride with her for pleasure. Very well, he had not sought her company. Let her think of him what she would. He was not interested in girls, anyway!

She had asked him to take the horses down by the hay shed. Did her mother know she was going to town? He suspected that she didn't, and that Esther wanted to get away without being seen. He rode down on the bay, leading Esther's black, and dismounted at the shed to wait. The twilight was deepening into night when she finally came.

"I waited till mother had gone to her room," she said, and Dane was satisfied that Mrs. Hughes knew nothing of the expedition.

They rode in silence down past the big cottonwood and up to the road.

"I may be taking you into trouble," said Esther finally, looking at him in genuine concern.

"I reckon I can take care of myself, ma'am," he smiled.

Her gaze shifted quickly to the road. They went on toward town at an easy lope, which both horses could easily maintain for the twelve miles.

"Have you ever killed a man, Mr. Dane?" Esther asked suddenly,

Dane met her gaze with a dreamy, speculative expression. "I don't reckon you'd want me to say yes to that," he evaded.

"But you are an expert with your weapon, are you not?"

"I was taught to be able to use it if necessary, ma'am."

"Do you *like* to use it?" she persisted.

Dane frowned. "I don't just know what you mean, ma'am."

She shrugged. "Please don't have any trouble tonight," she said. "I don't exactly know why I asked you to come, but you ride every night, anyway, and I suppose you might as well be riding into town as—" She stopped in confusion.

"Go ahead an' say it," Dane invited with a grin. "Anyway, she'd likely be in town to-night if there's goin' to be some doings."

Esther's head went up in the air.

They rode on, with Dane chuckling to himself and frowning by turns. Night had fallen, and the sky was blossoming with stars. A coyote slipped across the road ahead of them and headed north. Dane's gun was out in a twinkling, but he put it back.

"Why didn't you shoot?" asked Esther.

"Thought your horse might be gun-shy," he replied. "He seems high-strung."

"I don't believe you could have hit it," observed the girl.

"Maybe not. It was a smart ways off." He smiled at her. "Saturn!" he said sharply, as his horse stumbled. Then he held his face up to the cool, night wind.

"Is that your horse's name—Saturn?" Esther asked curiously.

"That's his name, ma'am. See him prick up his ears when you said it?"

"Funny name for a horse," she commented. "How did you happen to name him that?"

"Let's see. Saturn's the star that's got the rings aroun' it, ain't it, ma'am? Well, this gelding can run rings aroun' most horses, an' I guess that's how he got his name."

She laughed in evident amusement and delight. "Named for a star," she said. "I've watched you ride at night, Mr. Dane. You evidently like the stars."

"I like the stars because they're beautiful to me, ma'am," he replied in a voice that just carried to her ears. "I like the prairie cactus flowers, too, ma'am, an' the trees along the river, an' the flatlands rolling like a carpet to the mountains. I like the sky, too, ma'am, an' if we come back to earth after we die, as a lot of folks seem to think, I'd like to be an eagle an' soar aroun' up there an' watch." He paused, looking at her to see if she were laughing.

But she wasn't laughing. She was looking at him with astonished interest.

"Why, you are poetical," she said in a voice of surprise.

He looked away. “Maybe I am an’ didn’t know it,” he observed. “There’s the lights o’ town ahead, ma’am.”

She saw them glimmering faintly against the shadowy plain with the dark outlines of the Western mountains behind. Her gaze roved back to the man who rode beside her. He was more of a mystery now than ever. He had revealed a new side of his personality. He was a dreamer, too. Somehow he didn’t look at all like the sort of a man she took him to be. She caught herself up at this thought, compressing her lips, as she remembered the meeting she had witnessed in the bottoms. He had not returned next day. She hadn’t been told of the theft of the cattle.

Nevertheless she felt a sense of security, riding with him in this way in the night. Without intending to do so she compared him with the men she had met when she was at school in the East. He was an accomplished rider. Yet she had seen many Eastern men who were excellent horsemen. He evidently knew how to handle cattle. Yet that was his business—or part of his business. She glanced instinctively at the gun at his side. In that he was different. And in his dreamy, poetical viewpoint of life and nature he was different. And his calm assurance, his quiet confidence, as beguiling as it was convincing, that made him different, too.

What did he think of her, she wondered, with a vague thrill.

"We better ride along to the hotel first," he said, interrupting her thoughts. "I'll find out about the dance—where it is, an' one thing an' another, after I've taken you there an' put up the horses."

She readily assented. Now that she was nearly in town she was not just sure what she wished to do. Her main thought had been to be near Fred in event of trouble. What she would do in an emergency she didn't know. Now that she had come she realized that she had no plans, no method of procedure outlined. But when Fred saw her it most likely would have a steadying effect upon him.

They rode through town to the little hotel. Dane dismounted and held out a hand to aid her. She was surprised at his courtesy. They entered the small lobby.

"I'll leave you here a few minutes, ma'am, while I put up the horses and find out about the dance an' who's in town," he said, holding his hat in his hand. "I won't be gone long."

"Thank you," she said nervously and sought a chair.

She continued to stare at the door long after he had left.

What was there about this man that inspired her with confidence in him, despite what she thought she knew about him? Was she trusting him—it certainly amounted to that—because he, to all appearances, was working for her father? She knew this was not the case. Why did she resent his apparent infatuation for the dance-hall girl? Would that not be natural? Would not such a girl, indeed, be of his kind? Why did she think of him so seriously at all? She flushed, even as she asked herself this question. She was becoming silly!

It was nearly an hour before Dane returned. He appeared uneasy, removed his hat, and sat down in a chair near her.

"Did you see Fred?" she asked impatiently.

"Yes," replied Dane, "I saw him." He evaded her glance of inquiry.

"Well, where *is* he?" she asked impulsively.

"Why, he's at the dance, ma'am," drawled Dane.

"Of course," she said, compressing her lips. "That's what he came to town for. Who else is there?"

"There's quite a few there, ma'am; they came from all aroun', I guess. This is the last blow-out before the rodeo the first week in October. They all seem to be turnin' out for it."

"Very well, we'd better go," she said, leaning forward in her chair.

Dane seemed disturbed. He fidgeted about, cleared his throat. "I reckon you don't want to go to the dance, ma'am," he said finally.

"Not go! Why not? I came here for that

purpose." She lifted her brows in surprise. "Why shouldn't I go?" she asked sharply.

"Well, you see, ma'am, this dance ain't bein' staged in any regular hall."

She made a gesture of irritation. "Tell me what you mean," she said, leaning back in exasperation.

"They're holdin' this dance in The Palace," said Dane coolly. "I didn't know if you'd want to go there or not."

"Why shouldn't I go there?" she demanded. "If that's where the people of this vicinity dance, it must be the proper thing. Do you mean that there are no respectable people there? I don't hardly believe Fred wants to run with a questionable crowd."

Dane shrugged and rose to his splendid height. "As you say, ma'am. We might as well horn in."

She resented the way he put it but rose and passed through the door he held open for her. They walked in silence to The Palace. He pushed the swinging doors open, and they entered.

Esther stopped with a little gasp. The Palace was a blaze of light and a blare of sound. Festoons of bunting hung from the ceiling, partly obscuring the lamps, so that the place was bathed in a soft light; sprigs of evergreen and balsam branches were entwined with the bunting and draped about the few posts. The bar was strewn with glasses and bottles, lined with men. The reflection of the dancers and moving faces gave the mirror on the wall behind the bar a vivid, living reality; beneath it the iridescent gleam of a myriad of polished glasses flaunted the colors of a rainbow.

The place was packed. To the left the dancing floor was crowded. The orchestra played upon the little stage, with a large American flag draped behind and green branches at the foot. Solid strips of bunting in the national colors were stretched the length of the balcony above, and evergreens concealed the railing.

Evidently the gaming tables had been removed this night from the floor in the rear, and the space was given up to dancing. A movement in and out of the rear rooms testified to the fact that gambling had not been tabooed entirely, however. High stakes would rule on an occasion like this; and stiff games do not seek the general public.

The music of the orchestra was augmented by a queer medley of sounds which closely approached a din—shouts and laughter, women and girls shrilling greetings to each other, men renewing acquaintance with slaps on the back, the rhythmical movement of many feet, the clinking of glasses, the jingle of spurs, the loud voice of the man who called the dance numbers, the staccato of pistol shots from some celebrant without, and snatches of labored songs from roisterers at the bar.

Decidedly the crowd was an authentic representation of all the people living in the surrounding country. Cow-punchers, with flowing scarfs in brilliant hues and leather chaps and high-heeled boots, stockmen with great hats and heavy watch chains against broad expanse of vests, dry-land farmers, in their "Sunday best," looking distinctly different from the stockmen—less boisterous, too; pale-faced professional gamblers attired in somber tones; hangers-on and game "boosters" looking like prospectors in their affected rough dress; youth gay with the finery of ready-made, mail-order clothes; girls in fluffy white frocks, set off with pink and blue ribbons and sashes; matrons in sedate black and gray silks, with white lace collars.

Dane made way for Esther to the left and drew her to a place where she could have a good view of the dancing floor and the spectators.

It was not an altogether new scene to her; but she had been away for the better part of four years, and she was astonished at the progress which had been made since she last had attended a dance in the range country. The decorative scheme was better, more artistic. The men no longer wore their spurs while dancing. The youths were better dressed, and the girls, too. And the orchestra was playing jazz, while a majority of those on the floor danced modern steps! Truly in some ways her West had changed.

Dane, looking up, saw Fred Hughes and Marie on the balcony. Esther, following his gaze, saw them, too. Her face flushed, as she saw Fred and the girl laughing and talking quite as very good friends. Then the girl drew away from him, despite his apparent protests, and came down upon the floor, as the number ended.

Fred remained on the balcony, looking a bit gloomy. Dane saw Esther was watching the girl narrowly and in disapproval, as she came out on the floor. A man stepped quickly from the throng of spectators and walked toward her. Dane recognized Bunker, with a start.

The girl, Marie, looking very pretty in her white dress, stepped back from Bunker. Her eyes clouded.

Bunker said something with a leering grin, and she shook her head. The Flying W foreman spoke again, attempted to take her by the arm, but she evaded him. Then Bunker's face became dark, and his eyes flashed angrily. Words, which Dane could not hear, came quickly, and Marie raised her head haughtily.

Bunker, evidently wild with rage, leaped forward and grasped the girl by the arm.

There was a movement above the pair. Fred Hughes stripped the evergreens from a section of the rail, flung himself over it, hung for a moment above the floor, and then dropped upon Bunker's head and shoulders, breaking his hold upon the girl and sending him to the floor, with himself on top of him.

Esther screamed, and there was a sudden cessation of the sounds within the place, as Dane leaped out upon the floor and in two bounds reached the struggling pair.

Bunker, with his superior strength, was fast mastering Fred, and he was trying to get out his gun. Dane bent over them, and, as Bunker whipped Fred beneath him with his left arm, Dane reached down and jerked the Flying W man's gun from its holster, just as Bunker struck for it with his right hand.

He cursed in surprise and, rising, flung the youth from him. He found himself face to face with Dane. His eyes narrowed to slits, and the red flame of uncontrollable anger darted from them. Dane stood holding the other's gun in his hand.

"This ain't the time for a gun play, Bunker," said Dane in a hard, stern voice. "There's too many here that won't stand for you shootin' down a boy in cold blood. An' I take it there's some here that don't like your style on general principles."

His gaze shot past Bunker's purple face to where Fred Hughes was picking himself up and looking toward Bunker, a wild light in the boy's eyes. The youth's face was livid with a grimace of hatred.

"Fred—*don't draw!*" warned Dane, as Bunker whirled.

But Fred's gun was in his hand. His eyes were blazing. Even Bunker was taken aback. Dane was momentarily powerless to move because of what he saw.

Then the girl, Marie, white-faced, her eyes wide with fear, stepped deliberately between the boy and Bunker.

CHAPTER XXIII
STARTLING NEWS

Everyone in the room stood as if rooted to the spot, many on tiptoe, staring at the queer tableau. A silence, so complete and impressive that it almost could be felt, held the spectators breathless, in weird contrast to their revelry of a few moments before.

Looking into the girl's eyes Fred Hughes lowered his gun. A wave of emotion swept over his features, and the weapon clattered on the floor, released by nerveless fingers.

Marie smiled at him. "You are so queek with the anger, my Fred," she said softly in a low voice that nevertheless carried to those nearby.

Esther came hurriedly across the floor and, ignoring Marie, stepped between her and her brother. Fred's face regained its color in a flush of irritation. He scowled at his sister, as she put her arms about him and urged him to leave the place and go home.

Bunker turned on Dane with a snarl. "You've got the high hand again," he said in a thick voice which trembled with rage. "You're mighty lucky."

"There's your gun," said Dane, tossing the confiscated weapon to the other's feet.

Several men stepped forward, as Bunker stooped to recover his six-shooter. His gaze roved over their faces. Sturdy types of manhood, these; reputable men, evidently, who would not stand for any dirty work or gun play, or other acts of violence, when their women were on the scene.

Dane watched him like a cat as he picked up his weapon and thrust it into his holster.

"One of these days I'll run across you when you ain't carryin' a horseshoe," he sneered, darting a glance at Dane from eyes glowing with hatred. "When you see me again you want to be ready to draw!"

He turned and pushed his way through the crowd toward the door.

Dane saw Esther and Fred, but Marie had disappeared. He made his way through the throng to the stairway and went up to the balcony. He walked to the forward end, passed behind the curtain there, and knocked at the door to the rooms occupied by Marie. He had to knock twice before he got an answer. The girl opened the door hesitatingly, her eyes wide.

"Come in," she said when she saw who it was.

"Marie, what does all this mean?" Dane asked, as he stepped inside.

"Ah, Mistair Dane, you can see for yourself," she said, closing the door.

"No, I can't see," returned Dane sternly. "Why was young Fred so quick to jump on Bunker when he grabbed your arm? Why does Bunker keep after you? Why did you step between them when it looked like Fred would shoot sure before I could stop him? You might have been killed."

"Oh, I do not want to see Mistair Fred kill anybody," said the girl loudly. "He jump on Bunker because Bunker annoy me. It is you who save Fred, Mistair Dane. You are a big, brave mans."

She threw her arms about his neck suddenly and kissed him. Then she stepped back and laughed delightedly, while he stared at her in astonishment and perplexity.

"Why did you do that?" he asked, vaguely aware that his query sounded ridiculous.

"Because you save Mistair Fred," she answered, looking down.

"What's Fred to you?" Dane demanded.

"He ees ver' good friend," she replied, tossing her head.

"Look here, Marie, you've got to talk," declared Dane, now aroused. "Things are gettin' too serious to play this guessin' game. Where did you get my gun that you gave me the night you led us out of the bad lands?"

"I can no tell now—I am afraid," she said, her eyes avoiding his.

"You must tell me," he said sharply. "The man who got that gun, or the *person* who got that gun, is the one who shot Williams."

"No—no, it is not so," cried Marie.

"How do you know?" Dane thundered.

She was silent, her eyes downcast.

"You asked me not to hurt the hermit," said Dane sternly. "I ain't been near him. But I'll find him, an' I'll make him talk, if you don't come through."

"No!" she cried, grasping his arm. "You must not. You must have the trust for me—you must have the trust. Some time I tell you everyt'ing I know." She was speaking so fast it was almost impossible for him to distinguish her words. "I do not know who shoot the man, Williams—I do not know."

"Where did you get the gun?"

"I can no tell—it was by the accident. I give it to you to prove I am worthy of the trust."

"Where did you get the gun?"

She looked about wildly, clinging to his arm. Then she became calm and looked fearlessly into his eyes.

"From the hermit," she said quietly.

"Of course!" snapped Dane. "No wonder you asked me to handle him easy. He shot Williams an' tried to put the blame on me—or on Gordon Hughes. He rapped me on the head, so I couldn't see what was goin' on, an' then he took me to his cabin an' kept me long enough to pull the wool over my eyes. An' he's leadin' the rustlers in the bad lands in the bargain. A nice crowd you're in with! I believe you're one of 'em an' helpin' this scheme along. Don't ask me to spare the hermit after what you've told me to-night!"

"Oh, Mistair Dane, you no understand," the girl wailed. "It is no so what you say. Listen!" She spoke fiercely now. "Who tell you where your gun come from? It ees me—I tell you. Do you think I tell you if the hermit shoot Williams an' hit you? I tell you, an' I take you out of them bad lan's because I am the square. You must no hurt the—hermit!"

Dane shook his head in the negative. "He's the man that can clear up the shootin' business an' the cattle stealin'," he said. "I'm workin' for the Diamond H, an' I can't promise something I ain't got the right to promise."

"But you must," she cried wildly. "You are the beeg man. You must trust little me an' not break my heart."

"Break your heart!" exclaimed Dane, astonished. "Why, what does the hermit amount to in your life?"

She buried her head upon his shoulder.

"He ees my father!" she sobbed.

Dane stared straight ahead, disregarding the weeping girl. Her father. He remembered that the history of the old man and the girl was rather vague in that community. So *that* explained her rides to the bad lands! It explained why she had led them out by her secret trail. It was to place them under obligations to her so that she could ask that the hermit, her father, be protected. But the gun! She said it came from the hermit, but she denied that her father had done the shooting or had assaulted him. The hermit had said he had found him lying on the ground. Perhaps he had; but he had denied knowledge of the gun. And the fact remained that it looked very much as if he was operating with the rustlers.

"Are you tellin' me the truth?" Dane asked, holding the girl off, although she clung to his arms, and the tears continued to fall.

A look into her eyes, her shaken manner, convinced him that she had not lied to him.

The door was flung open, and Fred Hughes came in. He stared from one to the other, and his face darkened with anger.

"So this is it, is it?" he said to Marie.

"Don't be taking too much for granted," said Dane scowling.

"You!" cried Fred. "Dane, I think you're a rat!"

Dane's face clouded. He thrust the girl aside.

"I'm beginning to think what you need is a first-class lickin'," he said grimly.

"An' I'm thinkin' what I thought from the first," retorted the boy hotly. "You're a first-class double-crosser!"

"Don't say that again!" Dane warned him, his eyes narrowing.

Fred hesitated. He was boiling mad. "Oh,

bein' a gunman you've got me stopped," he said bitterly. "But guns don't get a man everything, Dane." His look was a mixture of cunning and hatred and rage.

"It wouldn't have got you anything if you'd shot Bunker," said Dane sharply.

"An' I'm believing you had more'n one reason for buttin' in on that play the way you did," snapped Fred, darting a scornful look at Marie. Before Dane could reply, Esther Hughes appeared in the doorway.

"Oh!" she said, arching her brows. "Is this some kind of a family gathering?"

Fred swore under his breath. "Sis, you're gettin' so you act like you'd left your brains back East," he said angrily and strode out of the room.

Dane smiled at her queerly. She sensed she had interrupted a tense situation. Marie stared at her with wide eyes. Tears still clung to her lashes. Esther averted her gaze haughtily.

"Maybe we better be goin' home, ma'am," Dane suggested in a polite voice.

Marie approached him, touched his arm, and looked up at him appealingly.

"You will remember?" she asked softly.

For a few moments he studied her. "Yes," he answered. Esther turned abruptly, and he followed her out. As they left, Marie dropped into a chair and buried her face in her hands. Dane led Esther through the crowd below. She breathed long breaths of the cool, fresh air, and then she shuddered, paused, and began to sway.

Dane caught her. "Are you feelin' bad, Miss Esther?" he asked with concern.

"No," she managed to say, closing her eyes, and fighting against the faintness which came with the reaction from her experience of the last half hour.

She steadied finally. "I wonder if Fred has started for home," she said wearily.

"I reckon he has—or will be startin' soon, ma'am," Dane replied. "We better go along to the hotel, if you're feelin' better. You'll likely want to rest a bit before we go back."

"Oh, it all was dreadful. I'll rest while you're getting the horses. I guess it was a good thing we came—that you were there, Mr. Dane."

He kept silent, as they walked to the hotel. He had many things on his mind. Marie's revelation had startled him—explained many things. Fred's conduct he dismissed with a frown. As for Esther, she was evidently sorry, but still unconvinced that he was acting in good faith. And he would not yield to the impulse to confide in her—tell her everything. She would have to find him out for herself.

He went for the horses and learned from the man at the barn that Fred had got his horse and ridden away. He took some time to saddle and take their mounts around to the front of the hotel.

He wished to give Esther an opportunity to rest.

They rode silently homeward. Overhead were myriads of stars, and a silver slice of moon rode in the high arch of the sky. Dane was preoccupied, and Esther, too, seemed busy with her own thoughts. They passed the big cottonwood and rode across the bottoms. They did not stop at the shed, but went on to the porch. Dane assisted her to dismount. She stood for a moment with the light of the moon on her face.

"I want to thank you," she said in a low, trembling voice. "And there's so much—I don't understand."

Her hand touched his sleeve, and she went hurriedly into the house.

For a brief interval Dane stood looking up at the star-filled night, his hat in his hands.

CHAPTER XXIV
TWO WOMEN

If Dane was puzzled, worried, undecided concerning the turn events had taken—uncertain as to what his next move should be, he was not in a more trying quandary than Esther Hughes.

The girl was not only perplexed, she was the victim of an insatiable curiosity. She didn't know what to think about Dane, and it aggravated her exceedingly to find herself wondering if she hadn't misjudged him. She was annoyed at him because he was so much of a mystery, yet she admired him for his quick action at the dance and confessed to herself that he had given her glimpses of a most interesting personality.

However, she had heard that dangerous characters in the West were often agreeable persons, even educated, and that the most dangerous were the ones who were slow to anger and slower still to resort to their weapons. But once they "went for their guns," the saying was that it "meant a funeral."

Dane could be a gentleman, apparently. Yet she had seen the look in his eyes, as he watched Bunker pick up the gun which had been thrown at his feet; and she realized with a shudder that the look had meant death for Bunker, if the Flying W foreman had then tried to use his weapon. She could not forget that look. She could not forget the scene in Marie's room. She could not forget that the dance-hall girl had asked him if he "would remember," and he had answered "yes."

And Fred! Why had he become so angry when she appeared. Her remark upon entering the room? She had meant nothing by it. Anyway, Fred had been acting strangely, and she condoned his impulsive speech as due to the exciting experience he had just gone through. But her lips tightened, as she recalled his presence on the balcony with the dance-hall girl before she had been accosted on the floor by Bunker. And Fred had undeniably acted as he had because of her. Marie could tell her much if she so desired, Esther concluded. At any event she might be able to tell her something about Dane.

Esther kept thinking of this all the day following their return from the dance. And in the late afternoon she saddled her horse and rode up on the bench land. Striking westward she rode until she passed the cottonwood tree in the center of the strip. There she sat her horse for some time, unaware that Dane was watching her from a ridge at the edge of the bad lands, where he had happened in the course of a fresh search for Marie's secret trail to the hermit's cabin. Finally, after turning back toward the ranch, she changed her mind and rode into the sunset on the road to town.

Dane rode out of the brakes and up to the road above the cottonwood, looking after her with a worried and puzzled expression.

Esther didn't ride fast. She wished to collect her thoughts. She wished to know thoroughly the purpose of her errand before she arrived in town *this* time. The twilight was spreading over the land, as she came close to Black Butte. She rode into the trees along the creek, dismounted and waited for dark. She wasn't exactly sure why it was she didn't wish to be observed, but she responded to some inner sense of caution. And she carefully planned her moves. She was glad no one had seen her leave the ranch, as she thought.

When darkness had descended she skirted the tree growth along the little creek to the point where it was nearest the eastern end of the town's short main street. Here she tied her horse and then proceeded on foot. She hesitated near the front entrance of The Palace and wondered wildly if there wasn't a way she could enter from the rear. The deep shadow behind the building, however, discouraged her, and, using all her will power, she entered through the swinging doors.

The decorations of the night before remained, but the crowd was gone. The place was all but deserted. As she looked around she saw a few men at the gaming tables, which had been reinstated in the rear of the big room, and a few others at the bar. Marie was not in sight.

Summoning her courage she walked rapidly to the stairway leading to the balcony and went up. She hurried along the balcony to the curtain and rapped on the door to the room where she had followed her brother the night before. The door opened, and the dance-hall girl stood before her.

"What do you want?" asked Marie in a tone far from cordial.

Esther bristled. Why should this girl feel antagonistic toward her? She held back the sharp retort which was on her tongue and pushed her way into the room.

"I want to talk with you a minute," she explained with a forced smile.

The girl confronted her, leaving the door open.

"What ees it?" she asked. Her eyes were wells of resentful light. Yet there was suspicion and curiosity in her gaze, too. And Esther divined that the girl was all too conscious of the difference in their positions.

She decided to take advantage of this.

"What was Mr. Dane telling you that made you cry last night?" she asked with another attempt to smile. She hadn't meant to put this question first, she realized, biting her lip; it had slipped out.

Marie laughed in delight. "You ask me? I tell

you I cry because of what I tell him. Why don't you ask Mistair Dane?"

Esther couldn't conceal her irritation nor her eagerness. "It is only right you should tell me what—what all this is about," she said with a note of pleading in her voice.

"Ah, an' so you want to know. You like Mistair Dane, maybe—like him ver' much?"

Esther's face flamed. "That isn't the question," she flared. "And it's ridiculous. Maybe you will tell me this: Why did my own brother attack that man Bunker because he was trying to—to dance with you, I suppose?"

"Oh," exclaimed Marie, "you are Mistair Fred's sister? How shall I know?"

Esther frowned at this. "I am telling you the truth," she said severely. "Why should my brother be so anxious to protect you?"

"He is the gallant," chirped Marie. "You would not want him to be so?"

"My dear girl, I am not finding fault with my brother," said Esther, changing her tactics. "But it is plain you have some sort of influence over him and Mr. Dane who is working on our ranch. I came here thinking perhaps you could tell me something of Mr. Dane—who he is, and where he comes from. Perhaps he has told you more than he has me. He seems to like you."

"A ver' fine man," said Marie, nodding her head several times. "Ver' brave. He knock that

Bunker down the stairs an' shoot ver' fast."

"So I understand," remarked Esther dryly. "Why did he knock Bunker down the stairs?"

"He try to be mean with me," answered Marie.

"I see," said Esther, raising her brows. "The main function of the men from our place seems to be to protect you."

Marie's eyes sparkled. "You are angry because so?"

"I have seen you meet Mr. Dane in the bottoms near the bad lands," Esther accused.

"You are a spy," flashed Marie with a fierce look. "An' he never meet me there, except one night when he catch me on the road an' ask me where I've been."

"I saw you ride down from the road to the shadow of the trees and saw him ride after you, and both of you disappeared," said Esther.

"Ah, but yes. It was so, *that* night. He look to see where I have gone, but he no find me."

"Then where did you go?" asked Esther skeptically.

"That I no tell," said Marie firmly. "Mistair Dane, he know."

"I thought so," said Esther coldly.

Marie frowned at her, and Esther immediately jumped to the conclusion that the girl was angry at her because she thought she was interested in Dane. She flushed again under the girl's gaze.

"You are think something ees wrong?" asked

Marie with a coolness which was disconcerting. “If you want to know something about your man you go to him an’ not to be asking other peoples. You can tell by the eyes if the man he ees all right!”

Esther’s face was flaming.

“You have no right to talk to me like that,” she began, but her words froze, as she heard a step on the balcony.

Then Dane appeared in the doorway.

Both girls stared at him—Marie with bright eyes, seemingly glad that he had come; Esther, disconcerted at first, then loftily, as it occurred to her that he was paying another visit to the dance-hall girl.

“I am glad you are come,” said Marie. “She ask about you.” She favored Esther with a side glance full of devilment.

Esther’s gaze fell before Dane’s questioning look. Then she tossed her head arrogantly.

“Don’t let me interfere with your visit,” she said, moving toward the door.

“I came here to get you,” said Dane evenly.

“Yes? How interesting. And how did you know I was here?”

“I saw you ride toward town. When you didn’t come back by nightfall I decided you had come on into town. I followed you an’ found you where I reckoned you’d be.”

“I do not like the idea of you spying on my

movements," said Esther, assuming a haughty attitude to conceal her confusion. "I will go now."

Dane stepped aside, and, as Esther passed him, Marie touched him on the arm.

"Mistair Fred—he ees mad with me?" she asked, her eyes glowing.

"He's peeved about something," Dane grinned.

"It ees because you are here when he come last night," she said in a bubbling voice.

Dane was about to say something, but he saw Esther hurrying down the balcony stairs, and he hastened after her and overtook her outside the front entrance.

She turned on him. "You needn't accompany me," she said.

"All the same I'm sure goin' along, ma'am," he replied cheerfully. "My horse is tied over in the trees by yours."

"You had no right to follow me," she flared.

"It ain't wise for you to be ridin' aroun' these prairies at night alone, ma'am," he said in an earnest voice.

"How about that dance-hall girl's night riding?" she asked, and then was sorry for it at once.

"A different matter," responded Dane, frowning.

"Quite naturally," said Esther coldly. Yet she pondered over the girl's denial that she had ridden to the bad lands to meet Dane. It was all so baffling. And she resented Dane's cool assertiveness, his domineering protection of her.

"I'll ride home alone," she told him when they reached the horses.

For reply he untied her horse and stood by while she mounted. She dug in her spurs, and the black raced toward the road.

In a few moments Dane was at her side. She spurred the black to his utmost, but couldn't shake Dane's bay. She gave it up and slowed to a swinging lope.

Dane's laugh sounded musically on her ears. She looked at him and saw he was smiling at her.

"Did Marie tell you what you wanted to know?" he inquired, his eyes sparkling.

She recalled the dance-hall girl's declaration that "you can tell by the eyes" if the man is all right. She looked away quickly and checked her mount to a walk.

"I think *you* are the one who should tell me," she said.

"Maybe someday I will, Miss Esther," he said softly, leaning toward her.

She could think of no answer to this. Moreover she felt a mysterious glow—a thrill—within her. Was it the quality of his tone, his words, the look in his eyes—the presence of him?

She upbraided herself mentally for her interest in him, an unknown. Perhaps an outlaw; more than likely an adventurer of the plains. Yet her very reasoning thus was an antithesis, and she found herself regarding him surreptitiously.

Perhaps the dance-hall girl was wiser than she knew! She pulled up her horse at the big cottonwood. "Mr. Dane," she said earnestly, "why do you persist in remaining such a mystery?"

He looked straight into her eyes.

"All the things aroun' us are a mystery, Miss Esther," he said whimsically. "The stars, the shadows that drift on these plains, this fine, big cottonwood tree, the mountains at our backs. We don't ask where they come from; we take 'em as they are. I reckon I'm a part of it. As long as we don't know all about the stars, or the trees, or the mountains, we'll keep wonderin' about 'em. If I was to tell you all about myself you'd quit wonderin' about me. An' I reckon I don't exactly want *that,* ma'am."

Esther drove in her spurs. She gave him her reins with a murmured "Good night," when they reached the porch of the ranch house.

Then she sat for an hour at her darkened window, thinking of his reply. And in time she came partly to understand it.

CHAPTER XXV
ON THE NORTH RANGE

For a whole week Dane kept strict watch throughout the day and part of the night on the bad lands. On two different days he maintained a vigil on the ridge above the hermit's cabin from early in the morning until midnight. But in all this time he saw no one in the tumbled country along the river except the hermit himself, who was living in his cabin as if nothing ever had happened, leaving it only for short intervals, when he disappeared in the direction of the river. Marie did not visit him on one of her night rides during this time, so far as Dane knew.

Dane was tempted more than once to visit the hermit to try to cajole or threaten him into telling what he knew about the rustling operations and the shooting of Williams, but the astonishing confession of Marie, that the hermit was her father, deterred him. Also he had implicit faith in his belief that the rustlers would again show their hand.

August now was well along. The green of the prairies had long since changed to gold. Gordon Hughes came down with a crew of men and put them to cutting the hay. When he was ready to return to the north range Dane announced that he wanted to go with him.

"I'm not gettin' anywhere here," he explained; "an' when the cattle thieves start workin' again they'll have to go where the stock is—up north."

Hughes readily assented. He was short of men, owing to the loss of those who had to put up the hay. When he left for the north range in the morning Dane rode with him. He asked for night duty, and Hughes agreed to this, also.

Dane soon was in excellent standing with the men. He found to his surprise that he had something of a reputation among them. Old Marty had spread the story of his encounters with Bunker in town and had aired his opinion as to what he thought about Dane's skill with his gun. Many of them called him Lightning to his face, and he merely smiled.

And he soon demonstrated that he was an experienced cow-puncher. While branding the fall calves he exhibited his skill with the rope, time and time again. Cow-punchers have specialties as well as men of other vocations. Dane's specialty won him the instant respect of every other roper with the outfit.

Not only did he stand his hours of guard at night, but he also helped with the work throughout the day. He never got more than four and a half hours of sleep. He was prepared to take on any extra task, or to do any one a favor.

The only thing he refused to do was talk, except for a friendly greeting, or a discourse connected with the work at hand. He sat by the fire, silent, moody, and almost forlorn, yet he heard everything that was said.

There was only one man with the outfit who paid him scant attention and purposely avoided him. That was Fred Hughes. The youth hadn't spoken to him since the night in Black Butte when he might have been killed, had it not been for Dane's quick action.

Dane pretended not to notice this singular situation. Yet, as time passed, he thought he saw a change in Gordon Hughes, also. The rancher did not appear quite so cordial, and Dane caught him looking at him several times in a peculiar way—half suspicious, half puzzled. Then one night it all came out.

It was a cool night in September, with a chilling wind sweeping down from the north. Clouds were scuttling across the sky, and there were indications of a storm. The cattle were uneasy, and Dane was singing. Fred was riding herd with him this night.

As they came in after midnight, Dane continued to sing softly, ignoring the boy who was riding close behind him.

Fred suddenly spurred his horse to Dane's side.

"You seem mighty cheerful," he said sarcastically. “Guess you ain’t worryin’ if we get the stock shipped or not.”

Dane ceased singing and looked at him.

“Worryin’ won’t get ’em shipped any quicker,” he observed wisely.

“No, an’ there’s lots of other things that mightn’t get ’em shipped,” said Fred. “We might lose ’em.”

“That ain’t likely with the bunch of men we’ve got,” said Dane.

“Well, we lost one bunch out of the back yard,” said Fred pointedly. “An’ it was funny you couldn’t find ’em when you was right on their heels.”

Dane considered. “Your father told you about it, I suppose,” he remarked dryly.

“Yes, an’ I’ll bet if *I’d* been aroun’ there they wouldn’t have got ’em across the river.”

“They didn’t get ’em across the river—*that* night or day,” said Dane with a dark scowl.

“Maybe not, but all we’ve got is your word for it.”

“You forgettin’ that Servais was along?” asked Dane sharply.

“No, but he ain’t so bright. He could be fooled—fooled as easy as some women I know. Like Marie, for instance.”

Dane was thoroughly angry. “Fred, you’re not talkin’ sense. I know what you’re gettin’ at. You’re tryin’ to say you think I had something to do with the runnin' off of that herd of a hundred head. An' you're hintin' that I'm hangin' aroun' Marie. You can think what you want about the herd, an' the other ain't none of your business!"

Fred's eyes flashed with anger, as his hand dropped to the butt of his gun. Then he stared with awed fascination into the black bore of Dane's weapon. He hadn't even seen the draw!

"An' you ain't got no business carryin' a gun," said Dane in a taunting voice, as they rode down to the wagon.

Nevertheless Fred's insinuations bothered Dane. That explained the changed attitude of Gordon Hughes. Fred had been telling him his suspicions. And Dane was compelled to confess to himself that it did look none too good for him. The cattle *had* disappeared from under his very eyes, almost. And Fred was undoubtedly jealous of the fact that Dane had aided Marie on two occasions. Why this should be he couldn't reason out. He wondered if Fred knew that the hermit was Marie's father. He was convinced none of the others on the Diamond H knew it.

The beef round-up was now on in earnest, with shipping day coming apace. Gordon Hughes was pushing the work as rapidly as possible. He had to ship by the first week in October to be sure of having the money to meet his paper at the bank. He knew he could not renew again with the boundary unsettled; he doubted if he could renew if the line were established. He had not attempted to fence it, as Williams was only just beginning to be about again. He didn't wish to make the Flying W owner think he had taken advantage of him while he was recovering from his wound. And he had had much to do. Now the haying was over, and he had all his men. When the beeves were rounded up he ordered Shay and a number of the men to remain with the other cattle. The balance of his force, including Dane and Fred, he selected to drive the beef herd to the shipping point, forty miles northwest.

On the first of October he announced they would start with the beef herd next day.

CHAPTER XXVI
THE ATTACK

It was a cool, bracing, typical autumn morning when they started with the beef herd. The cattle were in prime condition. The four-year-old shorthorns were especially good stock, larger than any of the Herefords and range breeds. While taking longer to mature, this breed, originally from the north of England, will average a larger beef, and Gordon Hughes realized that, since he had had to feed *all* his stock during two terrible winters, he had been fortunate in having the shorthorns after all. They would certainly command top price in the Chicago market and, with the other beeves, would bring more than the amount he needed to clear the pressing debt of the Diamond H and pay off his men.

There were six cow-punchers besides Hughes, Fred, and Dane, looking after the fifteen hundred head in the herd. The cook drove the light chuck wagon. They moved slowly, as Hughes did not wish to lose any more weight than was absolutely unavoidable. He had to bring his cattle to the market in excellent condition, and he had an enviable record with the buyers for so doing. He figured on three days to Highline, the shipping point. The cars had been ordered, and he had been notified they were waiting in the railway yards. He and Fred and four of the punchers were going East with the cattle. Allowing three days to Chicago, he expected to have his stock sold by October tenth at latest, which would give him four days and a half in which to return and settle his business with the American Bank in Black Butte—two days more than absolutely required. This, of course, providing Stevens, the banker, had not instructed that a draft be sent direct to him. In such event there would be plenty of time for the matter to be settled through the mails.

But time in this instance was indeed the "essence of the contract."

"Now don't try to trail 'em," said Hughes to his men, although this warning was hardly necessary. "Let 'em graze along. They won't lose any weight that way, an' some of 'em might pick up some. We'll hit water again to-night on the upper Muddy."

The herd was off the bedding ground shortly after dawn. Dane evaded both Fred and his father as much as possible. He would rather have stayed with Shay and the men looking after the other cattle in the north, as he believed the rustlers would strike there if they knew the beeves were being moved, and Gordon Hughes was gone; but the attitude of Fred had left him loath to ask for any special assignment from Hughes.

They proceeded slowly, the cattle grazing along, the men holding them in the direction they wanted them to go, but they made twelve miles that day and bedded down two miles beyond the upper Muddy Creek. Hughes was in charge and designated two of the punchers for the eight-to-ten night watch, Dane and another puncher for the ten-to-twelve watch, Fred and a puncher for the twelve-two watch, and two other punchers for the two-to-four watch. Breakfast would be ready at four in the morning.

Fetching their beds from the chuck wagon the men put them on the ground about the fire. Each man had two horses, and these were run in with the herd, making a wrangler unnecessary. The four horses for the chuck wagon were also put in with the herd at night.

Dane sat near the fire on his blankets, scowling into the blaze. He did not like the idea of being off the ranch; he was resentful of Fred's veiled accusation, of Gordon Hughes for evidently listening to Fred's charges, and he was irritated because Marie hadn't seen fit to tell him more than she had, and because he had been, as he thought, too lenient with her father, the hermit. He speculated, too, on what might happen while they were with the beef herd, and while Hughes was in Chicago. He would have to appear at the fall term of court, too, on the charge of having shot Williams. Could he clear up the mystery of that affair before he was called to court? Would Marie help him to do so? Or, after all, was the whole business a part of a scheme to get him out of the way and injure Gordon Hughes?

He went on guard at ten o'clock in a troubled frame of mind. When he came off at midnight he rode slowly under the stars for some time. It was half past two in the morning before he turned in for an hour or so of sleep.

They were a little late getting off the bedding ground that morning, but the cattle moved a little faster this day of their own accord. The shorthorns kept in the lead, with the white-faces showing an inclination to range farther out. They watered at some springs early in the afternoon and bedded down that night, thirteen and a half miles for the day, making twenty-five and a half miles on their way, with fourteen and a half miles yet to go.

"We'll have to make it to-morrow," said Hughes cheerfully. "An' we're lucky we've got the weather with us."

Dane talked quite a bit that night with a cow-puncher, named "Buck" Colter, who stood guard with him. When he went off at twelve o'clock, turning the guard over to Fred Hughes and another, he again rode out under the stars. The prairie here was more broken than to eastward. There were many small rises of ground and occasional coulees, where grew a few cottonwoods. They were nearing another creek in the north, where they would water in the morning.

As Dane rode along a gentle rise, his attention became fixed on a point north of the bedding ground of the cattle. He was some little distance west of the herd. He thought he saw a moving shadow near some miniature ridges on the north horizon. The moon had gone behind the mountains in the west at midnight, and the light of the stars was partly obscured by fleecy veils of cloud which were drifting in the night sky.

As he looked he made sure of the shadow, and then he saw others. In another moment he realized the significance of the shadows, when he saw them come racing down toward the cattle. There were nearly a score of them—riders bearing down upon the herd!

He gave the bay the spurs and dashed back toward camp. Shots now came riding on the wind from the riders nearing the cattle. The men had been closer to the bedding ground than he had thought. A shower of shots greeted his ears, and there were wild yells and shouts. He could no longer see the mysterious riders. He pushed the bay gelding to his utmost. The shots and yells continued. He could see flashes against the dark shadow of the herd. The riders were among the cattle. And now the big shadow at the bedding ground began to move. *The herd was on the run!*

Dane circled to the left and saw other riders coming toward him. In the dim starlight filtering through the screen of clouds it was difficult to tell friend from foe. And the cattle were stampeding *south.*

Instantly Dane realized it was the work of the rustlers. They were stampeding the beeves off their course, knowing it would mean a decided loss of weight and a big loss of time to rest them and put them back in condition. In half an hour of running, Hughes's chance of marketing the cattle by the fifteenth of the month would be gone. And it might be the rustlers had planned to split up the herd and run off a portion of it.

It was a bold undertaking. The rustlers meant business.

Fifteen hundred head of cattle were now on the dead run. Dane could hear Gordon Hughes roaring orders somewhere ahead of him. To the right of the stampeding herd he saw several riders firing their guns. Hughes's voice was drowned by the bellowing of the steers. He now was behind the herd. The riders who had been making toward him veered off to the north. Dane emptied his six-shooter at them without result, and they disappeared in the all-enveloping darkness.

He swung away to the right, where he could barely make out the forms of horsemen riding in close to the herd, frightening and maddening the cattle by shouting and firing their weapons. All of the rustlers must have gotten out of the herd by this time, he reasoned, reloading his gun. He raked the bay with his steel, as he rode down upon the riders ahead. Bullets whistled in his direction, and he swung in close to the cattle. The men ahead drew away, and he lost sight of them in the shadows about the forerunners of the herd. When he again caught sight of them he saw there were six of them. Again the bullets sang close to him. A steer to the left of him staggered and went down, several others piled upon the fallen animal. Dane turned out so that the bullets fired at him would not do further damage to the herd. He checked his pace. The odds were too great for him to attempt to rout the six rustlers ahead.

A rider bore down upon him from behind. He recognized Fred Hughes in the saddle. The boy was riding like mad, his gun held high. Dane yelled to Fred, as the latter drew near him.

"There's six of 'em down there," he called.

"An' you make seven," shouted the youth.

Dane whirled his horse in close to Fred's mount, causing it to rear and come to a sudden stop.

"Take your time about goin' down there," said Dane savagely; "unless you want to stop a few bullets. Don't you think those fellows can shoot?"

Fred's face was livid. His right hand came up with his gun. Dane's weapon streaked fire, and

Fred clasped his right wrist, as his gun went spinning.

"You're in with 'em," he screamed, his eyes blazing. "I saw you come from the west when they came down on us. You're tryin' to steal the herd!"

They were well behind the cattle which had passed on. Dane was about to give the youth a caustic reply and ride on, when three horsemen came plunging out of the shadows behind them, shooting.

Three shots came from Dane's gun almost simultaneously. One of the oncoming riders toppled from his saddle, and the other two separated to either side. Dane shouted to Fred to ride, as he spurred his horse and struck southward, firing at the man off to his left. The boy rode at his right.

Dane hastily reloaded. They were leaving their pursuers rapidly behind, for both were mounted on fast horses. They heard shots, but the menacing whine of the bullets did not come. They were out of range for accurate shooting. Fred was fumbling with the buckled strap of a second holster on his left side. Finally the gun came away, and he twisted in his saddle for a shot at the riders behind. But they were lost in the shadow. He looked at Dane queerly and saw that Dane was looking grimly ahead.

They caught up with the cattle, and a moment

later a rider loomed out of the shadows to the left. Dane waited for the spurt of flame which he expected to see. It didn't come. Evidently the other rider also was in doubt as to whether they were friends or foes. Then Dane recognized Buck Colter, who had stood guard with him. He looked about at Fred and saw the gun in the boy's hand for the first time. Fred evaded his glance, and Dane smiled.

"Come along," he shouted to Colter, and the three of them dashed down the right of the running herd.

The cattle began to straggle out and to slow their speed. Dane, in the lead, could see nothing of the six riders. He could tell by the movement of the cattle in front and off to the left that the herd had indeed split. And it was slowly, but surely coming to a stop.

However, the damage had been done. The effects of the stampede would be noticeable with the coming of daylight. The cattle would be nervous and restless, reduced in weight. It would take several days to bring them back into condition. Gordon Hughes would again be at the mercy of the banker, Stevens. They rode around the front of the herd, singing. The cattle had ceased to run. They saw another bunch off to the east. The herd had been broken up into sections. It was not improbable that the rustlers had made off with some of the beeves.

"Where's your father?" Dane called to Fred Hughes, although he realized, even as he put the question, that the boy hardly could be expected to know.

"He was over on the other side of the herd, I guess," said the boy. "The men likely was all asleep when things began to happen."

Dane sensed a subtle note of apology in the youth's tone. Buck Colter was swearing. Then Dane saw several shadowy forms cutting south from a point below the milling herd in the east. He pointed, put the spurs to his horse, and galloped in pursuit.

CHAPTER XXVII

THE WORTH OF A ROPE

Dane rode as fast as the bay could carry him. The cool wind whipped in his face, and the shadowy surface of the plain flowed under him. His horse had not been ridden the day before, as he had made a practice of reserving the bay for guard duty, anticipating, as he now realized, an emergency in the night.

However, it soon became apparent that the riders he was pursuing were mounted on excellent horses. They maintained their lead, and Dane soon was compelled to slow down the bay. He looked behind and saw Fred and Colter following him in the distance. The men ahead were riding at a swinging lope, heading southeast. They evidently were making for the refuge of the bad lands.

Dane rapidly figured the approximate distance. They had taken the beef herd some twenty-five miles from the north range above the Diamond H. However they had been heading northwest, and therefore they were not that distance directly west of their starting point, but were about twenty miles west and some few miles north when the attack had been made upon the herd. The cattle had been driven two miles or more south, and he had ridden another two miles. He estimated that he was about twenty miles from the bad lands. The men he was pursuing were about a mile and a half ahead of him.

In the northeast he could see another dark blotch upon the plain, which he assumed was a portion of the scattered herd. Once he thought he heard shots in that direction. Perhaps Gordon Hughes and the others were having a clash with some of the rustlers there. He reflected that there had been enough of the rustlers to keep Hughes and the men with him at the rear of the herd on the left side, just as he had been stopped on the right.

That the rustlers had not attacked the Diamond H men first indicated that their purpose had been primarily to stampede the herd. After that they probably expected they would have a chance to get away with a hundred head or so, which would not be noticed until the cattle had been counted some time the next day. That they might be able to do this in the confusion and the darkness, Dane well knew.

Fred Hughes and Colter caught up with him, and the three of them rode on the trail of the men ahead. They could make out four riders and knew that they, too, had been observed. But the fugitives undoubtedly had confidence in the ability of their horses to get them well into the bad lands in advance of their pursuers. They kept their steady gait, which was a fast one, but one that could be maintained by the horses to the edge of the brakes.

With the first pale glimmer of dawn in the east the band of color made by the autumn foliage of the trees in the bad lands could be seen in the south. The men ahead increased their pace. They could be seen plainly now, as they topped the rises of the plain, but Dane or the two with him could not recognize any of them.

"We've got to try an' catch 'em before they get into the brakes," said Dane. But, even as he said it, he doubted that they would be able to do this. He wondered vaguely about the others in the band; bethought himself too late that it might have been better if they had ridden east on the lookout for the main body of rustlers.

He spoke to the bay and urged him with the spurs. The horse dashed ahead in a last gallant spurt which soon left Fred and Colter behind. Dane made a considerable gain before the quartet realized what he was up to.

Then began a race for the edge of the bad lands, with all seven riders pushing their horses to their last bit of speed and endurance. Puffs of smoke came from the men ahead, but their bullets fell harmlessly out of range. Dane continued to gain and realized with exultation that the horses of the four ahead were nearly spent. They had been ridden some distance before the attack on the herd.

Although the odds were in favor of the fugitives, any cessation of speed on their part to engage in a fight would give Fred and Colter a chance to come up and get into it. The odds thus would be greatly lessened.

Gradually three of the rustlers drew away from a fourth, whose horse was fast playing out. Dane could see them gesticulating to him, and he was wielding a quirt cruelly. Possibly the others thought he would be able to make it into the brakes, or were not minded to stay by him, for they continued on.

The first tumbled ridges of the bad lands now were less than a mile away. The three men in the lead swerved to the right and rode toward the fringe of trees on the Flying W side of the strip. The fourth man, however, made straight for the nearest point, which was almost directly below the big cottonwood tree.

Dane flung out an arm, pointing toward the trio off to the right in the hope that Fred and Colter would see the signal and pursue the trio. He urged the bay after the lone rider ahead. He shot twice, as the man made the edge of the brakes and a moment after dashed in behind him. They were on the trail which he had traversed several times before—the trail over which the stolen herd had been taken, and where he and Servais had pursued the stallion.

He could see his man through the low-hanging

branches ahead. The reports of a gun broke sharply on the still, morning air, and bullets clipped the leaves about Dane, but he merely lowered his head close to his horse's neck and rode on. Then the vista ahead opened, as they came into a better piece of trail.

Dane saw his quarry twisted about in the saddle, facing him and raising his gun. Dane's own weapon snapped forward, but, before he could shoot, the plunging horse of the man ahead stopped suddenly and leaped to the left, sending his rider headlong upon a white surface which gleamed with ghostly pallor in the morning light—a soap hole.

Dane reined in the bay, staring grimly at the man who was struggling wildly in the oozy, sucking mud of the soap hole. He had lost his gun and was trying to crawl out, but, although he was only about six feet from the edge of the treacherous bog, he couldn't make any progress.

His feet and legs sank out of sight; he was nearly up to his waist when he turned his face, twisted in a grimace of deadly, horrible fear, up to Dane, who was sitting his horse and coolly shaking out his rope.

"Throw it," the man cried hoarsely. "I'm goin' down fast. Throw it—throw it!"

But Dane's movements were tantalizingly deliberate. His lids were narrowed over eyes in which shone a cold light of recognition. For the man in the bog was the man who had been with Bunker in The Palace in Black Butte and had tried to draw on the night Dane had knocked Bunker down the stairs.

By this time the man had sunk in up to his waist. He thrashed about, desperately trying to extricate himself, but his movements only served to hurry the deadly action of the sucking sands. An unearthly terror was in his face. He made queer, guttural sounds, and the sweat stood out upon his forehead in beads. His eyes shone with a wild, agonized look of doubt, as he fixed them upon Dane. He wet his lips and tried to shout, but all that came was a croak. He pushed at the surface of the mire, and his hands came away dripping with the black, slimy mud, streaked with alkali.

He was in above his waist. Inch by inch the devouring sands of the soap hole were dragging him down to the most horrible of all deaths feared by man. Dane held his rope ready in his hand. The man looked up at him in a frenzy of pleading. His face was ghastly. His lips twitched with the fear which gripped his heart; his hands opened and closed convulsively upon the yielding surface of the bog.

"Hold up your arms!"

Dane's rope was whirling.

A wild look of hope came into the man's eyes, as he weakly raised his arms.

The loop hissed through the air, settled over the man's head and shoulders, tightened under his arms. The bay braced back against the rope, as Dane took two turns about the saddle horn. Then he drew the man out of the mire up to his waist and held him there. The man drew a hand across his brow, leaving a streak of mud. The light of sanity had returned to his eyes, and he looked up eagerly.

"He can—pull me out," he said, recovering his voice with the return of hope. "Get me out—get me out *quick.*"

"I reckon there's about three questions you've got to answer before you can get out of there," said Dane crisply. "I'm hopin' you answer 'em, because if you don't I'm goin' to have to let this rope go back in with you."

The terror came into the man's eyes again.

"Who shot Williams in the back?" Dane demanded narrowly.

For just a moment the man hesitated. "That old witch doctor that lives in here," he said, clutching the rope with his hands.

"You mean the hermit?"

"Yes, the hermit."

"I don't believe it," said Dane, giving the rope a little slack.

"It *was* him!" cried the man, as he felt himself slip back into the depths of the soap hole. "I was ridin' herd there an' saw him in the trees with a rifle. I saw you, too, but the shot didn't come from you. Pull me out—I can prove it!"

"How're you goin' to prove it?" asked Dane coolly.

"It was a soft-nosed rifle bullet that hit Williams. I found the shell. I've *got* it."

The sweat was pouring from the man's face, as he clung to the rope which was drawn taut, holding the upper part of his body out of the bog.

"What became of the hundred head of cattle taken from the bottoms about two months ago?" Dane asked.

"They're in here somewhere, but I don't know where," was the answer. "They're cached. The hermit knows," he added quickly.

This coincided with Dane's own belief.

"Who's the head of this gang of rustlers?" he asked.

"I don't know anything about the rustlers!" cried the man. "I ain't been doin' any rustlin'."

Dane again gave the rope some slack, and the man yelled in terror, as he sank a foot above his waist into the sand.

"It didn't look like it to-night, did it!" said Dane grimly.

"I wasn't rustlin'," screamed the other, trying vainly to pull himself out by the rope which was gradually slackening. "All the orders I got was to stampede the herd!"

"Who gave that order?" asked Dane sternly.

The man looked wildly about. His face was ashen. Inch by inch he felt himself sinking—sinking.

"Bunker!" he shrieked. Then his head sagged upon the rope, as he fainted.

CHAPTER XXVIII
UNDER THE COTTONWOOD

When Dane had dragged the senseless man out of the soap hole he put his slicker about him, caught his horse, which had been standing with reins dangling at the left of the bog, lifted the man into the saddle and, with the bay following, started out of the brakes with him.

The man regained consciousness when they reached the bottoms, but was too weak to ride after his terrible experience, his frantic exertions in the mire, and the enervating reaction from his mental torture.

Dane took him on his own saddle and held him in front of him, as he rode to the ranch. There he was put in a bunk in the bunk house under the watchful eye of old Marty, who knew him for one of the cow-punchers hired on the Flying W early that spring.

"When Bunker came he put on a lot of new men," Marty told Dane. "Williams only kept four or five hands durin' the winter, an' Bunker didn't hire any of the old crowd when they showed up in the spring. This feller was one of the new ones."

Dane nodded in comprehension. He thought he understood why Bunker wanted his own crowd about him.

Esther came running out to ask Dane how it came he was back at the ranch. He told her a little of what had happened, but the girl could tell by his grave expression that it was more serious than his explanation indicated.

"You must come to the house and have something to eat," she said commandingly. "No, the cook shack is empty. The cook from here went up north when you took the other cook on the beef drive."

So Dane followed her into the kitchen, remarking that something should be sent out to the prisoner in the bunk house later in the morning.

Esther did not tell her mother what Dane had told her, or what she suspected. She insisted upon preparing Dane's breakfast, herself, while he sat in a straight-backed chair and watched her. Again in the possession of his normal health and strength, he did not feel any need of sleep. He pondered over what the man had told him at the soap hole. The hermit had shot Williams; the hermit knew where the cattle were cached; Bunker had given his men orders to stampede the beeves!

He smiled at Esther, as she placed food for him upon the kitchen table.

"I didn't know biscuits like these went with an Eastern education," he told her with a grin.

Esther flushed and regarded him disapprovingly. "You should have combed your hair," she retorted with a flash of amusement in her eyes.

"Well, now, ma'am, what d'ye think of that!" he exclaimed, wide-eyed and abashed. "An' here I'm all mud from draggin' that fellow out of the soap hole. I plumb forgot to fix myself up. I'm beggin' your pardon."

He started to rise.

"Sit right there and eat your breakfast," Esther said sternly, pushing him back into his chair. "Your hair looks better mussed up, anyway. Besides, you're not supposed to be a—a dandy," she bantered. "You bad men are supposed to look sort of fierce. Your beard's got to be an inch longer and kind of bristle out more before you'll look the part."

Dane's white teeth flashed in a brilliant smile.

"I reckon if I wasn't seein' you in a gingham apron for the first time you wouldn't be sayin' that, ma'am," he replied with a chuckle.

"S-o," she said, arching her brows and coloring. "You're becoming observing, too."

"I ain't exactly blind, ma'am; I like flowers an' trees an' all sorts of pretty things."

"Including dance-hall girls," Esther taunted, tossing her head.

Dane laughed boyishly. “Sure—you bet,” he chuckled. “But you see, I ain’t met many girls that was Eastern graduates.”

Esther turned away, confused. She looked at him slyly, as he was eating. That laugh and his natural humor hardly seemed in keeping with the supposed accomplishments of a gunman. Suddenly the pound of hoofs was heard without. Esther hurried to the door.

“Why, it’s father and some others!” she cried.

Dane left the table hurriedly and brushed past her, cramming on his hat.

Gordon Hughes and two other men were dismounting near the bunk house. Dane, hastening toward them, saw with surprise that one of the men was the hermit.

Gordon Hughes’s face was dark, and his eyes were snapping.

“Take him in the bunk house an’ keep him there till I get ready to tend to his case.”

He saw Dane, and his eyes flashed angrily. “Where have *you* been?” he demanded aggressively.

Dane drew him aside and quickly explained what had happened.

“I thought so,” snapped Hughes. “That old rat Williams an’ Bunker are behind this. I’ll make that man you got an’ the hermit talk, or I’ll snap their necks at the end of a rope!”

Hoofbeats again rode on the wind, and Fred

Hughes and Buck Colter came riding up to the little group.

"Lost 'em," said Fred to Dane. "Don't know where they went into the brakes. Couldn't find a sign of a trail."

Dane smiled in understanding. Very likely the men had taken the mysterious trail which Marie had used on her visits to the cabin of the hermit.

Fred looked at his father questioningly. The rancher was glowering about, apparently undecided as to the next move.

"I've sent a man for some of the boys from the north range," he ruminated, partly to himself. "They'll be here pretty quick. That crowd tried to get away with some of the shorthorns," he said angrily, turning to Dane. "Killed two of my men. We shot down three of 'em an' got the old fellow. Rest of 'em beat it."

Dane then explained how he had been restless and had been riding under the stars in the cool air of early morning when he saw the raiders come down from the north.

"I saw you come from the west," said Fred Hughes, his face turning a deep red. "I thought you'd gone out there to—to start the ball rolling. I guess maybe it was lucky you stopped me from tearin' down into that crowd." It was as much of an apology as the boy could make, and Dane made it easier for him by laughing and telling how he, himself, had been stopped by a shower of bullets, one of which had killed a steer.

Esther had joined them and was listening with her eyes wide and her lips parted in excitement.

"I'll teach Williams an' his crowd a lesson!" thundered Gordon Hughes. "A couple of dead weights swingin' from the big cottonwood will show 'em there's still a man-made law for rustlers an' raiders in this country."

There was a deep silence following his words.

"What're you aimin' to do, dad?" Fred asked soberly.

"I'm goin' to hang the prisoners at sundown!" Hughes exclaimed.

"Father!" cried Esther. "You can't do—*that.*"

"Go in the house," roared Hughes. "No one is goin' to tell me how to run this ranch in a time like this. It'll be a week before I can ship the cattle after last night's work, an' that'll be too late. I staked the Diamond H on that beef herd!"

He strode away toward the front of the house, where his wife was waiting on the porch. Dane signaled to Fred to follow him and walked toward the barn.

"Is that car of yours in runnin' shape again?" he asked the boy.

"Sure," said Fred, looking perplexed.

"Then get to Black Butte as fast as you can an' fetch Marie out here," said Dane.

"Why—what—" Again that smoldering, mysterious look welled in the boy's eyes.

"Don't ask any questions," snapped Dane. "Do as I tell you. If she wants to know anything, tell her what your father is figurin' on doin' at sundown. She'll come. Better take a couple of men with you in case you should meet anybody."

"But, dad'll think it's strange that—"

"Don't tell him," exclaimed Dane sharply. "This is right well important. I ain't got time to tell you why. I want to see you get started right away. Don't worry; I'm responsible. It's time you begun to show a little confidence in me, I reckon. Get that girl!"

Gordon Hughes evidently did not hear the car when Fred left for town, taking the little wrangler, Servais, and Colter with him. Dane went into the bunk house, where he found the man he had captured that morning, shaking with a chill and mumbling incoherently. He tried to make him talk, but couldn't. The man had been nearly frightened to death.

The hermit glared at him out of bloodshot eyes. His only reply to Dane's questions was a snarl. He clawed at his white beard and hair, and Dane looked at him, puzzled. He now looked as he had appeared on the day Dane had remained with him during the electric storm. The man who had come down with Hughes sat on guard in the bunk house, with a six-shooter on his knee.

Dane went to look after his horse and found Servais had put him in a box stall, worked his coat to a glossy finish, and blanketed him. He visited the stallion, as he had done many times since he had captured him in the meadow in the bad lands. He had advanced so far in making friends with the magnificent, big black that he could rub him on the nose and pat his neck without being snapped at.

Ten men arrived from the north range early in the afternoon. Gordon Hughes came out to them.

"Did Shay go over to look after the beeves?" he asked the cow-puncher he had sent with the message to the cow boss that morning.

The man nodded. "Took all the men in the north but these, an' two others that he left there, with him," he replied.

Hughes grunted in satisfaction. "Tell the men to get fresh horses out of the pasture an' to pick out the best," he instructed. "They can eat when they get back."

He returned to the house without noticing the absence of Fred and the others. Dane realized that Hughes had much on his mind.

They all ate late in the afternoon in the bunk house. Esther and her aunt served them. Gordon Hughes came out and, noticing Fred's absence, asked about him. Dane purposely ignored the query, and the others could furnish no information. Hughes finally decided with a deep scowl that Fred and the others had gone out scouting on their own initiative.

He tried to question the hermit, but met with no success.

"Get your horses!" he ordered the men.

Dane already had saddled his horse. He rode out of the barn, up to the road and looked anxiously in the direction of the town. Fred and the girl should have returned two hours ago, he reasoned. Even if Fred had had to wait for a time in town, he should have been back before then. But there was no veil of dust or other sign of the little car returning.

He saw a cavalcade of riders below him making past the barn and the hay shed. He rode slowly along the road to the cottonwood tree. The riders came up with Gordon Hughes in the lead. Dane saw the hermit and the man he had captured riding behind, closely guarded by Diamond H men.

Hughes ordered two of the men to throw their ropes over a limb of the cottonwood. The prisoners were brought up under the overhanging limb. There was a dead silence. Gordon Hughes's face was drawn and grim. Evidently he was determined to make an example of the hermit and the other. And, under ordinary circumstances, Dane reflected that he would be justified. It was the unwritten law of the West.

He rode close to the rancher.

"You goin' to give these men a chance to talk?" he asked quietly.

Hughes swung on him. “They can talk if they’re so minded,” he said. “But they’ve got to be quick about it, for I ain’t goin’ to ask ’em.”

“That man’s sick,” said Dane steadily, pointing to the man he had rescued from the soap hole.

“He ain’t too sick to talk if he wants to,” snapped Hughes.

“I reckon he is,” said Dane, looking the rancher square in the eyes.

“Are you goin’ to tell me what to do?” asked Hughes angrily.

“Gordon Hughes, I’m only askin’ you to use your own good sense,” said Dane in a loud, clear voice that rang upon all ears. “That man went through a lot this mornin’. I saw him. I kept him there till he talked. He’ll talk again when he gets at himself. Anyway I ran him down, an’ I fished him out of the soap hole, an’ I’m goin’ to say what’s goin’ to be done with him!”

“You’re goin’ to protect no cattle thief on this ranch,” roared Hughes.

Dane colored, but his gaze was steel-blue, as it burned into the rancher’s eyes.

“You’re puttin’ it the wrong way, Hughes,” he said firmly. “An’ I’ve a good reason why I don’t want to see that hermit hanged.”

He held up a hand, as Hughes opened his mouth to speak.

“Wait a minute!” Dane’s words were as sharp as the crack of a whiplash. “You’re wantin’ to put

the only two men who can tell us anything out of the way. Is that usin' good sense, Hughes?"

"They've got the chance to talk now," said Hughes, looking at the two prisoners.

The man whom Dane had captured was swaying in his saddle, shaking as if with the ague, dull and uncomprehending. The hermit was staring straight ahead, mumbling to himself. His eyes were bloodshot, lit with a brilliant fire in the contracted pupils. His hands fumbled at his sides.

"Scared to death—an' with good reason," said Gordon Hughes. "Put the neckties on 'em!"

"I reckon I wouldn't do that." Dane's tone was crisp, cold. "I'm still thinkin' we'd better wait."

"Then you're thinkin', an' that's all," said Hughes harshly.

Dane whirled the bay completely around. When he faced them the next instant he was a few paces farther away, where he could see every face. His gun was in his hand.

"I'll drill the first man that makes a move with the ropes!"

The group was so still it might have been marble. Gordon Hughes saw a look in Dane's eyes which he had never seen there before. The youthful-appearing countenance was suddenly grimly terrible; the eyes were lit with positive determination. There was the potent suggestion of utter finality in the menace of the gun.

Suddenly from the road behind them came

a hail, followed by many shouts. Dane saw the gaze of Hughes and the others shift to the road. Surprise was mirrored in their eyes.

A girl screamed.

Dane shoved his gun back into its holster, as Hughes turned his puzzled glance back to him.

"That's what I was waitin' for," he told the rancher with a queer smile.

A weird, guttural cry came from the hermit, as the girl, Marie, ran toward him, sobbing.

CHAPTER XXIX
THE CACHE

As the girl came up, Gordon Hughes dismounted, and Dane followed his example. Marie was crying, holding her father's hands, as he stooped over her and showed his first intelligent interest in the proceedings. Fred, Servais, and Colter joined the group.

Marie looked with staring eyes at the ropes thrown over the limb of the cottonwood.

"Oh, *what* was you going to do?" she cried.

Dane stepped forward. He saw Fred staring in astonishment. Gordon Hughes was frowning in deep perplexity.

"Marie," said Dane gently, "I reckon this thing has come to a show-down. Your father was caught this mornin' with a bunch of men who raided the Diamond H beef herd an' tried to make away with some cattle. There's some men been killed, an' it's a right serious business. I've protected your father as long as I can, an' I only protected him so this thing could be straightened out *some* time."

"Her *father!*" exclaimed Gordon Hughes.

"Ah, yes," said the girl tenderly, to the astonishment of all except Dane, "he ees my father. He ees not bad. It ees the men who bother him—that Bunker an' that Williams. They put the fear in his heart that they will tell he kill a man once—but it was *fair!* He would not steal the cattle by himself. They make heem help."

The hermit kept looking at her, wetting his lips with his tongue and mumbling.

"He ees the bad to-day," the girl continued with a sob in her voice. "He does not know so well. He ees by the tree when the lightnin' strike it an' knock him down. And since—" She tapped her head sorrowfully.

"A little off," said Dane to Hughes. He knew now why the hermit had been in such a mental state during the storm.

"He ees knock down by the lightnin' in the East, where we live then," resumed Marie. "My mother she die, an' we come to the West. We work for that man William before he buy the Flying Doubleyoo, an' my father he kill the man who try to—bother me."

There were tears in the girl's eyes, as she patted the old man's hands.

"Williams he bring us up here. An' then we leave because Williams he want to marry me. My father go into the bad lands, for hees head it ees not right. I work in the dance hall an' give my father money he need an' save so when he get so bad I can take care of heem. That is why I work there. Brady, he pay me well, an' the mens they give me money when I sing an' dance for them. An' I save for my father."

Fred Hughes had stepped to the girl's side. His face was strangely white. His father kept his eyes on the girl and listened intently. The reflected glow of the sunset lent a halo to her face.

"Then the man Bunker come," the girl went on in a low voice. "He ees ver' bad man. He ees know some men who take the cattle, an' he make my father watch them in a secret place, an' he say if he do not do as he say, Williams will have my father to the jail for the mans he kill. An' my father 'fraid, for hees head is bad."

Again she touched the wealth of hair beneath her cap.

"If he ees with the men who do bad las' night, it ees because Bunker tell him to go!" she said fiercely.

Hughes and Dane exchanged glances. The girl's statement coincided with that made by the man Dane had rescued from the bog.

"You are not goin' to hurt heem?" cried Marie.

"No." It was Dane who answered. Gordon Hughes remained silent.

"My father, he think Williams make me work in the dance hall, an' he ees ver' angry," smiled Marie. Her lashes were wet with tears.

"Marie, can you tell us who shot Williams?" Dane asked.

"No, no, I not know. My father say he found

you an' take you to the cabeen. You say you lose your gun, an' he go back an' find it. Then I take it an' give it to you for the proof that I tell you all thees some time."

"Why didn't you tell me before, Marie?"

"I am afraid of Bunker. He bother me." She shuddered, and Fred touched her reassuringly on the shoulder.

"Didn't your father tell you who shot Williams?" Dane persisted.

"I shot him!" Everyone started, as the hermit spoke. They saw him straighten in the saddle and pull his hands away from Marie's. His eyes were glittering points of fire. "I shot him," he repeated.

"No, no, no," cried the girl.

"Let him talk," said Gordon Hughes.

"I shot him, for he is a snake!" shrilled the hermit. "He should die. I will shoot him again!"

In a twinkling the hermit was out of his saddle. He stood in the center of the group, a wild figure, his white hair flying in the breeze, his face ghastly in the failing light.

"I'll shoot him again!" he shrieked and began to fumble at the saddle on the horse he had ridden, searching for his missing rifle.

Then he laughed, and Dane's blood froze, as he listened. He had never heard such a laugh. The hermit looked around with that glittering light in his eyes. His hands were trembling. Marie had stepped back and was looking at him in anguish.

With a wild shriek the hermit leaped forward, then Hughes and Dane and Fred bore him struggling to the ground. It was all they could do to hold him, while he writhed and twisted his body and raved. He quieted suddenly, and, when they lifted him up, he again looked straight ahead out of bloodshot eyes.

"It ees come," said Marie with a moan. "It has been too much—all thees trouble. Hees head—it—is gone!"

Fred put his arm about her.

"Take him to the bunk house," Gordon Hughes ordered. "And take this other fellow back, too." He turned to the girl, as the men set about carrying out his commands.

"You had better come to the house an' rest," he said kindly.

"He might have did eet," sobbed the girl. "He maybe did shoot Williams. He no tell me. Now he ees gone—it was the lightnin' that strike heem. It is *Bunker* who ees the snake!" she cried, clenching her small fists and looking straight at Dane. "He ees maybe in the place with the cattle," she cried. "I will take you there!"

"You must rest first," said Dane with a look at Hughes.

Fred spoke now for the first time in a trembling voice. "The car broke down," he said unsteadily. "We had to walk most of the way back. She has no horse."

Dane handed him the reins of his bridle, and Fred helped the girl to mount. They walked back to the ranch house.

The edge of Gordon Hughes's anger had been dulled by the story of the girl. Dane, too, had felt the power of Marie's argument which had been advanced not so much by her actual words, as by the hardship and sorrow she had suffered and the sacrifices she had made. Here was a dance-hall girl who was worthy of the respect of any man or woman; yet she had asked nothing of any one, had endured the scorn of her own sex, and had bravely bantered the men out of the attitude they were wont to assume toward one of her vocation.

Hughes and Dane entered the bunk house. The man whom Dane had captured and rescued, was tossing and turning in troubled sleep.

"He'll be all right to-morrow," said Dane. "He will have plenty to tell us yet. His story and the girl's agree, an' I ain't forgot he told me Marie's father shot Williams."

The hermit sat on his bunk, staring with unseeing eyes. He did not recognize them, and Gordon Hughes shook his head. The rancher appeared fascinated by the sight of the old man whose mental status had reverted to that of a young child. As they walked toward the house, Hughes looked curiously at Dane several times. He paused on the porch steps.

"Would you have shot if the men had started

to carry out my order?" he asked with a frown.

"Would you have gone through with the hanging if I hadn't?" Dane countered, smiling.

Gordon Hughes shrugged and led the way into the house. Esther met them in the sitting room, and Dane could tell by her expression that Fred had told her the story of Marie. She said the girl had been put to bed.

Hughes turned to Dane. "She's in no shape to show us the place where the cattle are cached now, an' I don't think they'd be likely to try to get 'em started out of the bad lands to-night. Have the men out before daylight, an' we'll go after 'em in the morning."

As Dane left the house, Fred came out on the porch. Night had fallen, but Dane could see the boy's grave face by the light of the stars. Fred held out his hand, and Dane grasped it warmly.

"Do you think *that* much of her?" he asked.

"An'—more," said Fred, as he turned back into the house.

Dane knew it was jealousy which had caused the boy to jump upon Bunker and to be suspicious of him. He smiled wanly at the recollection of the scene in Marie's room. For some time he stood looking into the night; then he sought his bunk.

They were up an hour before dawn. Marie, looking tired, but determined, did not ask to see her father before they started. Esther put her arms about the girl and kissed her as she mounted.

She rode in the lead, with Fred and his father on either side of her. Dane, Servais, Colter, and a number of cow-punchers rode behind. The dawn was breaking.

Leading them past the trail which Dane knew, Marie turned into the deep ravine on the Flying W side of the strip. When they came to the trees and bushes at its upper end, Marie pushed on through the tangle and came out upon the trail which had thus been so well concealed that Dane couldn't find it.

She led them to the meadow containing her father's cabin, then on to the meadow beyond where Dane had captured the stallion, and down the trail toward the river. When she reached the high, rocky ridge, which was nearest the river slope, she turned up it abruptly. On the crest she pointed below.

They saw a mass of stunted trees and bushes on the west slope and a connecting ridge between the bare ridge they were on and another wooded ridge west of them.

Servais explained to Dane in a whisper that he had been on the wooded ridge the first day they had searched for the missing cattle. Far below, the timber grew thick at the head of a wide ravine. Servais recognized the place. He had come up the ravine and had turned west when he struck the timber and bushes.

The girl was talking in a low voice.

"They bring the cattle up here an' down through the timber. There ees trails on both sides—look! One starts here. My father, he show me. It ees hollow under this." She pointed to the connecting ridge. "An' the trees they shut the place off."

Both Dane and Servais saw at once how the herd from the bottoms had disappeared. It had been driven up the rocky slope, the rain washing away the faint tracks as soon as they were made, and had disappeared in the timber by the time they gained the top of the ridge where the hermit had been shooting.

Hughes sent Dane with some men down to the timber barrier at the head of the ravine below. He sent Fred, Servais, and Colter to the other ridge, and, with two men, himself took the trail from the point on top the highest ridge. The orders were to "go in and let 'em have it." He delegated a man to go with Marie to a point of safety in the timber, along the trail by which they had come. They were to go in at the end of a quarter of an hour, and the watches of the leaders were set alike.

When the time was up, Dane led his men in through the thick stand of jack pines. He could hear the others on either side of him. In another moment all the riders broke through into a large meadow, the farther end of which was under the overhanging ridge. There they saw the cattle.

Swiftly they rode around the herd of cows and

calves and steers and, with guns drawn, charged the farther end of the meadow. But they found no one. A thorough search of the timber which screened the hidden meadow, failed to net results in the way of a fight or capture, or any signs whatever of the rustlers.

"They've beat it," said Hughes in a tone of disappointment.

Inspection of the cattle showed them to be mostly Diamond H stock. Hughes estimated that all the cattle stolen from him were there. Mixed with them were less than fifty head wearing the Flying W iron.

"Reckon they figured that gettin' three men killed, countin' the one you shot in the bad lands the time you chased 'em, an' losin' the hermit an' another captured, was enough," said Hughes to Dane.

Dane was looking about with a grim smile. "You know, Hughes, when an onery steer gets to rilin' up a herd an' makin' things troublesome, the thing to do is get rid of him," he said. "Same way with this rustlin' gang. We've got to get the one that's makin' all the trouble, I take it."

Hughes frowned. "There's Flyin' W stock here," he observed.

"I reckon Bunker or Williams wanted to protect themselves that a way," said Dane.

Hughes continued his inspection of the cattle and found they were in good shape. There was water in the big meadow, and evidently the cattle had ranged in the timber, also. None of the calves had been branded, and he surmised that the rustlers had intended to keep the herd until the calves could be weaned; then they would drive them south, with such beeves as they might be able to get away with, and use a running iron.

Hughes detailed five men, in charge of Dane, to drive the cattle back to the Diamond H bottoms, after the Flying W stock had been cut out. He told Dane, as he prepared to leave with Fred and the others, that they would take Marie back to the ranch with them.

Dane knew how to work cattle. He had the stolen Diamond H stock in the bottoms below the hay shed by early afternoon, and then he rode to the house. Esther Hughes came out on the porch, as he rode up.

"Where's your father?" Dane asked, swinging his hat low.

"He went to town with Fred and Marie and one of the cow-punchers."

Dane thought for a moment. There were enough men at the ranch to protect it in event of a raid. And Gordon Hughes had doubtless gone to Black Butte to have it out with Sam Stevens, the banker. The rancher might have other difficulties there.

"The sheriff was here—looking for you," said Esther.

Dane's eyes widened.

"But when he heard what dad told him he went off in his car with the man you captured," smiled the girl.

Dane looked gravely about, avoiding her eyes.

She stepped forward to the edge of the porch. "There—there isn't going to be any more trouble, is there, Mr. Dane?"

"I reckon I ain't able to answer that, ma'am," he said soberly.

Then he spurred his horse away from the porch, past the bunk house and barn, and up to the road leading to town.

CHAPTER XXX
THE KILLER

It was a Thursday and the first day of the annual rodeo, when Gordon Hughes, Fred, and Marie rode into Black Butte at noon. The town was filled with people who had come from miles around to participate in the celebration. The short main street was jammed with a colorful throng, the resorts were crowded, bunting and flags waved and fluttered in the breeze everywhere. The spirit of carnival was abroad.

Gordon Hughes felt none of this spirit. His face was set and grim; his eyes had the keen look of an animal's; he was like some lord of the forest at bay. He looked questioningly at Marie and Fred, as they drew up at the barn and corrals behind the hotel.

"I'll put the horses up," said Fred. "An' I'll look after Marie. She's not goin' back to The Palace."

Hughes gazed wonderingly as he saw the girl flush, although there was a look of pain in her eyes.

"All right," he said with a shrug, dismounting. "I've some business to attend to, an' then I'll come back to the hotel lookin' for you two. I'll help you get something better than workin' at The Palace," he added, nodding to Marie.

Fred dismounted with a smile which his father could not see, and as Hughes walked away, he helped Marie from the saddle, held her tight for a moment upon the ground, and told her to wait while he put up the horses.

Gordon Hughes went straight to the little building which housed the American Bank of Black Butte.

He found the bank open, despite the holiday, and stamped through the front room to the door of Sam Stevens's private office, where he knocked loudly. Stevens opened the door, started when he recognized his visitor, then invited him in with an elaborate bow.

Hughes flung his hat upon the banker's desk and pulled up a chair.

"Sit down, Stevens. There's trouble to pay," he said, without waiting for any polite preliminaries, such as the banker was wont to indulge in before beginning a business consultation.

"What is it?" asked Stevens, a frown appearing on his pasty face. Evidently he resented the rancher's peremptory manner.

"I can't market the cattle in time to get you your money by the fifteenth," said Gordon Hughes, looking the other straight in the eyes. "But I can make it by the twentieth or a day or two later," he added cheerfully.

"That won't do," said the banker shortly. "You know when your paper is due. Don't forget I've a mortgage on those cattle, Hughes. I trusted you to be able to attend to the marketing in time. I need *cash.*"

Hughes held his wrath in check by a supreme effort. "Wait until you hear what happened," he said in a voice which vibrated with intense feeling.

"I've heard what happened," said Stevens coolly.

"Where'd you hear?" asked Hughes in amazement.

"Those things get around quickly," replied the banker, idling with some papers upon his desk.

"An' maybe there's a reason for that," said the rancher darkly. "Those cattle were stampeded, an' an attempt was made to steal some of 'em. We shot two of the raiders an' caught another that's talked, an' he is ready to talk some more. An' we got the hermit—know him? We got him an' his story. It's Williams an' Bunker that's behind this thing!"

"What can you *prove?*" asked the banker in a hard voice.

Hughes was taken aback. "Don't you think we can prove anything with what we've seen an' two men confessing?" he thundered.

"The hermit's crazy, and it's the other man's word against the word of others," returned the banker coldly. “Williams has been losin’ cattle himself, he says. An’ now he’s lookin’ for men to get in his beeves. He claims you’ve run his men off the range.”

“He lies!” shouted Hughes. “He’s lost his men because they was stealin’ an’ stampedin’ my stock—takin’ a few of his for a blind. It got too hot for ’em, an’ they cleared out. It was through the hermit we found the cache of stolen cattle—nearly two hundred head of mine an’ less than fifty head of his.”

“I have nothing to do with that,” said the banker sharply, rising from his desk. “I’m running a bank. I’ve got to turn my paper into *cash.* If you’d got that boundary thing settled I’d have been able to realize on your paper with the county-seat banks.”

“An’ I can get you your money with only five days or so delay,” said Hughes, also rising. “I had to rest the beeves an’ put ’em into condition again. I can ship by the tenth, say, in a pinch.”

“Or you can sell them now,” suggested the banker, with a keen look at the stockman.

“Yes? Where? Is there a buyer here ready to take ’em off my hands?” Hughes spoke eagerly.

“Williams himself will give you seventy or seventy-five thousand dollars for them,” said Stevens. “That’ll clear you.”

Hughes clenched his fists. His face purpled with the force of his passion. He made as if he would spring at Stevens. The banker's face was white, but his eyes met those of the rancher squarely, as he drew an ivory-handled pistol from a side coat pocket.

"If necessary I will protect myself with any means at hand," he said, and backing to the door he threw it open. "Come in here," he called to the clerk in the cage.

Hughes disregarded the gun and the banker's call for a witness.

"Williams wants to buy the stock," he said in a low, trembling voice. "An' put the proposition through you. Seventy thousand—an' me stand a loss of thirty thousand or so!"

"My hands are tied!" cried the banker, a look of desperation in his eyes. "I need the cash, an' Williams can get it—where, I don't know *or care!*"

"Then, I'll ship the stock day after to-morrow," shouted Hughes, shaking his fist in the other's face. "I'll stand the loss in weight an' condition before I'll let Williams have the cattle, or let you two split a penny of my money!"

"I can hold up that shipment," said Stevens, his voice shaking.

"You can hold up nothing! You can notify Chicago to send you the draft for payment for the stock."

Gordon Hughes brushed the clerk out of his way with a force which sent him staggering to the wall and walked quickly out of the bank. He returned to the hotel, but could not find Fred or Marie. He sat down in a chair in the crowded lobby to think. He did not know where he could raise the large amount of cash Stevens wanted—even for the short period he would require it. Certainly it could not be raised north of Great Bend, the large city many miles south of the river; and he never had dealt with any banks there. No, he would have to ship the cattle. He would get them on the move again by the next day but one. He felt a hand on his shoulder and looked up quickly.

It was Dane.

Then he told Dane of his visit to the bank. Dane listened attentively, his eyes alert. When Hughes had finished Dane regarded him with a smile, which the rancher thought was queer.

"We can start the beeves again day after tomorrow all right, I reckon, if we have to," said Dane, his eyes glowing dreamily. "But it would mean a loss, all right. An' I've got something on my mind, too. Bunker was in town for a brief spell this mornin'."

"He hasn't gone?" said Hughes. "Thinks he's played safe?"

"He was drinkin' some," said Dane. "Brady told me he said he'd shoot me on sight." Again Hughes saw that peculiar smile. "An' Brady's worryin' 'bout Marie. I told him to forget it. I saw

Fred an' the girl dancing in the pavilion they've put up for the rodeo, an' I don't reckon Brady'll ever see her in his place again."

"Eh?" asked Hughes. "I guess Fred's tryin' to make her forget about her father. Fred ain't a bad kid. Bunker ain't here now?"

"Dunno," said Dane. "I'm takin' a little ride, an' I'll see you later."

Before Hughes could reply Dane was gone. Hughes went out looking for the dancing pavilion. He had made up his mind to stay in town that night.

Dane walked to the east end of town and into the trees where his horse was tied. He led the bay out of the trees, mounted, and sped eastward toward the Diamond H, keeping a wary lookout for other riders.

The knowledge that Bunker had not left the Flying W, but had had the temerity deliberately to enter town, was positive proof that he had no fear of the consequences of his move in ordering the stampede of Hughes's cattle. Undoubtedly he had been promised protection from the law by Williams. Or, and this was likely, he had confidence in his ability to take care of himself against any one, and he had become savagely reckless after the failure of the plan to steal part of the Diamond H beef herd. For Dane felt certain that Bunker was the man behind the rustlers.

Meanwhile his men had been frightened away.

As Williams was looking for men it was apparent that his force had cleared out. Dane remembered that old Marty had mentioned that Bunker had hired a new crew that spring. Surely the men he took on were ready to follow his orders and had doubtless been promised a substantial share of any profit accruing from the cattle-stealing operations.

That queer smile played about Dane's lips, as he remembered the warning of Willis Brady, proprietor of The Palace.

"He says he'll shoot you on sight!" Brady had whispered.

Dane reasoned that this showed that Bunker was enraged at him because he had helped to smash his schemes, and that Bunker had as well as said in so many words that his schemes were indeed shattered.

"An' maybe he thinks he'll have plain sailing again with me out of the way, if he can do it so it won't look too bad for him," Dane mused to himself.

He knew that in a case where two men drew their weapons the quicker shot could claim self-defense. It was a rule observed in all the courts of the northern range—in most of the West, for that matter. But the element of fairness would have to enter into it. If Bunker wanted to take an advantage, he would have to get out of the country. And, realizing that Bunker might not be averse to taking an advantage which would give him the revenge he craved, Dane was minded to be careful. He did not intend to be taken unawares.

It was late in the afternoon when he again reached the Diamond H. He at once sought out his friend, Servais.

"Servais, I've got a hard ride to make," he said briskly. "I've got to make Great Bend to-night!"

"Great Bend!" exclaimed the little wrangler. "Why so?"

"Can't tell you, Servais," smiled Dane. "I want to ride the stallion."

Servais's eyes popped. "The stallion? The big black, Jupiter? Dane, you're crazy!"

"No—no; I'm not crazy," laughed Dane, although his eyes were serious. "I'm not crazy yet, anyway. My horse can't stand the gaff for that distance. Besides, I've got to make time. The big black can take me there by daylight. He has the speed, an' the endurance an' the heart. He can turn the trick, an' it won't hurt him a bit."

"I know," said the wrangler; "but *you* can't ride him, Dane. He won't let anybody but me ride him. He'll bite an' fight you. It wouldn't be any use—you tryin' to make it on him."

"Servais, you're wrong," said Dane, laying a hand on the little wrangler's shoulder. "I've got acquainted with that horse. I've petted him for weeks an' made friends with him—been in the stall with him. *You've* seen me. He's seen us *both* in there, seen us together, knows we're friends. You can bring that horse out, and we'll both saddle him; we'll pet him; you can show him you want me to ride him, an' he'll let me ride him. You know horses, an' I know horses, an' that horse knows as much as the two of us. He'll take me to Great Bend."

Dane stood back and guessed by the look on Servais's face the struggle going on in the little wrangler's mind. There was, as Dane knew, another reason why Servais didn't want to let the horse go. The wrangler had been loath to mention this. The stallion was a thoroughbred and worth a lot of money. Gordon Hughes bought most of his saddle horses. He kept but a few mares, and those were thoroughbreds. This explained the number of excellent saddle horses on the ranch; these animals Hughes reserved for his own use and that of his family and for emergencies when hard, fast riding was imperative.

"I know what you're thinking about," said Dane earnestly. "If it wasn't mighty important, Servais, I wouldn't ask for the stallion."

Servais looked at him squarely. "All right," he said simply.

Together they brought out the magnificent horse and bridled and saddled him. Dane held him, rubbing his nose, while Servais got his own horse.

"I'm goin' to ride with you a ways to see you get along all right," said the wrangler.

Esther Hughes came out and was astonished at what she saw. Dane, with a knowing look at Servais, answered vaguely when she asked him where he was going, but confessed he was going to ride Jupiter. Then she insisted that her own horse be saddled so she could ride along and see the result.

Servais remained at the big black's head while Dane mounted. The stallion danced about a little, shook his head, as if in distinct disapproval, and then trotted off in obedience to Dane's voice and gentle spur.

Servais and Esther rode with him to the trail into the bad lands, followed him to the first soap hole, and then watched him out of sight, as he rode swiftly toward the river and the great stretches of prairie which rolled southward to the mighty Missouri and the city of Great Bend.

As the girl and Servais emerged from the brakes on their way back, a horseman came to a rearing stop before them. Esther caught her breath, as she recognized the rider. It was Bunker!

The Flying W foreman's face was dark with rage, his eyes gleaming red, his whole bearing apprehensive and sinister and recklessly bold.

"Where's Dane?" he demanded of Servais.

"I dunno," replied the little wrangler.

"You lie!" exclaimed Bunker.

"Ain't you sort of forgettin' there's a lady here?" said Servais, his whole body trembling with emotion.

Bunker ignored the question and the girl. "Dane's beatin' it out of the country for good!" he cried hoarsely. "He's yellow! An' you've give him the stallion to make his get-away sure, you little rat!"

"I reckon that ain't so, Bunker," said Servais in a voice so chilling that Esther shuddered with a fear which gripped at her heart.

She saw the look in Bunker's eyes and tried to cry out.

"You're a stinkin' little liar!" roared Bunker.

Servais's right hand struck just as Bunker's gun blazed in the falling dusk.

The little wrangler leaned forward in the saddle, toppled to one side, and dropped with a long-drawn sigh to the ground.

Esther screamed, as Bunker spurred past her into the bad lands trail.

She got off her horse, bent over Servais, and raised his head. By some whim of the fast-fading glow of the sunset a little ray of silver light played upon the staring eyes and set features. With sobs choking in her throat, she rested the head on the soft grass and covered the face with her handkerchief. Then she rode wildly for the ranch, welcoming the tears.

CHAPTER XXXI
NOT ON THE PROGRAM

The next morning Esther, her mother, her mount, and three of the Diamond H men arrived in Black Butte. They went to the hotel and waited while the men looked for Gordon Hughes. One of them returned an hour later with the information that the rancher could not be found.

Mrs. Hughes was very much upset. After the tragic happening at the ranch the evening before she feared that her husband might have been molested. She had insisted upon coming to town to learn why he hadn't come home. The men did not believe this, however, as they had heard that Hughes had been seen in town that morning, and it was ascertained that he and Fred had stayed at the hotel the night before.

Esther, too, was worried. She did not know why Dane had ridden away on the stallion, or where he was going. She couldn't help remembering Bunker's declaration that Dane was running away for good. And Servais was dead and could not tell how he had come to let Dane have the stallion. Esther's face became white, as she thought of the manner of the wrangler's death. Bunker hadn't given him a chance.

The three women were glad indeed when Fred appeared with a cheerful smile on his face.

"Dad went to the county seat in a car early this morning," he explained. "We had a room in the hotel last night. He had to stay over to see about some business with the lawyers up there. He's goin' on with the beeves to-morrow. He ought to be back by noon."

His eyes suddenly lighted up, as Marie came into the lobby. He walked to meet her. Both Esther and her mother greeted Marie warmly, although Mrs. Hughes appeared puzzled at the girl's high color.

Then Fred insisted that they all go out to where the rodeo contests were being held.

"They're bulldoggin' steers this mornin'," he said. "Dad should be along in time to eat dinner with us when we get back."

On the way through the crowded street Esther told Fred in snatches what had taken place at the ranch the afternoon and evening before. Fred stopped in his tracks and stared at her.

"Servais?" he exclaimed. "An' Dane *gone?*"

Esther said she believed Servais had let Dane have the stallion by her father's orders to go on some important errand.

"Never!" said Fred stoutly. "Dad would have said something to me about it last night, if he had. He didn't know *where* Dane had gone."

Both walked on in silence. Fred suddenly had

lost interest in the bulldogging. Had Dane fled? Marie pressed him about it until he told her.

"No, no," she said quickly; "he will come back."

Esther heard the girl's words and looked at her almost gratefully. She feared there would be more trouble if Dane came back, yet she wanted him back! She didn't pause to analyze her thought. She remembered Bunker's accusation that he was "yellow." And she remembered with horror the shooting of Servais. If she had been a man and a *gunman*—Her lips tightened, and her eyes flashed in a way they hadn't done since her return from the East. They went back to the hotel at noon. One of the men from the ranch approached Fred hurriedly.

"Dane's been combin' the town for yore dad," he said.

"Dane!" exclaimed Fred. "He's back?"

Esther's eyes were shining, and Marie smiled at her and nodded.

"Guess he wants to see yore dad powerful bad," said the man.

"What does he want with him?" asked Mrs. Hughes nervously.

"Dunno," said the cow-puncher. "Where *is* the boss?"

Fred started to reply, but was stopped by a little cry from Marie. She was pointing at the door. They turned and saw Gordon Hughes entering.

"Why did you come to town?" he asked his wife, as he joined them.

Mrs. Hughes and Esther told him what had happened, and why they were anxious about him. His face became dark, as he learned of Servais's death. Then his look gave way to surprise.

"But why did Dane take the stallion?" he asked. "He didn't tell me he wanted to use Jupiter."

"Well, he can tell you himself," said Fred dryly. "Here he comes."

Sure enough, Dane was coming toward them accompanied by a tall man who wore a businesslike air. Dane quickly introduced his companion as "Mr. Forbes of the Great Bend National Bank."

"I talked my friend Servais into lettin' me ride your stallion to Great Bend last night," said Dane to Gordon Hughes. "We came up in Mr. Forbes' car this mornin'. I'll have to go back down there an' get your horse."

Hughes looked mystified. "But why didn't you ask *me* for the horse?" he demanded.

"Because I'd have had to tell you too much," smiled Dane. "An' I'm sort of fond of surprises."

Mr. Forbes laughed merrily. "And I rather think you are in for a surprise, Mr. Hughes," he said in an agreeable voice.

"I looked everywhere for you," Dane said hurriedly. "Then I figured maybe they'd roped an' tied you an' drug you off, so we—that is,

Mr. Forbes—tended to some business for you. Maybe I had a lot of crust, an' I didn't tell you 'bout it ahead of time, for I didn't know if I could put it over. But I didn't want to see you lose—"

"Now what're you talkin' about?" Hughes interrupted, scowling.

"He's trying to tell you that the Great Bend National Bank took up your paper at the American Bank of Black Butte about an hour ago," said Forbes, smiling.

Gordon Hughes stared at the two of them, Dane and Forbes, in utter astonishment.

"And I might add that the Great Bend National Bank is prepared to grant you such extension on your notes as you may require to market your beef cattle," said Forbes.

"Mr. Forbes happens to be president of the Great Bend National," Dane put in.

Gordon Hughes found his tongue at last. "You—took up my notes—an' are goin' to extend 'em—loaned me some sixty thousand dollars without waitin' to see me?" Hughes gave it up. He couldn't understand it. He glared at Dane, suspecting some kind of a joke.

Forbes laughed again, then sobered quickly. "Yes, I took 'em up without waiting to see you, or give you a chance to say 'I, yes, or no'—and a mighty good thing I did."

"Eh, what's that?" stammered Hughes.

"A mighty good thing I did," Forbes repeated. "The American Bank hasn't been operating for half an hour. It closed its doors at noon to-day!"

"Closed?" said Hughes in an awed tone.

"Yes. I'm surprised the State bank examiner didn't close the American on the strength of its September statement. When I gave Mr. Stevens our check to-day to cover your notes he decided to close while he had a respectable cash showing. The depositors will realize something. A continued falling off in deposits and a too speculative policy of making loans, many of which are not properly secured, was responsible for the failure."

"That's why he was always talking about cash," Hughes reflected. "But I don't understand how you came to do this."

"Blame him," interrupted the Great Bend banker, pointing at Dane. "He rode all night and was waiting for me this morning when I came to the bank. He stated the case and bulldozed me into coming up here at once. I happen to know him rather well"—he frowned at Dane in mock severity—"and I also credit myself with sometimes being able to see a good business proposition. Your security was excellent, you needed only a short-term loan, and you were being pressed for reasons which I suspected, and which proved to be correct. That's all of it, except that we will be glad to have your business.

This north country, I believe, is coming back to a stock-raising basis, more or less."

Gordon Hughes held out his hand which the banker grasped warmly, with a smile to the others.

The rancher's face again was smiling and cheerful, as he patted his wife's shoulder.

"Oh, yes," he said suddenly, beaming upon Marie. "I got something for you up in Conard. A new job! My lawyer says he's willin' for you to come into his office an' learn to be a stenograffer!"

"I don't reckon she wants to be any stenographer," remarked Fred.

"Why not?" flared his father. "It's nice work, an' she's bright. She'll learn fast."

"Well, I don't need any stenographer," said Fred, in a quiet tone. "An', anyway, I won't have my wife workin'!" he added, putting his arm about Marie.

"Fred!" exclaimed his mother. "What are you saying?"

"Well, she isn't my wife yet," Fred said, looking at his father, "but she's goin' to be just as soon as we can fix her father up in a place where he'll be well taken care of, an' I can get a check for my summer's wages for a weddin' trip."

Marie moved a bit behind him. Her face was the color of roses.

The other members of the group stared at the

pair in dawning comprehension. Then the banker spoke.

"They say it's lucky to be the first to offer congratulations, so—" He shook hands with the two of them.

Then Mrs. Hughes and Esther took the girl into their arms, while Gordon Hughes's eyes kindled, and he shook his son by the shoulders.

"I never figured I'd want to pick a wife for you, Fred," he said soberly. "An' I'm not goin' to start complainin' now you've picked one out for yourself."

Dane shook hands with Fred, and the banker called Hughes aside.

"I want to talk business with you for about five minutes and get your signature on a couple of dotted lines," he said.

The rancher led him upstairs.

Mrs. Hughes took Marie into the little parlor, and Fred turned to Dane.

"You're a *white* man," he said enthusiastically. "I knew you took the stallion for some good reason an—" He suddenly remembered. Then he told Dane what had happened at the ranch after he left for Great Bend.

Esther saw Dane's face change. Grim lines took the place of the youthful look; anguish shone in his eyes.

"Bunker rode into the river trail," Fred concluded. "Did you see him?"

Dane shook his head. "I rode pretty fast, an' it was gettin' dark," he said with an effort. "Guess he didn't cross the river."

Fred hesitated to say more, struck by Dane's strange tone. Esther couldn't keep her eyes from him, and he didn't look at them. Buck Colter entered and walked over to them. He looked at Dane curiously and hesitated, as he saw the concern in Esther's eyes; then he spoke in a low voice.

"There's a bunch of the boys aroun'," he said to Dane meaningly. And then, as Dane looked at him quickly: "Bunker's in town."

The silence was broken by Dane's voice. "Thanks, Colter," he said quietly.

Gordon Hughes and the banker came down the stairs. Hughes was regarding Dane with a strange expression in which curiosity, respect, and perplexity were commingled. His look sharpened, as he noted the attitude of the silent group. Mrs. Hughes, her sister, and Marie came out of the other room to join them.

"When did he come in?" Dane asked Colter.

"Little spell ago," drawled the cow-puncher. "Thought I'd stroll down here an' tell you. The rest of the boys are up at The Palace."

"I'll be along shortly," said Dane.

Hughes had realized instantly by their tones and actions whom they were talking about. He confronted Dane.

“Don’t go out,” he said earnestly. “It ain’t worth it. Nobody’s payin’ any attention to what Bunker says, an’ he was drunk yesterday—maybe. We ain’t expectin’ you—”

His words stopped, as he met Dane’s look.

“I reckon you’re forgettin’ Servais, Gordon,” said Dane softly and turned away.

Fred followed him out. Hughes and the banker exchanged glances, and then they, too, went out. Esther turned to Marie with a choking cry, and the girl gathered her into her arms.

The dusty street threw the heat of the Indian summer sun into Dane’s face, as he walked slowly. There were few people about, as nearly all had gone out to witness the rodeo contests. Dane kept a sharp lookout, although his thoughts were busy.

He smiled at the impotency of Gordon Hughes’s speech. It was kind of Hughes to give him a loophole through which he might avoid meeting Bunker; but Bunker hadn’t been drunk when he had said he’d shoot him on sight, and he hadn’t been too drunk to shoot the little wrangler, Servais.

The man’s intense hatred of him had brought him to town. He was there for a purpose. Dane knew it. The others knew it. Colter had played the game when he had come to him with the news at once and had subtly conveyed the information that the Diamond H men were there to see fair play. When he had said the boys were at The Palace he had told Dane where Bunker was without saying it in so many words.

Dane knew what was expected of him. He had no wish to avoid it. Bunker was a menace—a ruthless, merciless killer. To-day, with his infamous plans blocked, his villainy disclosed, his vicious nature was given full rein, and he had made the meeting an absolute certainty when he had called Dane yellow.

Fred was close behind when Dane reached The Palace. Old Marty met him a few paces from the entrance.

"You here, Marty?" asked Dane in surprise.

"Sh!" cautioned Marty with a finger to his lips. "Bunker's in there waitin'. There ain't many aroun' 'cept some of our boys an' a few that's got wise. Ain't nobody between Bunker an' the door. He's standin' at the bar facin' this way. He ain't drinkin', either. Now be ready, Dane," said the old man in a voice that trembled. "He knows you're comin' and—"

Dane strode past him, kicked open the swinging doors, and leaped inside. Then came the roar of guns.

"Servais was the *last* one!" Dane's voice rang, as the echoes of five shots died away.

Dane half turned to the left, thrusting his smoking weapon out before him.

Bunker leaned against the bar, his gun hand dropping to his side. His eyes burned red into Dane's. Then a film seemed to shade them, his gun clattered to the floor, and he sank down with his head upon his chest.

"He—got him!" breathed old Marty in an awed voice.

Dane staggered back toward the door. Fred Hughes caught him in his arms as he was falling.

CHAPTER XXXII
THE DAWN

Bench lands and bottoms were a riot of shimmering gold and flaring crimsons. The sear, saffron-tinted leaves of the cottonwoods fluttered in the breeze and carpeted the space about the Diamond H ranch buildings. In the river brakes the deeper tones of choke cherries, aspens, willows, alders, poplars, and quaking ash showed against the enduring green of pines and cedar bushes. The mountains were clothed in a deep purple haze and crowned by silver minarets which gleamed in the sun.

Dane was sitting in a rocker on the porch enjoying the warmth of late afternoon. His left shoulder was bandaged where his flannel shirt was cut away, and his left arm was in a sling—mute evidence of the erring course of Bunker's bullets, aimed at his heart.

Marie was sitting with him.

"We are goin' to build a cabeen close by for my father," she was saying. "He will be all right where I can keep the eye on heem."

"When are you an' Fred goin' to get hitched up?" asked Dane with an amused smile.

They had become good friends, these two.

"Fred say when his father get back from sellin' the cattles in Chicago," said the girl, looking at him slyly. "An' you know hees father he get back yesterday."

Dane laughed with delight. "Then it ought to be right soon," he chuckled. "Fred's a fast worker, sure enough."

"It ees better than be a steneegrefer," said Marie, her eyes sparkling.

Dane's hearty laugh brought Esther Hughes to the porch.

"What are you two laughing about, Mr. Brentley?"

Dane appeared to scowl darkly, although he couldn't make his eyes work quite to suit his purpose. "You ain't forgot my first name, have you, ma'am?"

"No," said Esther cheerfully; "but I rather like to use your last name since father told us what it was."

"I asked Forbes to keep quiet," Dane complained; "but he had to spill all he knew."

"Oh, Mr. Forbes didn't tell us much," said Esther. "Just that you were fairly respectable, but a little wild and needed taming—and settling down."

They heard the purr of a motor, and Fred drove up with his father in a new car.

"Ain't I an old fool, mother?" said Hughes, as his wife came out. "I let this young whippersnapper talk me into buyin' him a new automobile for a weddin' present, an' it can go faster'n the other one. There won't be anything left when he smashes this one."

Fred looked cheerfully at Marie, as she came down the steps to inspect the new car. Hughes took the chair she vacated and sat down next to Dane.

"I stopped in at the county seat," he said. "Your man has told what he knew. Marie's father shot Williams all right, an' I don't know as I blame him. Anyway there won't be anything done about it. Bunker was doin' the rustlin' on his own hook. Brung in a bunch of his kind as hands over at the Flyin' W. But Williams was behind the stampede. Wanted to get my cattle cheap, an' the banker wanted cash quick. Hand in glove, the two of 'em, I 'spect. Guess Stevens was sore at me, too, because I talked right up at him."

He looked about at the circle of faces and grinned broadly.

"An' now Williams wants to sell out," he announced. "Don't want any law called in, an' that suits me. Told me himself to put the fence on the strip where I wanted it. Maybe we'll get some decent neighbors now, for the Flyin' W won't be hard to sell."

This news was the main topic of conversation at the supper table. Dane asked Gordon Hughes many questions of a business nature concerning stock raising in that vicinity, and the rancher was pleased with his knowledge.

"I reckon you'd make me a good foreman," he said to Dane.

Dane Brentley shook his head. "Guess you'll have to train Fred for that job," he said.

"You ain't thinkin' of moving on?" asked Hughes in a tone of disappointment.

"Well, that'll depend," drawled Dane, looking curiously at Esther Hughes.

The girl lowered her gaze, confused; then looked at him defiantly.

Marie giggled in sheer delight, and, as Esther glanced at her with elevated brows, the whole company laughed, Gordon Hughes loudest of all. Dane, however, did not laugh, and he thought Esther looked gratefully for a moment in his direction.

But after supper Gordon Hughes approached Dane seriously in the living room.

"I'd kind of hate to see you leavin' for other parts," he said in a very kindly manner. "I didn't have to be told by Forbes that you come of good, sound, Western stock. I spotted you the very first time we met—the day we was countin' the cattle in the bottoms—an' I didn't lose confidence even when things was breakin' the worst. I reckon we sort of understood each other, an' I think we understand each other now."

He gripped Dane's hand, and Dane saw the

same queer, baffling light in the rancher's eyes which he had noted once before. This time, however, he merely smiled and his answer was forestalled by the entrance of others into the room.

Five days passed, days of glorious Indian summer, which is at its best in the altitudes of Montana's north prairie country. Dane and Fred took several mysterious trips in the new car, and for two whole days were absent, returning in a car coated with dust, as if it had covered many miles. Fred brought back a ring for Marie and said he had bought it in Great Bend, the plains metropolis far to southward. Gordon Hughes appeared interested, but asked no questions.

And then one night Dane and Esther Hughes were sitting on the porch, looking at the stars and the gaunt branches of the cottonwoods weaving in the cool wind, talking sparingly of trivial things.

"I'm wonderin' what you think of me as a gunman by now," said Dane suddenly, during a lull in their conversation.

"Don't be silly," replied the girl. "Father told me he never hired you in any such capacity, and after I saw what kind of a man Bunker was, and what he did to Servais—well, you know I was *born* in the West, Dane."

"I've always been foolin' roun' with a shootin' iron, seems like," said Dane whimsically. "Sort of took to it when I was a kid. I can't remember my mother, an' I was thrown in with the men pretty young, seems like. When dad died, an' I sold our ranch, I guess I drifted with the crowd."

"But *why* didn't you tell us who you were?" asked Esther, puzzled. "It would have made things easier."

"That's just it," said Dane. "It would have made it too easy. I'd rather fight *against* odds than fight with 'em, I reckon. An' I've had a kid notion about bein' mysterious. The stars, or the wind, or the sky, or something has made me like to keep folks guessin'!" He laughed softly.

"I've been sorry I mistrusted you," said Esther dreamily.

"Well, I wanted you to do that," he said to her surprise. "Makes a better understandin' sort of, when things are straightened out."

She looked at him in the dim light of the stars. His eyes were sparkling, and she turned her head away. Again she remembered what Marie had said about a man's eyes. Marie was not a fool!

"Where are you going from here?" she asked, and she was astonished that she had put the question.

"Why, I've been scoutin' around lookin' for a location," he replied cheerfully. "I've got a little in the bank, an' Forbes down at Great Bend says he might be persuaded to take a chance on me if

I settled down, like you mentioned. An' I know a few about the cattle business." He rose and stood close to her chair.

"Esther," he said softly, "do you reckon you could live on the Flyin' W?"

She did not look at him. "Why do you ask such a thing as that?" she queried in a voice so low he could scarcely hear her.

"I was thinkin' pretty strong of buyin' the Flyin' W," he answered. "Don't you think you could sort of get along with me over there—Esther?"

And then she looked up at him with shining eyes. "With you and the stars, Dane," she whispered.

In a moment he had dropped beside her; his right arm closed about her shoulders, and he found her lips.

And while the wind played a symphony in the waving branches of the cottonwoods, he told her the story that's as old as the buffalo trails that still leave the imprint of the years on that vast, open land bounded by the skies.

"Beg pardon!"

They rose in confusion. Dane was scowling, and Esther was flushed and sparkling, holding to Dane's good arm.

"Just happened to be walkin' by an' wanted to say I expected you two'd wake up one of these days, an'—it'll suit the hull outfit to a T!"

It was old Marty, standing below the steps, his hat in his hand, the light of the rising moon silvering his hair and showing his wrinkled face wreathed in smiles.

Center Point Large Print
600 Brooks Road / PO Box 1
Thorndike, ME 04986-0001 USA

(207) 568-3717

US & Canada:
1 800 929-9108
www.centerpointlargeprint.com